Collected Stories

Volume II

David O. Zeus

This Edition 1.0 Published by DOZ
ISBN: 978-0-9955917-3-8

For Rose & Joe

CONTENTS

Foreword

Foggy Love Bottom 1

Scary Morning in the Woods 45

I'm Not Matt Damon 85

The Elephant of Marrakech 121

Book of Giants (Journal 9) 155

Sack Truck 189

A Life's Work 215

Acknowledgements 254

About the Author, Upcoming Titles 255

DAVID O ZEUS

Foreword

Not much to say here other than this is a small collection of short stories compiled in recent years while Nigel was musing on Beans. The stories are varied and, I hope, playful. There are more to come, but in the meantime, the stories enclosed are:

Foggy Love Bottom – a story of love and loss set in a little village with a peculiar name and history.

In *Scary Morning in the Woods,* the garden attack (described in *Scary Afternoon in the Garden)* leads the townsfolk to nervously take the fight to the creatures in the woods.

In *I'm Not Matt Damon* a lone human being is recreated by aliens (after the destruction of planet earth by asteroids) in their mistaken belief that he was once the great leader of humanity and finest representative of life on earth – Matt Damon.

The Elephant of Marrakech – a man retraces his steps to Marrakech to 'find the elephant' and make the decision he should have done seven years earlier.

Book of Giants: Journal 9 – a survivor's journal written eighteen months after an apocalyptic solar flare led to the disintegration of society and the re-emergence of ancient giants.

Sack Truck – a man loses his job as a result of the perfect storm of a confused memory (of a *Viz* comic character) and the fast-changing social mores of the modern world, all prompted by a reference to a 'sack truck'.

A Life's Work – a 100 year old New York mob-boss is released from prison after 50 years and is given the opportunity to reflect on his life as a gangster.

These are all standalone stories, but I anticipate a third outing for the 'Scary' stories and perhaps more outings (or 'Journals') in a *Book of Giants* series. *Collected Stories*: *Volume III* and *Volume IV* are being compiled and I hope to have *Nigel* out soon too.

The author

Foggy Love Bottom

Foggy: *adj:*

1. (of the atmosphere) thick or obscure with fog (cloud of tiny water droplets suspended in the atmosphere at or near the earth's surface which restricts visibility);
2. a state or cause of perplexity or confusion.

Love: *noun; verb*:

1. an intense feeling of deep affection;
2. a great interest and pleasure in something;
3. feel deep affection or sexual love for someone.

Bottom: *noun; adjective*:

1. the lowest point or part of something;
2. the ground under a sea, river, or lake;
3. a person's buttocks;
4. one of six flavours of quark;
5. (archaic) stamina or strength of character;
6. (archaic) a small settlement, generally one smaller than a village, at the base of a deep, narrow gorge.

– I – Foggy

After a restful night the fifty year old man, Peter, sat up in his bed to be met by the sight of nothing outside his windows. Literally nothing – just white nothing. At night the curtains remained drawn open so that on waking he could judge the start (and state) of the day, but on this particular morning he could not even discern the ivy creeping up the wall outside his bedroom window. The world outside was as pure and white as night is black. The previous evening had been clear of any hint of mist, so the presence of this pea-soup fog was curious. In the fifteen years he had lived in the cottage he had not seen such a thing. Sure, he knew he lived in a village called Foggy Love Bottom (the name must have come from somewhere), but the village was not overrun by bottoms (his or anybody else's), and love, well, let's not go there. So, why the fog all of a sudden? It was mid-October and the weather had turned, but normally you would get an inkling of weather like this.

Stepping on to his bedroom carpet was like stepping onto a dewy field. Cold and damp. Had the fog entered the room during the night? Peter did recall waking in the early hours and shivering at a distinct clamminess in the night air, but his little cottage was very old. The thick stone walls kept everything cold.

He showered and readied himself for his journey into Oxonville. Grabbing a quick bite to eat he saw the fog pressed up hard against the kitchen window almost as if it was trying to get in. He gulped his coffee and made for the door grabbing his pannier for the forty minute cycle to town and work, but on opening the front door, he stopped. There was no way he was cycling in this. The illumination from his cycle lamps would hardly reach a driver sitting on his back wheel. I'll take the bus, he thought.

With that, he emptied his pannier, threw his items into an old leather shoulder bag, pulled a long dark overcoat from the back of the cupboard – one he would never dare to wear on a bicycle for fear of the flaps being caught in a bicycle's mechanism – and left the house.

Nothing had prepared him for nature's gauze surrounding the house. It could have been the only house in the world. Wholly isolated from the trials and drama of a planet peopled by billions. The sun really is a unifier, he thought, as he trod carefully down the gravel path, through the garden gate to the village's main street – in fact, its one and only lane.

There was a single bus stop in the village itself, but it was not a regular service. He suspected the bus driver would be disinclined to manoeuvre down the narrow roads into the steep-sided gorge at the bottom of which the village itself was nestled. He shook his head in despair – he might have to walk up to the busy A-road at the top of the gorge.

Passers-by seemed to have similar ideas. Figures wrapped up tightly in scarves and long coats against the clamminess of the fog appeared suddenly in front of him before disappearing. Nothing was said. The fog had stripped the village of sound. It seemed strangely quiet, as if from a bygone age. Like the fog, you could almost reach out and touch the silence. It seemed to push up against him, insisting on contemplation. Eerie. He shook off his concerns and attributed his distraction to not having air rushing over his ears as he cycled. At least there was no traffic, everyone was being sensible.

Having taken two dozen steps down the lane he drew level with the front garden gate of his neighbour, Mr Goodban. What surprised Peter was that the seventy-year old widower was rarely seen outside his home and in such a smart state of dress. Spruced up in jacket and tie, Mr Goodban stood to attention clutching a bouquet of home-picked flowers. Peter nodded to his neighbour in acknowledgment, but received nothing in return.

'I suspect the bus won't make it down into the village today,' said Peter rolling his eyes and waving at the fog in the spirit of good neighbourliness.

Again, nothing. No reaction. Mr Goodban was lost to the fog. Both the fog and silence had indeed laid claim to any human interaction in Foggy Love Bottom that morning.

Peter left his neighbour and within a few steps was lost to the whiteness himself. Other than the murmur of a loved-up couple talking on a corner, he saw nothing as he made his way out of the village in the hunt for a bus.

– II – Bottom

Peter had moved into Foggy Love Bottom at a time when he wanted to bring about a change in his life. He hadn't been at rock bottom, but it was a bottom of sorts. A low-lying plateau, perhaps. Moving house, out of Oxonville, would stir things up. It would require him to cycle forty minutes to his workplace in Oxonville itself, but, he had concluded, eighty minutes of cardiovascular exercise five days a week would be good. His thighs and lungs would benefit the most, closely followed by his spirit and heart. It had been a sensible buy – in terms of property he could have got more for his money the further out of town he moved. The name of the village had amused him and it seemed 'kinda appropriate' considering his then-circumstances, but he didn't dwell on it. It was only after friends and family starting asking him why he was living in a village called 'Foggy Love Bottom' that he decided to conduct some research. The postman shrugged and replied: 'Because it's foggy sometimes?' The shop assistant looked blank and replied: 'Because it's always been called that?' And the local bobby replied: 'It was named after someone?' (It was good thing there was little to no crime in Foggy Love Bottom.)

Eventually he tracked down the oldest woman in the village. She couldn't help, but she did suggest he spoke to the oldest woman in the next village who had been born in Foggy Love Bottom nearly one hundred years before. And so he did. He learnt that the village had acquired its name because: i., it was often foggy; ii. the village sat snuggled at the bottom of a small gorge or valley hence 'bottom'; and iii. it was a place where lost loved ones could reunite, albeit briefly.

His interest piqued, he sought out local senior citizens and quizzed them on their views. He scoured local libraries and community centres for publications that might give him a fuller picture of why Foggy Love Bottom was called Foggy Love Bottom. Not only did he read articles on weather systems and local climate, geological rock formations, the ice age, but also antique parish magazines and letters and poems compiled by long-forgotten local community writing guilds.

He learnt that indeed the village was positioned in a sharply-inclined valley formation that had been cut by retreating ice sheets twelve thousand years earlier. The thick strip of limestone running southeast to north west for twenty miles had meant the ice had been able to cut deep into the landscape, making a one mile wide and third of a mile deep scar on the landscape. In effect, a large crevasse. The surrounding granite gave steep sides to the sunken pocket in the landscape. Geologists had also estimated that the formation had sunk further as the ice retreated as the different rock strata reacted to the change in weight from the retreating ice. With regard to the fog, that was the result of cold air sweeping across southern England from the Atlantic but warming in irregular patterns as it passed over the peat marshes of Wessex. As it reached the Cotswolds the great mix of air would fall into the pocket, suddenly cool, and create thick, thick fog that could last for days.

Reports of thick, thick fog in the 16th-19th centuries had been commonplace, especially at a time when the River Thames would freeze over in the mini ice age of the 1600s – a time when London would became famous for its winter fairs on the river. But the weather in the twentieth century had been relatively mild and occurrences of deep thick fog were not so commonplace.

References to a settlement at the base of the steep valley or gorge dated to the fourteenth century, but for some reason the settlement had not grown beyond a dozen houses and a pub. It had remained the smallest of villages (or 'bottom' – an evolution from the Old English word 'botm' meaning bottom, ground, abyss – 'valley bottom') of no more than eighty residents at any one time according to the census going back to 1643. Local historians had speculated that the occurrences of fog had put people off moving to the area owing to the fear of robbers on roads leading into the 'botm'. It seemed perfectly plausible. Interestingly, some historians had referred to a story that the 'botm' (bottom) also acted as a pull on lost loves. Peter learned that at one time local superstition held that the fog suspended time. Or rather it enabled all Time to be present. The fog acted as a barrier to the laws of the natural world, suspending them for as long as the fog stayed. Hence the reference to the fog as 'God's cloak' (also the name of the settlement's one pub). The cloak was God's own way of giving one tiny 'botm' time off from His laws of Time and Nature. Time out from the trials of life. What happened in the fog, stayed in the fog. The Almighty willfully withheld His gaze for just a few short days of fogginess.

Peter came across reports of the 'fog fairs' of the 18th and 19th centuries. He read that widows and widowers would be drawn to the location and be found wandering the gorge and the village for hours, if not days, at a time. It was said men and women would meet their deceased loves and walk as they had once done, side by side, until the fog cleared. Between 1690 and 1756 fog fairs would happen every year. Chapels were built on the ridge circumference of the valley-gorge, and there was much demand for people to be buried in the region in the hope they would one day reconnect with their lost loves. Such was the demand that local churches decided only those meeting an early death (under 30 years of age) could be buried near Foggy Love Bottom. Not that it mattered; all true loves could meet fleetingly in the fog until they were reunited for an eternity in the after-life.

In local parish newsletters there were stories of old men and women found quietly sobbing in the fog. Reports seemed to peak after the Crimean war (1853-1856) and Boer war (1880-1881), and more recently, the decade following the First World War at the beginning of the twentieth century. But with the Second World War, modernising ideas, changes in climate and a greater transitory population, the reports declined as the practices seemed to have slipped away.

He came across hand-drawn illustrations in old publications of fog in the unusual geological formation. He recognised the church spires on the circumference of the gorge formation and what appeared to be a lake. It had become a lake of fog. Almost like a loch. A lake into which one could dive and roam the landscape of lost loves.

It reminded him of his grandmother's references to fog being the manifestation of love. She had grown up in the Wessex area so perhaps she had consciously or subconsciously called upon the memory of stories about Foggy Love Bottom. She had told him that love is a fog – it pulls a man and a woman together in mutual security, but can dissipate when the sun pushes hard. To find someone in the fog, is to be bound to them. You can always find your way back in the fog, because it removes all distraction. By losing your way, you find a way.

And then he forgot about it. At least for a dozen years until a foggy, foggy day in mid-October.

– III – Love

Peter reflected on his research as he travelled in the bus to work. The fog remained thick and gave an eerie calmness to the surrounding countryside. Everything had slowed – slowed almost to a point as if time were standing still. And if time was standing still, then one could move one through it. The real world was suspended and anything could happen. The fog did not relent for the twenty minute journey into Oxonville. The bus dropped him into a part of town he barely knew. Coupled with the fog, it was a struggle to walk the unfamiliar route into work. Other commuters seemed to have a similar problem. They too were moving slowly and unsurely.

His working day was confined to an office and a keyboard. Having picked up a sandwich on the way to work, there was no need for him to leave the building at lunchtime. He made the decision to work through lunch and leave a little early, no one would complain. In fact some of his colleagues had phoned in and used the fog as a reason for a day's absence, so even the office had an unusual calm about it.

The working day done, he walked out of the building into a world of the same softness. The fog had not eased. The whiteness, emanating a gentle glow, hung in the air as he made his way to the centre of town. Once again passers-by became muffled shadows wrapped up against the cold. Being a cyclist he was not familiar with the location of bus stops and therefore found himself walking up and down the high street gazing at posts and bus signage looking for his ride home. Eventually he found a tatty old sign announcing a pickup for Bus 2A via Little Hintock to Foggy Love Bottom. I hope they are laying on more buses, he thought as he saw the line of passengers grow. Surely the bus companies have contingencies for busy times owing to inclement weather?

Having been used to the convenience of jumping on a bicycle he was reminded of the frustrations of waiting in a line of strangers. Ten, twenty minutes passed as he shuffled from foot to foot. The only thing fighting against the clamminess of the cloud was the welcome aroma of proper coffee being made in the covered market just behind him. What I would do for a coffee, he thought. He knew that no sooner had he stepped into the bistro to order his latte than he would lose his place in the queue and a speedy journey home.

Of course he did not know his fellow passengers-in-waiting. Perhaps they were all cyclists. They had the same idea as him – keep warm and wrap the scarf around their faces. All that is, but one. A woman eight feet away from him, he noted. He did a double-take. She looked like someone from his past. A woman called Fabiana. Um, yes, Fabiana. It was indeed a long story.

He looked again.

There was no doubt that it was indeed Fabiana. He knew because various bodily organs instinctively reacted – his heart jumped a few times and started beating erratically, his stomach fell, his brain misfired and a chill ran through his largest organ – his skin. He looked as closely as he could, as discreetly as he could. Perhaps he would spot something that would disqualify her from being his old friend. But no, there was nothing. It must be Fabiana. Surely. She hadn't changed. Had she seen him? Should he avoid eye contact? The last time they had communicated had been fifteen years earlier and arguably in strained circumstances. (If a three-page letter of confession could be described as strained.)

Just as he was pondering the implications of looking closer, she turned her head and her eyes met his.

Fifteen years is a long time; time to move on.

His brow was furrowed in thought and his eyes – wide in unblinking surprise and muted terror – masked the remembered excitement of a younger man. All he could discern in her expression was, well, nothing. Maybe a lot of things had happened in those fifteen years and memories of a handful of summers together had fallen first into shade then into shadow. Out of instinctive politeness he offered a smile of recognition rather than a smile of friendship, but to his surprise a full welcoming smile was returned.

Perhaps this isn't going to be all awkward and bad, he thought.

As if on cue, they both started to shuffle towards each other to exchange a few words without trying to give up their places in the queue.

'I was hoping to see you,' she said, without prompting when they could share quietly.

'What are you doing here?' he asked.

'Unfinished business,' she replied quietly, her eyes fixed on his.

'Where are you headed?' he said falteringly, wanting to know how much time they would have together.

He heard a bus approach out of the fog and brake to a halt behind him. Sensing the prospect of a warm home and removal from the immediate clamminess of the high street, the crowd started to press towards the bus. Fabiana nodded towards the vehicle, its doors now opening.

This is bizarre, he thought. She has not aged at all it seems.

'How long are you here for?' he asked over the heads of a few masked passengers realising time was not on his side.

'As long as I need,' she said winningly.

'Okay, well, we should meet up,' he heard himself say, albeit with some trepidation.

'Definitely,' she replied.

She smiled warmly and nodded towards the bus again. Passengers were pressing around them trying to gain access.

Was she nodding to him to get on the bus or was she nodding that she too was getting on the same bus? The bustling crowd moved them on. Now separated by a few feet, he understood it to mean they were both getting on the bus and they could continue their discussion on the vehicle.

'Now is good for me,' she volunteered over the shoulder of a grumpy man in a dark overcoat.

He nodded back and motioned towards the bus. She nodded and smiled, and, if he wasn't mistaken, in her smile he could detect relief.

He boarded the bus, paid his money and shuffled down the bus. All the seats were taken. Everybody seemed to travelling. He stood halfway down the bus watching Fabiana as she waited in line a few places behind him, artfully holding her place in the line from being usurped by anybody who tried to push their way onboard. For a moment he thought she would not make it on to the vehicle. The boarding of the bus by a young woman with a pram and an elderly woman added to his suspense. If Fabiana didn't make it on to the bus they had at least agreed to meet. Should he make efforts to disembark himself? But he was trapped now. Such was the moisture generated by the breath of sweaty passengers inside the bus it was almost as if the fog had breached the confines of the vehicle.

No matter, to his great relief, Fabiana was the last passenger to board the bus before the driver waved a grumpy 'no' to the unhappy crowd outside, closed the door and engaged a clunky gear setting off slowly in the fog.

She smiled and waved from the front of the bus. He smiled and waved back.

Where was she going, he thought? What was she doing over from Spain? Visiting family friends again?

He mouthed the words 'today? Or definitely tomorrow?' and pointed at her as if confirming the arrangements.

She nodded and gave the thumbs up. She looked beautiful. That smile…and the twinkle in the eyes. Peter hadn't seen the smile for fifteen years and, having not had any response to the letter he had sent to her, he had assumed he would never see its brilliance again.

– IV – Fabiana

To make a long story short: Fabiana and Peter had met in the Turf Tavern twenty years earlier. As was typical in late summer, Oxonville was full of tourists and language school students, therefore seats at a central pub on a warm evening were at a premium. Much to his dismay Oxonville publicans did not, as a rule, reserve seating for residents, therefore it was a rather disagreeable Peter who met his two friends in the Turf that evening. Some considerable irritation resulted from standing behind excitable twenty-somethings speaking in various tongues at the busy bar before he was finally able to purchase a drink and join his two friends outside in the beer garden.

Feeling indignant that he was expected to stand on a Friday evening in his own hometown, he toured the premises looking for space on a table. Finding one table with space for six occupied by one young Spanish woman, he strode up and grumpily pointed to the five unoccupied places, mumbling, 'Is anyone sitting here?'

'No,' came the cheerful reply, accompanied by a bright smile and twinkling eyes. He grudgingly noted her attractiveness, but chastised himself for recognising the appeal of another human being. He was in the pub to catch up with old friends, not succumb to the appeal of tourists intruding on resident-exclusive space in his homeland. Alerting his friends to the available seating, they joined him at the table alongside the Spanish girl's friend now returned with their own drinks. The two sets of friends spent most of the evening engaged in their separate conversations and he inwardly applauded his friends for similarly ignoring the two Spanish ladies. Until that is, one of them broke ranks (two hours later) and enquired after the reason they were visiting Oxonville. And so, two conversations became one.

Eventually Peter was broken down and what had begun as a reluctant polite conversation became a thoughtful interaction. Almost veering off into what might be described as muted enthusiasm, he managed to pull himself back from the brink. On somebody's suggestion, there followed a night-time walk that ended in further melting of frosty relations in an ice cream parlour. There were many meet-ups with Fabiana in subsequent weeks before her unwelcome return to her native Spain. The friendship, that he had assumed was fleeting, was revived on an annual basis by Fabiana's visits to Oxonville and were even complemented by his own visits to Spain. But any tender feelings that he might had had for her were complicated by the creep into (and firm encampment in) the 'friend-zone' and her (apparently dysfunctional) on-off relationship with a boyfriend back in Spain.

During Peter and Fabiana's brief meetings over the years Peter's attempts to break out from the stalemate were thwarted by circumstance or him alone. The sorties ended in a failure in the form of polite hugs and kisses at the end of the evening. Like a war of attrition he was unable to raise the wherewithal to break the misery of friendship. Until, that is, one summer fifteen years earlier (and five years into his misery).

Informed by Fabiana of the dates of her visit to Oxonville that fateful year, he committed himself to one last sortie out of the lowlands of the friend-zone and make a break for the valley of love. (Yes, this articulation made him feel sick too.) He anticipated (even planned) a walk with Fabiana along a canal or meandering stroll in a local meadow and the sharing of his secret – the lifting of the weight from his shoulders. He intended to explain that he had slain the demons of youth and was looking now to a new part of his life and he needed to explore the possibility of a life shared – with her. He would acknowledge she might have commitments at home and so, should his advances be politely declined by a startled Fabiana, he would, though hurt, survive and be able to move onwards with life, to oblivion.

Unfortunately, for whatever reason, they did not meet that summer which left him somewhat aggrieved. The 'for whatever reason' was of bother to him. Perhaps she was ill and cut the holiday short. Perhaps someone else was ill and the trip was cut short. Perhaps a change of itinerary was forced upon her, perhaps she was…. Perhaps, perhaps, perhaps.

Anyway, she did not come, they did not meet. He had no word. Rather than leave it for another year, he decided to maintain momentum and act upon his plan of revelation. He wrote a letter.

He began by apologising for the letter itself and suggesting she remain seated while she read it. He wrote that he had hoped to express the thoughts contained therein to her in person, but her non-appearance meant that a letter was required. The second paragraph contained the whammy. He liked her, a lot. Always had. From the moment of meeting in the pub five years earlier. He regretted finding himself in the friend-zone, over the years he had assumed the physical distance between them would mean that she would fade from his memory, his thoughts, his heart. But she hadn't. In fact, she had dug in, much to his annoyance and he had come to the conclusion that there was not much he could do about it. That was, until now.

He referred to particular instances over the years when he realised what she meant (and could mean) to him. Simple acts of walking her home, sharing a goodbye, would leave an impression on him. It was only when he was walking home alone that he would he feel a peculiar and unfamiliar 'emptiness', as if a chair had been vacated beside him.

He explained that he was writing to say he needed her to know how he felt and that consequently he needed to know how she felt in return. Wanting a form of closure, he gave her two options: respond to the letter in the affirmative (the feeling was mutual), or, if she was not interested, he asked her to slip away without a word to a place where she would only exist in the haze of his distant memory.

Forty-eight hours after she had been scheduled to return to Spain, the letter had been dispatched to her Spanish home. She would receive it on her arrival home. She would have time to mull things over. He gave her a week, then extended it to two, then three weeks. There was no reply. She had heeded his request and his feelings were not reciprocated. She was going to withdraw from their friendship quietly and without drama. Even though it was what he had requested, his feelings had been carpet-bombed. He realised he was no soldier of love. Such acts of wanton violence did not leave him battle-hardened, just shell-shocked. He would follow her example, he would withdraw. He needed to move on, so move he did. Away from Oxonville. To a village far removed from his memories of Oxonville summers. And so he had found himself in Foggy Love Bottom. A place to let him forget. That was fifteen years ago.

So, what was she doing back here in Oxonville? After all this time? And on his bus?

– V – The Journey Home

He looked down the vehicle. Occasionally their eyes would meet and there would be smiles, smiles of anticipation at the prospect of catching up after fifteen years. What was she doing here? Again, why was she getting on this bus anyway? What was the 'unfinished business'? Was it her intention to disembark with him at Foggy Love Bottom?

He was jolted out of his musing by the bus scrunching to the halt. Where, he did not know, the fog was as thick as brandy butter.

He could just discern shadowy figures lined up on the grass verge outside in the murkiness. Not more passengers, he thought to himself as the front doors opened. There's no room, he muttered, but the driver obviously didn't think so.

He watched with concern as he saw the woman with the pushchair, the elderly woman and a few middle-aged men push their way through the insides of the bus towards the exit. Fabiana, polite as she was, shuffled towards the door before disembarking the bus in a clear attempt to make way for the alighting passengers. Concern turned to horror as he watched a handful of queuing passengers push their way onto the vehicle leaving Fabiana stranded at the step onto the bus.

Within moments the vehicle was full of bodies again and Fabiana was left stranded outside. The grumpy driver then did what grumpy drivers do, he closed the door. Halfway down the packed vehicle Peter shamefully did not summon the power to protest. He thought he saw Fabiana knock on the door but the driver waved and the bus slowly moved off.

Peter's immediate impulse was to get off the vehicle, but there was only one door to the bus – at the front by the driver. Most modern buses had a door at the front and a second further down the bus for people to disembark. He was trapped behind twenty bodies more than halfway down the bus. He looked for a bell. There were normally bells embedded in the metal railings, but there was nothing except for a pull-cord high in the corner that was again obstructed by throng of grumpy commuters.

He berated himself for selecting an old bus, but he was a cyclist and how could he know he would end up in this situation? Forcing his way to the window and leaning over disgruntled and bemused commuters Peter watched as the vehicle slowly trundled past Fabiana. A stampede of thoughts raced through his head like a herd of oxen as he waved at her. With waves and gestures of pointing he hoped he communicated his plan to disembark the bus at the next stop. If she boarded the next bus going in the same direction they could meet at the next stop and travel on together. No sooner had he communicated this plan, he backed it up with another plan to return to her bus stop using the next available bus, but he quickly abandoned it thinking they might both end up boarding buses going in separate directions. Fabiana seemed be taking some of his plans on board and was gesticulating and pointing herself. Finally, just as she slipped from view enveloped in the fog, he mouthed 'tomorrow, tomorrow' and pointed in the direction of the bus stop at the beginning of their journey. His relief at seeing her mouth the words 'tomorrow' and 'definitely' accompanied with a nod should not be underestimated. For good measure, he returned to a few gestures implying he would not give up on meeting up that evening, but she was gone. The fog had claimed her.

The fog had claimed him too. He did not know where he was. The bus was rumbling along into whiteness. Not familiar with the bus's speed-of-travel, he was remained oblivious and took a deep breath trying to recall the sequence of his gesticulations and what Fabiana might have of made of them. After a few minutes (too many) he heard the bus's engine change down a gear. And then another. The bus was stopping. Decision made, he pushed his way to the front of the bus and disembarked with a handful of other passengers. He didn't know where he was. He was a cyclist and never paid attention to bus stop signage. Before he could ask any of the passengers they too had been swallowed up by the fog in all directions. He was even denied the indignity of knocking on the bus's door, gaining re-admittance and asking the driver because it too had rumbled off into the white stuff. Within moments he was left alone in the quiet, clammy white darkness of an October night.

I'll just have to wait, he thought. She would have climbed onto the next bus.

So wait he did. He stood fixed to the spot. Though his heart was pounding, it was not enough to pump the blood around his body and keep him warm, so he began to walk in circles. How much time did pass? Ten minutes? Twenty minutes? He did not know.

Straining his eyes for the sound of a bus, he found himself imagining things. Occasionally an old car would pass, but traffic was light. Eventually a sound he was about to dismiss as a false alarm grew. It must be a bus. Its diesel engine an approaching muffled echo in the fog. Then the lights...and finally the changing down of mechanical gears and braking of a vehicle. The bus was illuminated and, in the hope of being easily spotted by Fabiana, he stood close to the bus sign and scoured the insides for her familiar profile. The vehicle was full but the bus was stationary long enough (allowing passengers to alight) that he was confident she was not on the bus. Besides, she would make herself visible knowing he might be waiting at the bus stop.

She was not there. The bus moved off and was again swallowed up by the fog.

His heart, though lively, was not pounding at the pace it had once been. Why does life have to be like this, he cursed under his breath.

The sound of the receding bus never quite receded altogether. It seemed to hum then ever so slightly increase. Had it turned around? The sound was coming from both directions and he realised he was being approached by both a bus coming from town and a bus heading towards town. The bus heading from town drew to a halt in front of him again full people, he scanned its insides and made sure he could be visible to anyone looking out. He resisted the urge to board the bus because the opportunity to return to the previous bus stop was not lost on him. Aware time was the master of the moment not him, he scanned the insides of the bus one last time and, satisfied as far as he could be that Fabiana was not aboard, he dashed across the road to a bus returning to Oxonville. Just in time he boarded and paid for a ticket for a few stops and settled in for the short ride.

The fog was relentless. The bus moved slowly its lights illuminating the swirling monster around them. His heart pounded as he doubted himself and his actions. Should he have stayed put? By chasing after her, what should he expect? It had been fifteen years. Was he subconsciously chasing an old life, a lost opportunity? He didn't want to feel like this again. Don't people grow out of this, he thought? His heart sank further as a number of other vehicles rumbled past going in the opposite direction, away from town. Were they buses? Had she jumped in a taxi? Or given up and jumped on a bus heading back to Oxonville?

He disembarked at the next stop and crossed the road to the point where he had last seen Fabiana. It was empty. She had gone. But where? Thus did he find himself alone and isolated in the fog in the midst of the countryside. His heartbeat slowed, and the clamminess of the fog began to creep inside him. His life as he had known it these last fifteen years was beginning to return. A sort of acceptance of a fate he had not chosen and no one would choose. The absence of an urgency, of vulnerability. An earthly compliance to middle-to-late age, not concerned with higher, lighter things.

Peter stood at the bus stop for another hour ignoring the invitation of a journey home from two buses, but after a full hour, and once the fog had finally claimed his warmth, a third one arrived bereft of passengers. The doors opened.

'I'm the last one,' said the driver, 'we're finishing early. The fog. Where you headed?'

'Foggy Love Bottom.'

The driver nodded and the fifty year old man wearily stepped into the vehicle and sat for the remaining fifteen minute journey home swearing to himself never to take the bus again. He would cycle tomorrow whatever the weather.

The bus dropped him at the top of the gorge, the bus driver advised him that they would not be driving down into the gorge and to the village itself. Pleased to be outside once more he slipped out into the fog and, using the torch from his smartphone, slowly strolled down into the gorge along the route he had cycled for so many years. On foot, at a walker's pace and though the fog, it was a different world. There was no air rushing past his ears, no need (or possibility) to scour the roads and bends ahead for approaching vehicle or pedestrians. All was quiet.

The world was sleeping. Not just the people, the animals in the hedgerows and the birds in the trees, the sun, moon, the stars and Time itself had all departed. Rather than being disconcerting, it engendered a profound sense of peace and stillness. It was not as if the world and its dog had absconded, no, it was as if the all things animate and inanimate had withdrawn out of a sense of respect for the occasion. A respect that was almost tangible.

He entered Foggy Love Bottom. Any sound (he could discern none) had been wrapped up in the thickness of the fog and lost. Villagers had hunkered down in their homes, heavy curtains blocked out the foggy world. The street itself was barely illuminated by a few old lampposts. He passed a number of couples moving quietly through the fog, their hushed talk absorbed by the moisture of the air. Reaching his own home he noted the house of his neighbour, Mr Goodban, was dark. The curtains were not drawn. He was not home.

– VI – The Following Day

Peter rose the next morning early still determined to cycle. The fog was brandy-butter thick again, but local radio reports suggested there was only 24 hours left. He knew from experience what 24 hours might mean for the region, but the Foggy Love Bottom gorge might have an additional day of it. Loading up his bike with an additional complement of lights from his spare bicycle he set off from the village pleased to be spared the trials of being enclosed in a public transport. He waved to Mr Goodban who stood again to attention at his garden gate dressed up in jacket and tie, but received no response. He took his time on his journey into town, sometimes pulling off the road altogether onto the grass verge if he thought a bus was approaching him from behind. Initially he congratulated himself for being old and not foolish, but he soon found himself scanning the insides of each passing bus and becoming overwhelmed by a sense of foolishness. Perhaps foolishness is something that is never banished from the human condition. It just takes different forms. This is what memories of a past life do to you. Senior citizens really are survivors.

Taking the bicycle made sense. It gave him options. He would honour the rendezvous with Fabiana at the end of the working day. It had been intimated that it would be at the same bus stop and it was perfectly logical place to meet. She didn't know where he now lived. He had no idea where she lived. His best hope was that she would wait at the town bus stop where they had met the previous day – thinking it would be on his journey home. She had often teased him for being too logical when assessing any given situation, so she knew him well enough to know that he would think it the logical place to meet. Having his own means of transport would mean that he was not dependent on catching a last bus home especially if, like the previous evening, the buses stopped running earlier in the evening. They could retire to an old favourite pub or restaurant and catch up on the lost years. Perhaps the Turf Tavern where they had met in, what was now, a previous life. Or maybe The Bear Inn, or The Eagle and Child. Maybe he would revisit the matter of his letter and request, nay demand, a reaction. All in good humour, of course.

His working day disappeared into a fog of its own. For a second day colleagues had phoned in their absence so he felt perfectly justified at leaving the office nearly two hours early.

'Long cycle home in the fog,' he muttered to colleagues as he departed, rolling his eyes.

'You're cycling in this?' some said, alarmed.

'Yep,' he replied, rolling his eyes again for good measure.

He had left the building by 3.30 p.m. and walked his bike to the same bus stop by the covered market by 3.50 p.m. Locking it up nearby he felt pleased that he was leaving nothing to chance. He had done everything he could. Now, all he had to do was wait.

The fog was still thick, so he planted himself against the cold stone exterior wall of one of the town's oldest building within a dozen yards of the bus stop itself. Although he might not be able to make out the facial features of any of the bus commuters lining up for the bus, he could certainly discern their profile and Fabiana's profile and shape would certainly never be lost on him.

He had bumped into Fabiana soon after five o'clock the previous day, so he assumed the optimum time was between five and six o'clock. He was ready for the long wait.

He did not move from his position leaning against the wall over the following hour and shuffling from foot-to-foot for the second hour. With no sign of Fabiana by 6.00 p.m. his optimism began to sink and, with it, the warmth of his insides dissolved. The clammy fog was laying claim to his spirits. But he was not going anywhere. He would wait this one out. She had certainly not been waiting in the queue or its near vicinity for the six buses he had observed. In fact he had no way to contact her.

He didn't have a phone number, he once had an email address but had purged all her contact details a year or so after the non-arrival of a response to his letter. He wasn't on social media and suspected she wasn't either. He recalled that Fabiana had a local Oxonville friend but all he knew was a first name – Jennie. At a push he might be able to find the house where Fabiana had stayed when visiting Oxonville years before having walked her home a number of times, but it was in a part of town he was unfamiliar with. He might be able to limit the search to one street or another. But that was fifteen years ago. He would have to knock on a dozen doors.

The last time he had met her was in fact in Spain. She had invited him to visit for a long weekend. It had been almost a test for himself. And he had failed. He knew the matter had to be broached. He had been encouraged by the receipt of the invitation, but the flight to another time zone did not move him out of the friend zone.

By 6.45 p.m. the stone wall had done his business, he was cold to the core and having resisted the aroma of the coffee shop from the covered market entrance for over two hours he succumbed. A strong coffee would pick him up before the establishment closed at 7.00 p.m. Taking the two dozen steps into the entrance of the covered market, he could shuffle a dozen steps back to monitor the figures at the bus stop. Having lost his place in the coffee queue a few times and aware the establishment was about to close its doors and kick out those few remaining customers from the tables outside, he committed himself to waiting in the queue for coffee.

It was at this point that from somewhere amidst that clatter of crockery being washed, shutters of other shops in the market being pulled down that he heard the words 'Fabiana Lopez'. For a moment he thought he might have been imagining it. It must surely be his internal voice vocalizing his thoughts. But no, it was the voice of a young male and Fabiana's name had been uttered as if part of a conversation. Grabbing his coffee he turned and identified the speaker – a young man in his late twenties talking to a female bystander.

'Excuse me,' he asked the young man not sorry to interrupt the conversation, 'you mentioned the name of a Fabiana Lopez?'

'Yes,' the man replied taken aback somewhat.

'She's a friend of mine. We are supposed to be meeting. Round about now.'

'Oh,' the young man replied, a curtain of concern suddenly falling over his face, 'Are you family?'

'No, as I said, I'm a friend.'

The covered market was closing and staff of the shops and the market security were escorting members to the exit leading to the high street. Within a few steps they found themselves on the street. The young man was pausing to think and was hardly being forthcoming.

'Are you a friend of hers yourself?' Peter asked.

'No, I'm a reporter with the Oxonville Gazette,' the young man said falteringly. 'I just mentioned her name in the context of a court case I am reporting on.'

'Oh, I see.'

Perhaps this was the unfinished business that had brought Fabiana to Oxford. Perhaps the court case had delayed her arrival at the bus stop. An end-of-day meeting with solicitors. He was right to stay around. The coffee would help.

'You said you were meeting her?' the young reporter asked with a confused look on his face.

'Yes, here, at the bus stop,' Peter replied turning and nodding towards the bus stop two dozen yards away.

Suddenly, blessed by the momentary parting in the throng of commuters boarding a bus, he saw Fabiana's unmistakeable profile as she stepped onto the 2A bus.

Gripped both by relief that she had honoured her promise to meet and panic that he was about to lose her again, he turned and thanked the reporter and ran towards the bus.

To his horror it was departing. He cursed the crowd of commuters still queuing who were no doubt themselves frustrated at being unable to board their bus home. The faster he ran the faster the bus seemed to pull away. A desperate flash of hope flashed across his mind: if he stopped running, would the bus stop? In his madness he knew it would not make sense. But as the throng thwarted his progress, the bus continued to accelerate until it was consumed by the fog, soon leaving only swirling whiteness caused by the disappearing vehicle.

No, surely, I don't believe it, he whispered to himself. Please, no.

She was gone.

I'm not having this, he thought, and spun round on his heel and raced back up the street. Never had he been so relieved to meet a stranger before.

'I need to go,' he said to the young reporter with some urgency. 'Do you have a business card? Something I can use to contact you?'

'Sure,' the reporter replied pulling out his wallet and handing over a card. 'My contact details at the Gazette.'

Thanking the reporter, Peter turned and raced down the street towards his locked bike, pulling out his own wallet as he did do. Placing the business card deep inside his wallet he was making as determined an effort as possible not to misplace the only means by which he might be able to reach Fabiana if his pursuit of the bus failed.

On his bike, racing down the High Street, he assessed his chances of keeping up with the vehicle. He concluded that his chances were good – the bus was occasionally slowed by traffic, the fog and the need to halt at successive bus stops. It was a forty minute bike ride to Foggy Love Bottom which is far as he would go. He did not know where Fabiana might alight, perhaps at the bus stop where they parted the previous night or the one following. Being a man of middle years, he knew he could not race for too long. He needed to pace himself. He could only do his best.

It was tough. Chasing something you cannot see. How far was the bus ahead of him? There were a handful of inclines on the route leading out from Oxonville – no problem for a bus, just a gentle push on the accelerator, but for the cyclist, it burnt the thighs and pushed the lungs. He raced past the first bus stop, nothing. Empty of bus and bodies. He pushed on to the second, then third. Similarly, nothing. Now outside the town he was in the countryside. He had to be careful. He was not too conscious of the location of bus stops and kicked himself for not paying attention to street furniture when cycling on the way home over all these years. But then, out of the gloom he saw what he thought were two red lights suspended a few feet above ground level. As he approached he saw the yellow glow of the illumination of the bus's interiors. Signage on the back of the bus stated '2A'.

He pushed on determined that the lights would not retreat and be eaten by the fog. For the first time in twenty-four hours he was grateful as he rounded the bus and came to a stop directly in front of the driver. His thighs on fire and physically exhausted after nearly twenty minutes of hard graft on the bike he climbed off his 21-speed and made enough eye contact with the driver to prevent collision should the bus pull away too soon. There was no need, there was no rush. He walked his bike round to the door and surveyed the passengers disembarking. He was satisfied that he had not missed other alighting passengers. Nothing. No Fabiana. He then walked slowly the length of the bus studying the insides for any sign of his old friend. She was not to be seen. He double-backed and double-checked. Again nothing.

Passengers with pushchairs and walking sticks were still climbing off the bus. There was no time to waste. Sometimes buses overtake one another along the route as they drop off and pick up passengers. He jumped onto the bike and sped off into the gloom. Now it was his turn to disappear.

For another five minutes he raced through a world cut off from anywhere, anything. The coldness bit into his face, his hands beginning to freeze on his handlebars. She must be on the next one, he thought.

Once again he saw the red rear lights of a large vehicle emerge ahead of him. It was slowing towards the junction on the country road. If only I can get ahead of it, he thought. He knew there was a bus stop fifty yards beyond the junction. He could pause and wait for the bus.

He raced down the inside lane of the bus looking into the interiors as much as he dare as he navigated the uneven grass verge bordering the road. Within moments he had passed it and slipped around a car the bus had been waiting to pass. With all his might he accelerated his race to the bus stop (the same one he had first alighted at twenty-four hours earlier) and heaved himself off the bicycle and turned. With some relief he saw the faint headlights of the bus labour around the corner. Maybe old buses were not such a bad thing. They move slowly after all.

He threw his bike into the grass of the verge and waited patiently, the bus was obliged to stop, he was a potential passenger after all. It did indeed stop. A few passengers disembarked, but no Fabiana. This time, rather than walking the length of the exteriors, he purposely climbed on to the bus and surveyed the insides with a confidence not to be messed with.

'Where to?' asked the driver.

Buying time as he searched the faces of every single remaining passenger, he mumbled, 'Foggy Love Bottom'.

'We're not heading down to the village today, too foggy,' came the reply.

'Right, okay,' he mumbled in reply, his heart sinking as he surveyed the interior of the bus for a second time. No Fabiana.

'We can take you close, but can't deliver you home.'

The driver's words were lost on the dejected man as he stepped off the bus. Finding himself back in the cold wet air, Peter rattled his memory of the buses that had picked up passengers before his coffee. How many buses might there be currently on route?

Feeling the need to press on he retrieved his bike from the grass and continued on his way. It was another twenty minutes before he would reach the descent into his village. He did stop on a few occasions when he discerned a vehicle approaching him either ahead of him or from behind. He pulled his bicycle up onto the safety of the verge and thanked the fog for slowing down the passing vehicles. He intently surveyed the illuminated interiors but saw nothing.

By the time he was on the slow descent into the village he was becoming accustomed to the idea of another missed rendezvous. At least he had been assured she had been true to her word. In fact, 'Definitely,' had been her word.

Once again the fog in the gorge around the village became thicker. He was indeed isolated from the world. In fact, it had become so thick he climbed off the bike and walked in the silence. At least he had tried. And he had the contact details for the reporter. He would track him down first thing tomorrow when the reporter returned to his office and perhaps get a message to her through her solicitors. And so it was that he reached a stillness in the whiteness.

With just the gentle sound of his footfall on the tarmac and the gentle whirr of his bicycle chain, he entered Foggy Love Bottom. It was as quiet and still as the night before. Sometimes a couple of walkers, lovebirds even, would appear wrapped up and holding each other close against the chill, but they were gone as soon as they appeared. As he approached his own home he heard the gentle hum of a vehicle and saw what he thought were two red dots suspended a few feet above the road.

I thought buses weren't coming down to the village? He strolled further, passing his neighbour's, Mr Goodban's, cottage. Again, no one was home. The curtains were not drawn. It was then that he saw a displacement in the whiteness of the fog. It was a figure crossing the road in front of him and approaching what he had concluded was a bus waiting at the bus stop opposite his home. There was a familiarity to the profile of the figure as it moved to the bus's steps and climbed on board. He knew the profile. The movements of the woman. It was Fabiana. His throat tightened, his stomach fell. The figure, Fabiana, had emerged from his own garden gate. She had had been visiting his home.

He threw his bicycle down and ran towards the vehicle, as he did, so did the bus's diesel engine fire up as it began to move off away from him.

'Wait, Fabiana. Fabiana,' he shouted as he approached. Almost as a direct retort the diesel engines fired harder drowning out his cries.

He ran faster and faster. Just like he had done in the town earlier that evening. It was as if an invisible force both connected him with the vehicle but kept him at a distance. The harder he pushed into the fog, the harder the fog pushed the bus on its way, its old engine still drowning out his cries. There were no echoes in the street. All surfaces were damp and absorbing.

However, he did reach close enough to see the illuminated interiors of the vehicle and saw that it was indeed Fabiana making her way down the aisle towards the back of the empty bus. If only she could see me... Again, he cried out her name with all his life force. Again the engines fought his pleas. Had she heard him? She stopped for the briefest of moments starring out of the rear window. She brushed the hair away from her face and smiled. In her hand was a folded piece of paper. Again, was she looking at him, or just at her reflection in the rear window? He could not tell. She looked happy, or rather, content. At peace. Untroubled. Satisfied, perhaps. And that was the last he saw of her as she took her seat, her back to him as the fog once again swallowed her, and everything around him, up.

How long he stood there he did not know. Time had no call upon that place. It was only when the clamminess reached his bones that he turned, retrieved his bike from the road behind him and wheeled it through his garden gate and into his home.

How had she found him? Why was she visiting? She must have done her homework. He had moved jobs and house. He was not a presence on the Internet or social media. She must have been keen to meet, for sure.

– VII – The Fog Clears

After a long night of rest Peter rose to a different day. Rather than a clamminess hanging in the air and a white softness outside the window, there was a golden hue filling his room. Looking out of the window he saw the sun pushing hard through the last remnants of the whiteness. The fog had been replaced by a light mist which itself would have lost the battle to the sun's rays by mid-morning. The weather might have lifted but his heart remained heavy.

The journey into Oxonville would be clear once he had ridden out of the gorge. He checked his wallet for the reporter's ragged, old business card and was confident the contact details of Fabiana would be in his hand by lunchtime. The fog would hinder their meeting no more.

The cycle ride into town was indeed clear of fog and he had returned to his usual practice of ignoring the passing buses and their passengers. He arrived at the office a little early and rattled off an email to the reporter referring to their brief conversation the previous night and explaining he was trying to contact Fabiana Lopez. Keen not to get rebuffed he also said he would follow up with a phone call.

The email bounced back immediately with an error message. He checked the email address with the business card – it was not his mistake. Shortly after nine o'clock he dialled the number on the business card to be met by a dead tone. He checked the card again. The number did appear to be short of a digit. There being no alternative mobile number on the card Peter conducted an internet search on the Oxonville Gazette and reached the contact page of their website. The business card was indeed lacking one digit at the beginning of number. He remembered the region had brought in additional numbers to cope with demand many years earlier. He hoped, with some caution, that the reporter demonstrated a greater degree of competency in his work than his business card suggested.

He dialled the newspaper, reached the reception and politely asked for the reporter by name.

'He's a reporter?' the young woman at the end of the line replied to his enquiry.

'Yes, at the newspaper,' he replied.

Then silence. Peter allowed her time to check her lists, her computer, her anything, he wasn't going anywhere.

'I'm new here,' she said, before returning to silence.

'That's okay,' he replied, patiently.

'Um, I can't find him on my list, but Brenda is the expert, she comes in at lunchtime. Can you call back?'

'Sure. In the meantime, however, it would be helpful if you passed the details of this call on to Brenda so she is ahead of the game when I call.'

The receptionist agreed and they signed off. Peter was not encouraged. Things did not bode well. Perhaps the reporter was a long-term wannabe freelancer who took liberties with his work profile.

Nevertheless, he felt calmer. Gazing out the window during various meetings what once had been a yellow hue of the moisture was now the faintest wispiness of white and a different world from forty-eight hours earlier.

Peter wondered what a rendezvous would bring. Would the old familiarity return? It reminded him of the days following his meetings with Fabiana twenty years before. At that time there had been no SMS texting, no social media to follow up on their nights-out. A follow-up on an evening out required a phone call to a landline at such a time as to coincide with her presence at the other end. Occasionally her English host and friend, Jennie, would answer his call and he would do his best to appear the gentleman. It seemed to work. His messages would get through to Fabiana and she would return the call.

He left it to the early afternoon to call the newspaper and Brenda. She sounded much more like the old hand the other receptionist had described, but he was frustrated and concerned at her first words about the reporter.

'He doesn't work here anymore. Hasn't done for a number of years. Is he passing himself off as an employee here?'

'I was after contact details and he handed me a business card. Maybe he was confused, it was a bit of a rush and it was foggy.'

'No excuse,' she muttered.

He was beginning to wish he would have more success with the young new receptionist.

'Do you have contact details for him? It is rather urgent and would be much appreciated,' he said as a last ditch attempt to make progress.

'I'll make one attempt to find a contact email or number and email you before the end of the day,' Brenda mumbled.

He thanked her and hoped for the best. In fact he spent the rest of the afternoon hoping and considering alternatives. Resolving to skip away a little earlier to pay a visit to the courthouse and also the bus stop between five and six o'clock just in case Fabiana (or the reporter) would make an appearance.

Brenda was as good as her word and an email arrived at the end of his working day. Pleased, he delayed his departure and dispatched an email to the reporter thanking for his brief recent conversation near the covered market and asking to speak to him about Fabiana Lopez. The less information the better at this stage, he thought. His emailing meant that when he reached the courthouse it was closing for the day. It also meant he was slightly delayed at reaching the covered market. It all looked different in the daylight. He could now see a series of bus stop signs rather than just the one post rising and disappearing into nothingness. He stepped inside the covered market to the small coffee shop. In contrast to the improved street furniture outside, the coffee shop looked more decrepit than the previous evening. He wouldn't dally and wait on the off chance the reporter dropped by, the email should do it. He would have Fabiana's details by tomorrow.

Checking his phone before midnight he received a reply from the reporter. The email, short and to the point, gave no answers (not even referring to Fabiana herself) but rather seemed to be touting for business – the provision of services at competitive rates. The email's signature referred to a Media Services company that was based in a business park on the outskirts of Oxonville. Feeling the personal touch was required once more, Peter resolved to rise early and pay a visit to the reporter himself at his place of work.

– VIII – Foggy Memories

Arriving at the business park on the outskirts of the town by eight o'clock Peter positioned himself in the sun to keep himself from shivering too much during the forty-five minutes before the offices formally opened. He watched everybody arrive thinking he might catch the reporter before he entered the premises. Peter could plead his cause and employ his senior years to glean more information, otherwise what was the use of all those additional years if it were not to be waved in the face of a much younger man? Looking at the uninspiring, prefabricated building, Peter reflected on Brenda's musings that the reporter was possibly embellishing his standing and credentials. Perhaps the reporter had gone one step further and was also embellishing his career by listing the Media Services company's premises as his base. Not having seen the reporter arrive, Peter slipped into the building to investigate. Arriving at a counter Peter rang the bell and waited. A few minutes later a middle-aged man appeared.

'I'm looking for Stephen?' asked Peter politely with a smile.

'Yes?'

'He replied to my email last night. I just happened to be passing on the way to work and thought I would drop by and save us a handful of emails.'

'Yes? What was it regarding?'

'He hopefully has the contact details of an individual involved in a case he was reporting on. He mentioned a 'Fabiana Lopez'?'

'Oh, yes, I remember,' the man replied with the hint of an acknowledgement in his squint.

Peter paused, momentarily thrown. Did the reporter work as part of a team? Had Peter sent the email to a team member, his reporting partner? Did the business card that had been handed over to Peter in fact belong to a colleague? Had Peter been naïve to assume the so-called twenty-something reporter was playing a straight bat? Did they all duck and dive, play the game? Peter's confusion must have been apparent because the man standing opposite him continued.

'I have not had a chance to check my records.'

Or was Peter possibly talking to the reporter in question? There was an echo of the younger reporter's facial features in the man standing opposite him. This man was fatter and tired-looking though. The flush of youth had been well and truly flushed from his features and demeanor. Peter racked his memory of the foggy night a few evenings before in the covered market trying to recall details of the reporter's face. Perhaps his youthful appearance had been the result of the animation of reporting on an interesting case? Perhaps his age had been disguised by a woolly hat and a closely wrapped neck scarf.

'Look, can I call you later? My records are pretty good and if we did meet and discuss the matter then I certainly should have a record of the case at least; though possibly not our meeting.'

Now thoroughly bemused and before he embarrassed himself further, Peter decided to withdraw. If the man at the counter was indeed the reporter in question, the information on Fabiana had been promised and should arrive later that day.

There was no reason to doubt it. In the meantime, Peter would try some Internet searching or grit his teeth and explore what social media might throw up.

Later that day, the phone rang. Peter answered.

'I'm sorry,' said the person at the other end of the phone, 'your memory is obviously better than mine. I have checked my old records and, yes, I did report on the case of Fabiana Lopez.'

The listener, Peter, was much relieved and pleased that the caller, whether he was Stephen (the reporter) or not, had got back to him the same day. 'Oh, good, thank you.'

'I remember it now. She was murdered fifteen years ago by her ex-boyfriend. Her body was found on a grass verge in the outskirts of Oxonville.'

'I'm sorry. I don't understand,' Peter muttered down the phone, his head swimming. 'I saw her two nights ago, boarding a bus on the High Street.'

'Well, perhaps you mistook another woman for her.'

'But we spoke,' Peter whispered quietly into the mouthpiece. 'I spoke to her, Fabiana, the night before.'

'Ah, well,' the reporter said sounding even a little relieved that he was not the bearer of bad news, 'then it must be another Fabiana Lopez.'

Believing the fact that hearing about the murder of someone with the same name as a loved one must be shocking, the reporter filled the silence by reading a few more of his notes.

'But if you are mistaken, I have contact details for the family friend here in front of me. Would you like them?'

'Please,' Peter replied somewhat breathless, relieved to have one piece of information with which to correct the error. He scribbled the details down.

The call ended, Peter sat at his office desk staring at the scribbled notes in front of him – Jennie Trent, 72 Trinity Street.

For the fourth day in a row Peter left the office early, but there was not a wisp of fog on which to lay the blame. At approximately five o'clock he found himself standing in an unfamiliar part of town in front of a brown door at the end of a terrace.

He had never met Jennie, so he would not recognise her. How would she recognise him?

The doorbell did stir movement inside the house. He saw a figure moving through the stain-glass in the front door as it displaced the light which came from the back of the house. The door opened and a late sixty-something woman, in relative good health, stood before him. He hadn't prepared his opening line, he was still distracted, even in shock from the conversation he had had earlier in the afternoon. The few days of fog seemed to make complete sense compared to these new days of sunshine (and clear nights) now visited upon him.

The woman stood motionless in front of him. Her expression turned quizzical and then just as he was about to force a greeting from his lips, she softened in a moment of realisation.

'You're Fabiana's friend, aren't you?' she sighed.

'Yes,' Peter replied, breathing out in relief. At last, some sense.

'I'm Jennie. Please, come in,' the woman said quietly with the warmest of smiles and standing aside to let him pass.

They sat and talked for three hours. By end of the evening they were old friends. Old, dear friends. It was a shame they had never met in the company of Fabiana herself.

Peter learned that Fabiana had indeed been murdered fifteen years earlier while on a visit to Oxonville. Her body had been found on a grass verge in fields outside the town and her murderer apprehended swiftly, found guilty and imprisoned. He committed suicide in prison five years later.

A checking of the dates suggested that Peter had moved away from Oxonville a few months prior to her murder and a few months before his move to Foggy Love Bottom. He shook his head in disbelief. He was shaken to the core. How could he not know? How could he not have heard? He grudgingly acknowledged it was at a time before smartphones provided news-in-hand from a multitude of sources. He wouldn't have reviewed local papers nor watched television news at a time of his own personal upheaval. His family and friends were not really aware of his Spanish friend, so there was no reason for him to hear on the grapevine.

'You knew about me, Jennie. Why didn't someone, the police or you try to contact me?'

'Initially it had nothing to do with you. The family and I did not want to give your name to the police (not that we had your full name) in case it undermined the prosecution of her killer. We wanted to protect her memory. The defence might have used you as an excuse, a provocation. The less anybody knew about you, the better. It was important that he was put away for good.'

'But what about afterwards?'

'We did try to reach you. A reporter on the case claimed that you (or someone like you) had made contact with him and he had passed over his details to you. We guessed it was you. Apparently, you said you would be in touch, but you never followed up. He said he tried to find you but hit a brick wall, couldn't track you down and the police weren't interested in complicating any appeal by her convicted murderer. To them it was a straightforward case of ex-partner abuse. In time, we eventually assumed you wanted your own space to grieve. You would get in touch with me or the family if and when the time was right.'

'I did not know. I did not know,' he said shaking his head in disbelief. 'This can't be true. I saw her twice this week getting on the bus. I spoke to her.'

Where was the clarity of the fog when he needed it? All he felt was Jennie's reassuring hand on his arm. 'It was foggy, perhaps you mistook this woman for Fabiana.'

'What was Fabiana doing here in Oxonville anyway?' he asked turning to Jennie.

She came over for a long weekend and spent it here with me. She wouldn't tell me why explicitly. She just said she had unfinished business, here in Oxonville. It obviously upset her ex-partner, he must have suspected something, and he followed her here. She was last seen boarding a bus on the High Street. She was never to be seen alive again.'

Jennie was obviously upset. It had been fifteen difficult years for her. He suspected that in fifteen years he might well feel no less bereft than she did right now. After regaining a degree of composure, she turned to him and fixed him with a purposeful look.

'She was carrying one folded piece of paper. A letter. Your letter to her. A sympathetic detective kept it off the radar and passed it to us once everything was done. It was buried with her.'

'Where is she buried?

'In Spain. In her hometown, by the sea.'

'Was she coming to see me?' Peter asked tentatively.

Jennie raised her eyebrows hoping it would be enough of an answer.

'But why?'

'Why do you think?' Jennie replied.

He left. Felt sick. And headed home. He didn't know if he wished for the return of the fog or not. Yet he had felt happier, more vital in that fog than he had done for years. Did happiness return for other people? Did peace return to those Crimean and Boer war widows? Had the fog returned for his benefit? Should he move away? To a place far away from the prospect of fog? If he stayed in Foggy Love Bottom would he become like Mr Goodban? Would he now forever be waiting for the return of the fog? Were the events of the last few days meant to be closure, for him? For her?

– IX – Iberian Haze

In early spring of the following year, Peter rose early from his small family-run hotel near Sitges in Catalonia, Spain, and walked along the quiet seaside village's street to the edge of town. Following the scribbles the hotel owner had made on the tourist map he climbed an incline on a well-kept track to a graveyard on a cliff top overlooking the sea. It was cold. The sun had risen and hung over the sea piercing the morning mist. After a little bit of hunting he found Fabiana's headstone and laid some flowers on her grave.

'Thank you,' he whispered. 'And sorry.'

It was funny to think that, on a massive ball of cooling rock called earth floating in empty nothingness, there was a patch of disturbed soil, eight foot by three foot, that would probably define his own three score years and ten. Nobody would know that within that patch of soil, hidden as it was from the heavens, was part of him. A part of his own existence. It was ironic to think that his own resting place would be of no consequence to him. Anybody wishing to learn something about him would have to visit this small patch of earth on a cliff top overlooking the sea. A patch of earth with buried treasure. Lying here beneath this soil were two lifetimes, not one. It was a sacred place where his love would rest until the universe would be no more.

He raised his eyes and gazed out to sea. Squinting in the brightness it seemed as if the sea and sky had become one. There was no horizon. There was a blurring of the line between earth and heaven. He smiled. Fog – a silent witness, a quiet facilitator.

Never again would he be irked by the prospect of clammy air. As he watched the moist air roll and swirl far out at sea, he knew he would be ready for when it wished to return and make landfall once again. Whether he would live out his days in Foggy Love Bottom, he did not know. There might come a time when he would move on, but, looking at the fog roll out at sea, he knew that, for the time being, he would remain in the village and take a keener interest in local events when the autumnal nights closed in. In fact, he could picture himself later that year standing to attention at his garden gate in the early hours, bouquet in hand just like his neighbour, Mr Goodban, listening out for the light step of visitor or the rumble of an approaching bus in the hope of spending a few fleeting moments in the company of an old and dear friend.

DAVID O ZEUS

Scary Morning in the Woods

– I – Wow, I'm famous

Wow, I didn't think things could move so quickly. Just a short while ago I was ignored by grown-ups, but now everybody knows me. I'm not saying I'm famous, I just happened to be in the right place at the right time. I was there to witness the two creatures from the woods tear Nick, Jonny and Sam's bodies apart that scary afternoon in the garden (my garden). When my mother heard me say this (that I was in the right place at the right time) to Nick's younger brother at Nick's funeral she whispered really angrily (but loud enough for other grown-ups to hear) that I was not in the 'right' place nor at the 'right' time. She said I was in the wrong place at the wrong time. But I quietly begged to differ. (Quietly enough for her not to hear.) It was Nick, Jonny and Sam who were in the wrong place at the wrong time; it was me who was in the right place at the right time to witness it. After all, if I had been in someone else's house or garden I would have been in the wrong place. I wouldn't have seen anything. And if the creatures had come when I was at school, then it would have been the wrong time, because I wouldn't have been glued to the conservatory's windows watching the gory showdown (between men and creatures from the woods) but at my school desk writing about the war we were supposed to be fighting with other men. It seems bizarre – go to school and learn about all the heroics the men are doing in faraway lands, but don't watch the attempts to be heroic going on in your own back garden!

I kept all this to myself, of course, I wasn't nearly twelve for nothing. I had learnt some things. I don't know if it is a woman-thing or a mother-thing, but women (or a mother) can scowl in a way no man can. Or, in a way that I have never seen a man scowl. Not like the man I know best – my dad has never scowled. Not at me. When I try to imagine my dad scowling it doesn't really work. It would be just sad. No, my dad just rolls his eyes and sighs. Like he is tired and almost giving up. I don't know. Sometimes my mum and dad have even done it together. It is very rare, but it does happen. When it does there is the danger you can get trapped in a circle of scowl, eye roll and sigh. There was one occasion when the tortoise was asleep and wouldn't wake up. So I buried it and told my dad it had died. He seemed confused at the time, but let it go saying, don't tell your mum she'll be upset. When my mum asked what had happened to the tortoise, I looked at my dad who said it had escaped. Now it was my mum's turn to look confused. 'A tortoise escaping?' she muttered looking at my dad. Helping my dad out, I explained that it had escaped then died so it wouldn't be coming back. (This all happened before the scary afternoon in the garden, so I was much younger. If I had been smarter I might have said it escaped then was chased into the woods and eaten by the creatures.) Anyway, my mum went a bit quiet and thoughtful – you could tell by her face. It wasn't a scowl at this stage, more like the furrowing of the brow when she asked my dad, 'are you sure it wasn't going into hyper-sleep?'

I didn't know what hyper-sleep was and judging by the look on my dad's face, he didn't know either, but he fudged it (quite well, I thought) and replied, 'No' with a slight twitch and a shrug.

Apparently scientists are working on hyper-sleep which is sleeping for a long time. (Not like the local policeman who, as my uncle says, is forever asleep on the job.) I don't understand it. What's the point in living for a hundred years if you are asleep for most of it? Only the very rich people want to do it. I don't know why. Do they think that when they wake up people will be pleased to see them? Normally people are pleased to see them only because they have money. The danger would be their money would either be stolen when they were asleep or would all be spent keeping them asleep. I still really struggle with the 'logic' of adults.

My mum turned to me and said, with a slight scowl, 'Why didn't you tell me it had died?'

'Because you would have been upset and wouldn't have been able to cook dinner,' I replied.

That was when she delivered her first proper scowl which I thought was unfair. My dad wasn't going to get away with it that easily.

'That's what dad said,' I added.

I don't know what came first: the second bigger scowl (directed at my dad) or my dad rolling his eyes and sighing. After that things moved swiftly. It was quite bizarre. Scowl, eye roll, all in quick succession and it became a circular motion. Much like a whirlpool. Anybody watching who was prone to dizzy spells would have probably fallen over. Every time my mum or dad said something to break the circle, it seemed to make the circle move faster.

My dad tried loads:

'Relax' which actually did the exact opposite.

'You're a great cook' which I thought was a good line (because it is half-true and she tries so hard) and could work, but it didn't. I don't know why it didn't and, again, judging by the look on his face, nor did my dad, because he rolled his eyes and sighed.

But my mum tried saying things which only resulted in my dad rolling his eyes and sighing (sometimes he closed his eyes and just breathed). She said:

'Perhaps paying more attention to what your son is doing might be of benefit to him,' she said (with a scowl of course).

On one level I didn't understand this. It was the tortoise that had died. Not me. I was fine. Perhaps she meant – if he had paid more attention to the tortoise it would have been of benefit to him (it – the tortoise). That would have made sense. But, I suppose, her comment on another level was sensible, even 'logical'. (Logical in the sense that it was compatible with grown-up logic). How could I not benefit from a dad who paid more attention to me? But I didn't need much attention – I was nearly a man.

So, for this reason, I nodded (quite vigorously) in support of my mother, or what I thought was supportive of my mother because for some reason she then scowled at me. What had I done? I had just agreed with her.

Anyone, it went on. It was like being trapped in a vortex. (A vortex – I had to check this at school – is a mathematical term used to describe circular motion to impending doom.) Anyway, it was like a vortex of death or hell, whichever is worse.

Sometimes the scowl or eye roll would happen just as the other had started speaking when it was impossible to know what they were going to say. I am a little ashamed to say that by the end of the evening I had started to roll my eyes and sigh too. Perhaps because I was a boy. My younger sister was also nearby, she just looked confused. But given time, perhaps her confusion would become a scowl (or at least when my dad opened his mouth).

– II – A Big Meeting

Truth be said, sometimes my parents are a pair of clowns. I wouldn't say it to their faces. Not yet anyway. I'd wait for the right moment. There would be the danger they would punish me. Parents like to think they are smart and in many ways they are, but how do you outsmart a smart parent? By being smarter. That is one thing I have learnt. At the moment (my age – still technically eleven, remember) I have to work hard at being smarter, but I think I will get smarter as I grow older. So I might save the "you're a pair of clowns" quip for a few years in the future. Put it 'in the bank', if you like and withdraw and deliver it some rainy day.

Anyway, they think they would punish me in a way that would make me regret what I have done. For instance, they might prevent me from going to see a projection picture story with my friends or refusing me ice-cream on a hot Sunday. But the way you would outsmart a parent would be to call them a pair of clowns when you know there is nothing on at the projection picture story house that you want to see or when you are bored with ice-cream. If you are really clever (I suspect this will be when I am well past twelve in my case) I would even plan the clown-quip by saying a few days before that I wanted to go and see a projection picture story on Sunday afternoon after the Sunday lunch and pudding and ice-cream. The trouble with the planning and the delivery of the quip is that sometimes it would not time well with the reason to call them clowns. Plan too much and madness follows. It is a dilemma that I am struggling with in my brain in quiet times.

I was thinking about this ('plan too much and madness follows') when I attended the meeting for the trip in the woods. After the scary afternoon in the garden there had been a great furore in the neighborhood and the town. Everybody was complaining and the mayor was being criticised for not doing his job. (Which was no different when he was being criticised for doing his job.) 'Why aren't you protecting us, you have to do something. You have to keep our children safe. You need to address the problem of the creatures in the woods. What are you going to do? Do your job!' and many more questions and complaints.

Anyway, a big meeting was planned late that afternoon. Someone from the mayor's office came to our house and I heard him in the hallway whispering urgently to my mum and dad. I suspected it was about me and the scary afternoon in the garden. I was trying to be as quiet as I could as I sat at the top of the stairs listening just round the corner out of sight. I had to be careful because there were creaky floorboards at the top of the stairs. So I lowered myself down into a sitting position carefully. The urgent discussion went on longer than I had thought. I heard things like: 'he has to appear, he is the only one who saw what happened; he is too young; what can he add to the discussion; he is traumatised by the experience; not from what I have heard, he has been drawing pictures of the scene and promised his school friends he would write it up in full detail and sell copies for a shilling a piece'. (This annoyed me. I don't know what the man from the mayor's office knew, but he should have asked me first. I know it would have annoyed my mum for some reason and I hadn't agreed the pricing structure anyway.)

That said, the discussion went on for a long time. The trouble was I had been drinking a lot of the new fizzy drink that morning. My body wasn't used to it. The fizzy bubbles were filling my stomach and gas was trying to escape from me at both ends. I would normally move away so I could release the pressure in a secluded part of house (or outside in the garden if I were ever allowed to go in the garden again). 'Remove yourself from company,' my mum used to say which wasn't fair, I thought, because I knew my mum also had to manage her own gas, but she was well-practised and could manage silent and controlled releases. My dad less so, but, fair play, he did remove himself to another room, but I still heard it. My little sister also would succumb to biology, often much to her own surprise, but my mum never said anything to her, partly because my sister usually burst into tears when she let go a pop.

Anyway, that moment at the top of the stairs was a catalogue of errors – a perfect storm.

I tried to adjust my sitting position gently – being careful to make sure the floorboard didn't creak – to allow a mother-type passing of gas, but as I moved, the floorboard did creak which broke my concentration on controlling the pop. My body relaxed to avoid further creaking, but this only resulted in a short but effective burst of bottom-pops along with lots of floorboard creaking. I instinctively tried to adjust my position to block further explosions which only resulted in a massive floorboard creak. This shocked even me and, now totally distracted, gas travelled the other way culminating in noteworthy bouche-burp. I had given my position away. All three adults looked up at the top of the stairs, I peeked around the corner to see them not sure which sound had caught their attention. Their conversation was over as all three stared at me. The man from the mayor's office and my dad just looked confused. My mum's scowl was either from annoyance or embarrassment. I'm not sure. Perhaps both. Normally when she looked like that she would say – 'I can't take you anywhere'. She didn't say that this time, I suppose because I was at the top of the stairs at home.

– III – Town Hall: Part One

Later that afternoon I found myself heading into town to attend the meeting. Apparently the meeting had started early that morning and was still going on. We arrived as it was getting dark. My mum had dressed me in my best clothes (for her benefit or for mine, I don't know). She muttered it would distract people from the noises coming out of me. She had hidden all the fizzy drinks that morning. Not that it did much good, my nerves at the thought of being in front of a crowd of logical grown-ups had the same effect as the fizzy drinks. In those six hours I had had to practise being a woman more than I had ever done so in my life. Gosh, it must be hard being a woman every day.

Before we entered the town hall building for the meeting my mother grabbed me by the arm and took me to one side. My dad stood behind her in a show of support (for her, I think).

'If they ask you questions, always be polite and honest,' my mum said, sternly. 'This is polite society.'

'What do you mean?'

'You know what polite means.'

'Yes, but what does polite mean in "polite society"?' I said, genuinely confused. (It had been one of the things bothering me in recent times.)

'I don't understand,' my mum said, looking confused.

For a terrifying moment I consciously had to stop rolling my eyes – terrifying because I knew it would annoy my mum but also terrifying because I thought I was turning into my dad. I don't mind turning into my dad at some point, but I thought that would be in a hundred years. I want to turn into myself first because I thought it was a pretty interesting prospect (not only for me, but for others too).

Anyway, back to my mum's confusion.

I'm surprised she didn't understand. Politeness is all about avoiding the truth (that is what I had observed), so to tell the truth, be honest, in a society that avoids the truth seemed to be a bit weird. Or is it in fact ironic (a new word I had to look up and think about for a long time about when to use it)?

'What will you say when they ask about what happened?' my mum said.

'I will tell them Johnny's insides were torn open, Sam was bitten to death and Nick was a fool to prod the creature with a fork and get his head ripped off. All three of them didn't have a hope of surviving; the creatures from the woods were the most effective killing machines I have ever seen.'

A wave of tiredness swept across my mother's face (almost as if she couldn't manage a scowl). A blankness remained as if she didn't understand what she had given birth to.

'I'm a boy wanting to tell the truth,' I said filling the silence.

'Now what would you say if you wanted to be polite?' she said through gritted teeth.

I focused my eyes on her eyes. My eyes were twitching – almost begging to roll backwards and upwards. I sighed.

'They were brave. It was scary. It was horrible,' I moaned.

'And?'

'And there was a hell of a lot of blood. It was spurting...'

Her eyes narrowed.

'But I didn't hear anything,' I mumbled, sad that life as a grown-up was probably going to be so depressingly polite.

She stood upright, put her hands on her hips in such a way that suggested she had made a decision.

'Best to say nothing, I think,' she said firmly.

'Truth hurts,' I said. 'They need to get used to that.'

'Some people have been hurt enough,' she said quietly.

'But truth doesn't kill.'

(I don't know where that line came from, but it felt like a pretty grown-up response and accurate, which is ironic, because I don't think a grown-up would have said it.)

'Polite society is destined for a bloody death,' I muttered.

'And you'd like that wouldn't you?' she snapped (a little).

'As long as I had a ringside seat,' I snapped back (quietly, in a murmuring sort of way).

And we left it at that. For about ten seconds.

I still love my mother and always will, but sometimes it is so much work, even stressful, listening to her and trying to abide by her rules. There should be a movement, a support group for boys with mothers. Jelly Gosh, sometimes I wish I was an orphan.

'We don't say that in polite society.'

'What? The truth? Is it polite to lie?'

'No, but it is polite to suppress certain instincts,' said mother.

'Suppress the instinct for truth?'

'Is there anything called a 'truth society' dad?' I asked, looking at dad trying to bring him into the conversation.

'Never heard of it,' he mumbled, shrugging.

'It is like 'polite society' but deals with the truth,' I said.

My dad just looked confused then looked upwards at the sky. (There was nothing up there.)

'Ask your mum', he mumbled.

'Is there anything called a 'truth society' mum?'

'Your father will explain.'

This is why it is sometimes important to have a conversation when both parents are present otherwise you just end up going in circles. Sometimes I just want to cry out: 'I'm eleven, I don't have time for this, I do want to get on with my life.'

That said, sometimes I do have conversations and the same thing happens. I ask a question, my mum doesn't answer and tells me to ask my dad; I ask my dad he says the same thing – ask your mum. But they're sitting at the same table. Do they think I'm stupid? Or are they stupid and I have evolved beyond them and I can see their stupidity but they can't?

(Anyway, if anybody reading this knows if there is such a thing as a "truth society" (and if it can exist at the same time as a "polite society"), please write to me at my parents' house. I will probably live there for a few more years.)

I had never been in the town hall before. I'm not sure why. It never appealed I suppose. Why would any young boy with his whole life ahead of him want to go into a dreary building where people gather and talk in a dreary way. I wasn't disappointed. The building was indeed pretty dreary and dark. Weak light came from old lamps hanging from the ceilings and from wall lights illuminating paintings of dead people, most of them fat and all of them pretty ugly. I do wonder why places like town halls have pictures of dead people, looking into the distance and pretty lifeless. I know they contributed to the town and community when they were alive, but why not have pictures of living people? Or even pictures of young boys (like me) and young girls (like my sister) who are going to shape the future? We should be celebrated, not the dead. Imagine having pictures of Sam, Nick and Johnny on the walls, it would still be pretty depressing (even though they weren't fat). If I had my way I would ban dead people from the walls of the town. That's not to say Sam, Nick and Johnny shouldn't be remembered, but any picture should show how they died; it should be a battle scene, with pitchfork, stick and the creatures tearing at their bodies. That would be an interesting picture to look at. It could be titled, 'the butchering at no.12'.

Failing that, they should hang pictures of young people like me and my sister – we are not fat and grown-ups keep telling us we're cute. I hate it, grown-ups grabbing my cheek and giving it a wiggle or patting my head, stroking my hair and laughing. It's usually the women who do it. I think it is a form of control. Trying to impose a hierarchy when boys are too young to know better, but I am old enough to know. Mark my words, there will come a time when no woman will grab my cheeks or stroke me.

Everybody sat around the tables in the big hall. I counted – there were 42 people around the table in the shape of a horseshoe. In the middle (at the top) were the fattest and oldest. There was a slimmer man but he looked as if he hated food – his face was pinched and there was a snarl, almost as if the thought that was in his head was distasteful. (Perhaps the thought was dinner.)

Around the tables were rows and rows of normal people (who had not pursued power) grouped and leaning against walls and pillars and chatting quietly. The whole hall was full of normal people – people who did most of the living in the town and never had any ambition to have pictures of themselves hanging on the walls when they were dead. They seemed tense, though. The mayor and other elected officials sat and also seemed tense, but I think it was more about having the audience. Most people ignored the elected officials. Now that they were being watched and had to make decisions, they seemed lost – just like Gary Murphy before he took a spelling test and I knew he hadn't done his homework.

My dad kept a firm grip on my shoulder.

The fat mayor banged his hammer on the table and asked people to quiet down. The quietness (or something) pleased him.

He welcomed people to the meeting and thanked them for coming to the final session of the day. He read out a list of things he wanted to discuss. Suddenly, as I was thinking about other things, I suddenly heard someone shout out something from the crowd. The mayor waved and nodded:

'Yes, we will be talking to the boy, perhaps at the time when we have reached a decision on what to do.'

Some people disagreed, shouting they wanted to know now, but the mayor hadn't been elected for people to tell him what to do. He was in charge, that was the most important thing.

It went on for hours. And I mean hours. The first part was trying to agree what had happened. How had the creatures travelled out of the woods and reached the back gardens without anyone sounding the alarm? Were there supposed to be lookouts? Were there supposed to be plans? First these questions were general and directed to the group. Later my dad told me these questions were 'rhetorical' which meant it was a question someone asks oneself and is not supposed to be answered. I agreed that if that was the correct word, then it was accurate, because nobody answered it. And what is the point of asking yourself a question that is not supposed to be, or expected to be, answered? What's the point? It sounds like a cop-out. Anyway, soon the rhetorical questions were dropped and the questions were directed to the mayor who began to look flustered. I realised the group were beginning to question why he had not put in place plans to deal with the creatures. He had let things slip.

As I've said, he was fat. And one thing I have noticed is that fat people are slow. Slow to move. There was this guy at school – and his name was actually Guy – who was known as the 'fat guy'. In fact he was quite a nice bloke but I didn't realise how someone could get so fat. Some boys were a bit mean to him and asked him how he got so fat. He said he was born big-boned, but once I was chatting to him quietly and he said that he wasn't big-boned, he just liked to eat. He ate when he was happy and he ate when he was sad. There were also a few fat girls at school too. I never asked why they were fat but wondered if it was because they were happy or sad. But one thing I did notice, was that they too said it was because they were big-boned. At that moment I wondered whether the idea of polite society was invented for fat people.

Anyway, the fat mayor was probably used to working in this polite society, but things had changed. Three boys were dead and the parents were having none of it. So, not only was he not in a polite situation, but he was slow to change. This left a vacuum and anger filled it. He was feeling pressure so quickly started making excuses and even started to blame others. And who did he blame? Sam, Nick and Johnny, of course. They were not there to defend themselves. Trouble was their mothers were. It wasn't pretty.

The discussion soon moved on to what should be done. At first it was slow, because I think the committee was used to 'talking about things' and discussing what to do. Then the 'what-to-do' would be written up in an essay saying the committee had discussed what-to-do and what-to-do was going to be discussed again at the next meeting once the cost of what-had-to-be-done had been examined. My dad told me to watch the cakes and buns on the ends of the horseshoe table. Nobody touched them during the first half of the meeting even though there were a lot of buns. Nobody wanted to be first, I suppose. My dad shook his head in disgust. They were expensive buns and pastries.

'That's where the money goes,' my dad muttered to the man next to him.

'Committees are expensive to run,' the man replied. 'You can't expect indecision to cost nothing.'

My dad nodded.

The man next door then muttered, 'but I'm here and a honorary committee member' and he stepped through the crowd leaned forward and grabbed a bun.

'Hey, they are for the committee members,' said some of the committee members.

'I'm here and getting hungry because you are taking too long. Besides, you get expensive buns every week.'

And with that suddenly everybody else starting stepping forward and in the time it took Sam's insides to be opened up, the plates were cleared. The committee members hadn't had any. They looked shocked.

The mayor said: 'that's not proper'.

'I'll tell you what's proper,' the first bun-muncher said, 'get on with a decision and we can all go home and eat. If you wanted a bun, then grab one and eat. Don't keep thinking about yourselves and how it will look. We all know you like buns. Especially you, Mr Mayor. Besides, you don't want indigestion if you are going to lead this group of councilors out into the woods tomorrow.'

That shut the mayor up. He looked shocked and hungry. And then everybody started shouting.

There were two groups of women and there were two groups of men, but all mixed up. One group of women was saying to the men: just go into the woods, hunt the creatures and kill them. One group of men said: we need to plan and think. Let's sit down. Another group of women said the creatures are dangerous, I'm not putting my husband or son in harm's way. The second group of men said, let's just go out into the woods now.

After much thought I think that it all came down to 'love'. The women who said don't go to the woods were thinking of their loved ones (most probably their sons – like Johnny, Nick and Sam); the men who didn't want to go to the woods (who wanted to plan) loved their lives as they were (why disturb the peace?); the men who wanted to go to the woods wanted to be loved (by the women – either type of woman would do most probably); and finally the women who did want the men to go to the woods did so because they were grumpy and had given up on love.

– IV – Town Hall: Part Two: I speak!

Then my mum turned up with sandwiches. She had disappeared earlier (before the bun fight) knowing people would be hungry. It was early evening now and there was a short break to eat. I could see my mum and dad talking quietly. My mum looked worried. I wondered – is dad going to go into the woods? The meeting started again, by which time people had seen me and were getting impatient.

'Let's hear from the boy,' someone cried out.

'Yes, let's hear from the boy,' shouted another.

'Yeah, he's the only one who saw what happened.'

'Okay,' said the fat mayor and motioned towards me.

Now lots of things happened at the same time but I cannot describe them quickly. So as I describe them, remember that they were all happening at roundabout the same time. They also include thoughts and feelings. There are quite a few thoughts, but not too many feelings because I'm not a girl. (God knows how long this story would be if it were written by a girl.)

Firstly, the moment the mayor motioned me over it seemed as if the whole world stopped. Everybody, and I mean everybody, turned and looked at me. That has never happened to me before. Let me tell you, it is weird. Maybe one hundred and fifty or two hundred people, turned and looked. And they were not looking at me like I was in a school play or I had scored some points in a ball game. They looked at me as if they could learn something from me. I was an expert. They were looking for answers and they were looking at me.

Secondly, I felt my mother, who was standing behind me, grip my shoulders preventing me from even thinking of moving. Through her grip I could feel that her own body was rigid. My dad, who was standing beside me, was in shock. I glanced up at him and all he was doing was looking forward his eyes wider than usual (even when listening to mum).

I took a few steps forward. There was resistance from my mother, but sometimes you have to step forward to be a man. But then (from the corner of my eye) I saw my father rest his hand on my mother's forearm. I waited for a moment for the message from dad to mum be processed and then I felt her grip lessen. Taking my cue I stepped forward and broke free of the grip of womanhood. Feeling my shoulders free at last I had to physically and mentally stop myself punching the air with both fists. But in that instant I knew in a predictive sort of way that the 'boy who saw' punching the air as if he had indeed scored winning points in a ball game would send all the wrong signals. I don't know where this predictive sense came from, one thing I definitely knew was that it was an adult thing – an adult response – and was possibly the beginning of my expression as a man in society.

I stepped forward to the edge of the horseshoe. All eyes remained on me. Although my mother's hands were not on me, I felt her presence. That is where she wanted me to stop. So I did. But it was not enough. I was the star witness at this trial of the killer creatures of Johnny, Sam and Nick. They needed to know what had happened from the horse's mouth. (I don't know where this saying comes from, horses don't speak, but I don't know of any other speaking animal.) I stepped forward and moved directly into the centre of the horseshoe table and directly in front of the mayor. I was in the front of everybody. I hadn't known it at the time, but there was a spotlight right in the middle of the ceiling above the horseshoe meeting table. I was now right under that light.

Everybody was quiet.

'Tell us what happened,' said the mayor in a hushed tone.

Although my mother was now standing in the shadows, I still felt her presence and remembered her words.

'In your own words,' continued the mayor.

"In your own words" meant not my mother's words – that is how I took it. It was a relief. I took a deep breath.

'Blood, lots of it. It was incredible. The most amazing thing I have ever seen. The creatures are killing machines…..'

And so I started the story and explained everything in detail. Nothing interrupted me, not even the little muffled cries of women, or the muffled sound of men being sick. I've never made a woman cry before or made a man throw up, I suppose it was yet another milestone of growing up that I experienced that day.

I know my mother would have been – in her words – 'aghast', but I knew it was the one and only opportunity I would have to tell it. I've heard grown-ups (especially really old, decrepit grown-ups) talk about not having regrets. I knew in that moment I was not going to regret not telling it (the story of the scary afternoon in the garden) as it was. It was oddly satisfying. Grown men might have felt sick, but I felt proud.

Eventually my story came to and end and I had said everything I could. I ended on a personal note:

'I've never seen actual human guts before. It was amazing. Truly. And scary. But I didn't scream.'

There was silence in the hall. Nobody said anything. While I had been talking I had not really concentrated on what people were doing or looking like because I was so engrossed in telling my story. Now that I had stopped I started to look at them. Lots of people looked pale.

'Well,' the mayor said, 'er, thank you.'

I smiled and nodded.

Suddenly the hall erupted in noise. Through the hum I heard people shout – so what are we going to do? Who is going to go? People seemed unhappy with the fat mayor.

'We want a leader. Where is our leadership? Where is your courage?'

I could see that people were suggesting that the fat mayor should lead any group into the woods. He was shaking his head and laughing awkwardly as if people were making a joke, but they weren't. They really did want to the mayor to go, perhaps to teach him a lesson – that leadership should be by example. I was also looking at the council members. I guessed that they were torn, some would want to be rid of the mayor, others feared that they too might get nominated to lead the group into the woods and hunt the creatures.

Then I heard a voice.

'Maybe the boy should lead us. He's the brave one.'

'Is the boy going to go into the woods?' said another.

I didn't actually hear my mother scream, but before she did I felt a welling up inside and took a step forward. 'Yes, I will go into the woods. I know what the creatures looked like.'

'You don't know what you're doing,' said one council member – a podgy woman.

'I'm the one person who does know what I'm doing,' I said.

'Who's going with me?' I said.

Suddenly the hall fell silent.

A few seconds passed and then I felt two hands on my shoulders. It was my mother.

'Wait,' the mayor said. 'Wait, please.'

My mother halted. I know she didn't want to (I could feel she was irritated), but that is what happens when you bring a truthful boy to a gathering of polite society.

'Do you think a group of men and women could catch and kill these creatures?' asked the mayor.

I paused and thought. I even soaked up the moment, then stopped myself in case I started to develop a liking for political ambition. Perhaps that's how the fat mayor had started on his journey – somebody had asked him a question as a child and then stupidly let him speak. I found myself conflicted. Anyway, the answer was clear to me:

'Yes, I think so, if they are well organised, well-led and brave.'

I knew I was in trouble with my mum. I also knew my mum didn't like the mayor and was annoyed that I had been pressured into appearing at the council hearing. So I put the two thoughts together and did something for my mother:

'I think you would be a good leader, Mr Mayor,' I added.

The mayor looked like he had been shot by a gun.

Another chubby councillor jumped in. I guess he was a supporter of the mayor: 'And if it goes badly? When you told your story you sounded unsure whether you could out-run a creature. Do you think a grown man could out-run a creature?'

I turned and looked at the pale mayor. So did everybody else. We all knew he wouldn't be able to out-run a creature from the woods.

'When you say "grown man", how grown?' I replied, quietly looking at the mayor. There was a murmur around the hall. I didn't know if my mum would be pleased or angry.

'Someone needs to identify the creatures – the boy can identify the creatures,' a man cried out from the crowd.

I nodded, quite excited. I could feel my mum's eyes burn into my back.

'The boy shouldn't be punished,' a woman called out.

'It's not punishment, it's leadership. Better than anything we are getting from the mayor and his cronies,' another voice cried out.

Again, I nodded, unaware that people were watching me.

'I could identify the creature,' I said over the hubbub. 'The main bad one – black with golden feathers. And I think I could escape. It's only punishment if the creature thinks I am tasty then catches and eats me. But there is less meat on me and I'm not a slow runner. Just ask Gary Murphy.'

There was another murmur around the hall. This time the mayor looked like he had been slapped with a wet fish – annoyed, but not physically hurt.

'I think I'll be okay. I'm not scared,' I said. 'I'm not slow, I'm not fat and I'm not tasty.'

It was only after I said it (and after the gasps and laughter of the men and women) that I realised I was putting the mayor in the spotlight. It was if my mouth was moving faster than my brain. But why shouldn't I put the mayor in the spotlight? He wanted to be there at the centre of the horseshoe table. Again, if you bring a boy to meeting, expect to be told the truth – the mayor was fat and probably slow.

I paused and didn't say anything else because I got confused. I kept telling myself it was true but I was in polite society. (Can it be polite society if people are shouting with each other and disagreeing?) Anyway, just when I thought mum would be super angry, I felt her hands on my shoulders. She spun me round and she slipped her arm around my shoulders and whispered, 'that's my boy', then she marched me out without anyone noticing. There was a lull in the hubbub as I was being led out. It was this lull which made the following question asked by a nervous woman all the more memorable.

'Won't it provoke them?' she said.

The hall fell silent.

She continued. 'If the creatures are intelligent and expert hunters, as the boy says, won't they feel threatened and attack the town? Then what do we do?'

There was another nervous murmur, but this time louder. Then it died down and everyone turned to the mayor. He shook his head,

'They won't attack the town. If they're intelligent, they are not stupid.'

Grown-up logic, again. If ever anyone had an excuse for rolling their eyes, it was right then. My opinion of grown-ups – especially ambitious grown-ups – was deteriorating rapidly. And with that, I left the hall. Stepping out into the coolness of the dark night I was glad, but not encouraged. I had no desire to return to the town hall (unless it was to unveil one of my drawings of the scary afternoon attack). Fierce and nervous looking men stood guard outside the hall. Flame torches were burning on every street corner. My town was changing.

– V – Planning!

I ended the last story with my mum arriving at the garden and with me holding the severed head of Nick. That was only because my mum immediately ordered me to go to my room (which I did and wrote the story down). I thought everything had finished, but in some ways it was just beginning. After the events of that scary afternoon loads of men and women started coming around to our house. There was lots of noise and wailing. The men, I guessed, a bit like me, wanted to see the dead bodies, but were trying to be grown-up about it. The women cried (some wailed) and started hugging each other. Anyway, all the noise and crying soon got boring, but I noted that if anyone wanted to see the difference between a man and a woman get a creature to bite someone's head off and see how they react.

As I was falling asleep late that night after my appearance at the town hall meeting I heard the front door open and close as visitors came and went – just like the scary afternoon. There was lots of hushed discussion, but I was too tired to care and fell asleep. I woke early to much commotion going on downstairs. I could write lots about what I heard when I crept halfway down the stairs. My sister soon joined me. I told her to be quiet. I learnt that many people from the town were preparing for a trip to the woods that morning at ten o'clock (three hours later) and that my mum was disagreeing with my dad. They covered lots of topics – fear, bravery, danger, wisdom and carnage.

My mum always complains about dad not listening. I'm not sure she is correct though, because he does listen, but I now know that he just doesn't agree. But he is not fool enough to say he doesn't agree because that opens a whole different can of killer worms.

Mum was angry that apparently other people had wanted me to join a group going to the woods. My dad was saying the whole trip was off if I didn't show my face. (Nice, I thought, as long as a creature didn't tear it off.) Apparently my presence would shame council members and some men into attending. My dad explained to my mum that he had an arrangement with ten men that as soon as the group entered the woods he would bring me back. My dad explained that he had borrowed a horse. My mum said that was crazy. He explained that there had been talk of using motorised vehicles and tractors, but he thought a horse would move quicker and adapt to danger more easily. I think I am right in saying that my mum's anger got worse – sometimes it is difficult to tell. She started making all sorts of suggestions and it all got a bit confusing. I think that is one reason why the men didn't want any women on the trip, because in those circumstances (in the woods) literally listening to a woman and agreeing (or not agreeing) could mean certain death.

A few hours later I found myself crossing the field from the end of my garden towards the woods. It was several hundred yards between the wall at the end of my garden to the tree line and the slight incline was quite bumpy. Nothing used the field so nobody had flattened it properly. It was just a bit of wasteland. And it wasn't really a battlefield either. People were saying the battle would be in the woods which I thought was a bit crazy – the creatures would have the advantage and know the attack and escape routes between the trees. It would also mean that if we needed to make a hasty escape then it would be a bit slow as we weaved back out through the wood. Nevertheless, I was determined to be brave however scary it was going to be and it would give me amazing stories to tell.

I sat behind my dad as we rode up to the group gathering at the edge of the woods. I watched tractors and motorised vehicles also crossing the field to the same point in the tree line. The tractors were pulling trolleys with wooden trailers. Some of the trailers had a tarpaulin drawn over what looked like a cage. They seemed strange and flimsy. Why were they doing that?

Judging by his furrowed brow my dad obviously had the same thought. As we rode up to the tractor-trailer one of the canvas panels was pulled back to reveal eight men, holding pitchforks and sticks, sitting looking scared. My dad's face must have said it all.

'You have a problem?' asked one of the men (I'll call him 'angry-man' here).

My dad didn't say anything. He just let his eyes do the talking – and they said a lot. He just rolled his eyes like he does with mum (but not in an abstract way) as he reviewed the tent-like thing covering the back of the trailer. I wanted to do the same and I had my opportunity. No sooner had my dad finished his eye roll when angry-man looked angry and turned to me. So I just did the exact same thing – I let my eyes roll following the shape of the tent. I was afraid I would not do it as convincingly as my dad, so added another expression. I scrambled about in my head until I found an image of a shepherd's pie that had fallen off the table and was lying in a squishy mess and then imagined the fat mayor on his hands and knees eating it up. It was a look of disgust. I don't know what images other people use in their heads, but I reckon my mum has quite a few good ones. Anyway, by rolling my eyes and thinking of a fat man eating a meat pie off a dirty floor doesn't mean that I am turning into my dad, it means that I was just supporting him. That said, I had heard people say that children turn into their parents, but I think if a child is conscious and works hard to develop their own images in their own head, then their expressions will be different. So, at that moment, I promised I would never ask my mum what is in her head when she is listening to my dad.

Anyway, it worked. The angry-man in the trailer got angrier.

'The creatures won't see us, but you they'll see you a mile off.'

Then I realised he was talking about the tent – the tent thing was part of a camouflage disguise. But I thought it was stupid. The creatures have noses. They could smell fear. Besides, trying to make a speedy escape in a trailer from the woods across the bumpy field to the edge of the houses was risky. A horse would manage it so much better.

'Why is the boy here?' the angry-man in the trailer spat.

I think the man was trying to make my dad feel bad. I don't know what my dad felt and, I confess, I didn't really care, I was too excited and nervous. One thing I did know – the creatures didn't care who won any argument either.

'He's bait,' said another man (I'll call him 'bait-man') from behind as he was getting to his feet and joining the angry-man's side, 'for the mayor – to embarrass him into joining this madness.'

'Once the mayor's here, I'll take him back,' said my dad.

'But you might need help in the woods,' I said.

'Or luck. He survived the last attack,' muttered bait-man.

A third man ('stick-man') appeared carrying a long stick.

Other men arrived, some on foot, most in similar trailers pulled by tractors and other motorised vehicles. They carried sickles, pitchforks, long knives, axes. One had a crossbow. Another carried a musket.

Soon a tractor arrived carrying the fat mayor. He tried to climb down from his seat, but his spinning and puffing was taking too much time so he stayed put. He stood up and looked as if he was about to give a speech but I think his fear made his mind go blank.

'On your way,' said the mayor, waving to the woods.

Nobody moved. They just stood waiting.

Bait-man pointed at me. 'He's going into woods,' he shouted.

My dad then jabbed the horse with his heels and we trotted off in front of the mayor's vehicle towards the entrance to the woods. We're going into the woods? Mum would go crazy. But dad stopped at the very edge, turned the horse around then shuffled back a few steps giving space at the entrance for a vehicle to squeeze through. My dad turned and looked at the mayor expectantly. I did the same.

Other vehicles then backed up and formed a line behind the mayor's tractor. The men on foot did the same. We all sat or stood there for about a minute. The mayor was muttering to the driver of his tractor. Suddenly, its engine revved and it trundled forward, then passed us and disappeared into the woods.

– VI – Attack!

You know when something isn't right. It was my primitive sense. It was as if the woods themselves quietened down, like an audience in anticipation of a show. We had only gone about one hundred paces into the wood when we reached a clearing. We were never supposed to go into the woods but other tractors and trailers had waited for my dad to follow the first vehicles into the wood, but I could tell he was going to peel off when the going got tricky, but here we were almost immediately at a clearing.

I think everybody felt that something wasn't right. My dad seemed to make a decision. He steered the horse over to a big strong tree whose branches hung just within my reach when I stood on the back of a horse. He pushed me up, I grabbed the lowest branch and started climbing just at the right time. There was a sudden rustle of bushes and trees. Then, like stage curtains, the greenery parted and the play began. I was still climbing when it started – the running, the screaming. I don't know where my dad rode off to, but I couldn't see him. I settled into my seat. Again, it was perfect and ringside, I saw everything! I counted four creatures that attacked at once all from different directions. There was so much to look at. There was some manly shouting (that you could tell was scared), but then there was some girly shouting (mostly from the councillors I think). It was a good thing the women weren't there, they would have been very disappointed.

Some of the councillors tried to climb the trees like me. But they were fat. The mayor jumped off (or rather rolled off) his seat in the vehicle and made a dash for some heavy, thick bush that I suppose he thought would protect him. I say 'dash', it was like running on the spot and then a stumble quickly followed by a tumble forward. It was a great advert for not eating too much. After what seemed ten seconds he stumbled into the tree and wrapped his arms around the trunk in a hug. I knew there was a reason fat people would never survive in the wild. They only survive in towns.

There was one councillor who was trying to fight off the black and golden feathered creature; even the creature looked confused, tilting its head this way and that way wondering what the podgy man was doing waving his arms about. It was the same councillor who had said in the council meeting that he was not the right person to go. I think he was the deputy mayor (so close to being the full-fat mayor). Here he was meeting the real world. Why aren't leaders brought up in the real world, to fight beasts and dangerous creatures and to develop courage anymore? I think the deputy mayor came along to show he could be a leader. He knew he was less fat than the real mayor, so he probably thought he could run faster. It was still a risk going into the woods, but if he made it out he might make it to leader.

Before long I saw four of the creatures tucking into the insides of other men – they tended to be the fat slow ones, so it was probably meant to be. There was one large man who was trying to hit a creature with a stick. He was trying to be brave, but I wondered – what was the point? There would be no one around to witness it. No one would write about it. (Unless I did. Would it be left to me to write everything down again? I hadn't finished writing up the story about the scary afternoon in the garden. And I have other things on my plate – I'm still at school. Do they know how much homework Mrs Austin gives me? He shouldn't assume I would do it. People have lives.)

The creature bit his arm as he tried to hit it with stick, but it wiggled its head trying to shake the arm free from his body. I could tell it was working because the man was off his feet, flailing about and screaming. The creature must have had a good grip. Not that I was surprised. Its teeth were pretty spectacular.

It was then that I saw the red-backed creature (who had visited my garden) attack another councillor. I say 'attack' it was more like a quizzical stroll up to the stationary man.

Meanwhile the mayor was lying in the bracken – playing dead, I think. Trouble was, because he was fat and unfit his chest was rising and falling as he breathed heavily. A creature strolled over and bent over him looked quizzically at the heaving lump of lunch on the ground. Then with a sudden movement it grabbed at the body a few times with its talons, moving it around. Then as the mayor struggled and tried to wriggle away, the creature grabbed the mayor head in its jaws and started to chomp away, shaking its ugly head this way and that, trying to bite the mayor's head off. I saw everything in slow motion although it probably happened pretty quickly. The creature bit off the head and for a moment the mayor's head was in its jaws but turned looking at me (still sat high in a tree twenty yards away). It was funny, I was trying to determine the look on the mayor's face – it was a look of surprise. I wondered was the mayor still conscious? Was it a genuine look of surprise – like, 'what is happening to me? Can this really be happening? Why is my head in the jaws of a creature from the woods? Will I survive?'

I could tell he wasn't going to survive – his body now had no head. I had to stop myself from shouting 'no, you're going to die. It's bitten your head off.' But I didn't, partly because it was so noisy (which was to be expected) and no one would hear me because all the creatures were hissing and gurgling and all the men were screaming like they never intended to impress a woman again.

How long does a severed head take to 'die'? What was the last thing the mayor ever saw? Was it the image of a boy sitting in a tree watching a head about to disappear down the throat of a creature from the woods?

Then what? Would the head roll down its throat and land in its stomach and all sorts of liquid stuff go up its nose? And into its eyes? And because the head was severed, there was no finger to wipe the eye? So the head would be thinking – I need to wipe my eye, but where is my hand? I need to blow the gunge out of my nose, but where is my breath? And wouldn't the head get stuck in the creature's throat? How does the creature know it can swallow the mayor's head whole?

Earlier in the summer, on a Sunday, I was eating a cooked Sunday lunch of meat and vegetables. I was looking hard at a Shire sprout as it sat on my plate. I had no intention of eating it whole but my mother must have seen me looking at the sprout on the plate and said: don't try and swallow it whole, you'll choke.

Why do mothers feel they have to watch their children eat? Is that how the 'tradition' (as she calls it) of family mealtimes developed? It's not a tradition, it's a form of control and oppression.

'No, I won't choke,' I replied.

Mum looked at my dad in a demanding sort of way.

He sighed and rolled his eyes without actually rolling his eyes (a trick I was keen to master too).

'You'll choke,' he muttered.

I shook my head. I didn't want to repeat myself.

Anyway, I gulped it down in one go, without cutting it up first. A moment later I was choking. Next minute my dad was slapping me hard on the back and it soon popped out and rolled across the table. Nothing was said – but in a shouty sort of way. (Which was, I thought, a 'sophisticated' woman's way of saying 'I told you so'. Sometimes I wished I was being brought up in a less sophisticated family, in a less sophisticated time.)

Back to the woods: the mayor's head slipped down the creature's throat (I think I saw a little bulge in the creature's throat as it moved down through its neck to its stomach). Looking at the creature's expression I thought – that's not a Shire sprout, that's a strawberry, a strawberry covered in creamy, half-melted ice-cream.

The creatures carried on. It was a picnic to them. I swear I saw one of them burp. I had to stop myself from shouting – don't rush, you'll choke.

It was curious, it made me think how creatures and people are different. Creatures don't have manners, they just woof food down, just like I do when mum is away for a weekend and dad just plonks some stuff down on the table in front of us. Even my dad woofs it down when my mum is away. Does this mean my mum, and even women in general, are a civilising force – *the* civilising force? I tried to imagine the creature being more evolved and civilised. They would eat slower. Or perhaps they evolved to be first class hunting and eating machines because their mums weren't around.

– VII – Carnage!

I sat there high in the branches of the tree gazing at what was going on around me. It must have been like this in olden times, great big battles. This would definitely end up as a picture hanging in the town hall. 'The Picnic in the Woods.' Would the artist show me, a boy, sitting in a tree watching it all? The sole survivor? I wasn't a survivor yet, but I thought there was a pretty good chance. Although I was quite high up the tree, one of the creatures spotted me, trotted over and tried to jump up at me. At one point it even tried to climb the tree. But its arms were rubbish and it struggled. They had probably never needed to learn how to scale a tree. They had dominated life on the forest floor for millions of years. No animal was going to chase them up a tree. Maybe boys were the perfect example of a survivor. They had the brains of a man, but the nimbleness to escape up trees when necessary. And, like the creatures, boys were not plagued by a grown-up's pride or ambition or stupidity. And they weren't politicians. None of my friends had ever wanted to be a politician. Boys were the ultimate survivors.

When the creature realised it could not reach me, it turned and trotted off to feast on some of the other men. Immediately afterwards my dad appeared on the horse below me. (For a moment I thought – was my dad waiting for the creature to decide not to eat his son before coming to get me?) He shouted at me to get down from the tree. We were going to escape the carnage and get back in the house, he said. He rarely shouts, but I could see he meant it from the strained look on his face. I had a look to see if there was danger out there in the wood clearing – there was danger, but it was looking the other way. The creatures (there might have been eight of them now) were tucking into the men. Some other men had been hiding and now some of the men were running back the way we had come and back to the field. I thought: good luck – even if you make it to the field, it is a big and then even if you cross it successfully you will reach the walls of the gardens (like mine) which are pretty high. My dad shouted again, I climbed down and jumped on the horse and wrapped my arms tightly around him.

Suddenly we took off and were galloping through the undergrowth and swerving in and out of the trees. We were also swerving around men from the town racing the same way back to the field. They were going so slowly or we were going so fast, I'm not sure. I will never forget the look of fear and desperation as they looked up at me as we raced past on the horse. I say that, but, in fact, I think I probably will forget it when more exciting and frightening things happen to me. I am sure I have seen frightened looks on people's faces and other things that I thought (at the time) 'I'll never forget that', but now, I can't remember anything. It has all been wiped clean by the excitement of the past week. That, or it has just become another usual memory. Much like Nick's head getting torn off last week in the garden. Now, it's just normal. So, now whenever I think of Sam, I think of him without a head. It's weird, to know someone for years with a head, then you see it being removed, and now he will be forever Nick without a head. As we raced past these desperate, running men, I knew they would not survive, so I wanted to give them one last happy image, so I waved and smiled.

We broke cover and my dad and I galloped across the field. I could tell the creatures were following. I could hear their throaty calls to each other – 'our breakfast is getting away!' I imagined them saying. It seemed to take forever to cross the field. I knew more men would die on the way, but how many?! My dad was riding the horse as fast as he could. It wasn't much of a running horse but I think the creatures had scared the horse too. Everybody and everything was scared that morning. It was incredible. My heart was beating so fast, I'm sure everybody's else's (and the horse's heart too) were beating fast. How could anybody live like this? This must have been how the ancients had lived especially when their society had descended into chaos and the giants attacked.

Before long my dad and I were getting closer to the wall at the end of my garden. We were closer to my garden than we were to the woods. But we weren't safe yet. What was annoying was that I knew lots of stuff was going on behind me but, because I had to cling so tightly to my dad, I could not look around. After a minute of heavy galloping we crossed the field and arrived at the wall at the end of my garden. Ever since I was young I had been accustomed to be grateful for such a high wall, but now it looked a bit daunting. My father pulled up the horse right beside the wall and told me to climb quickly to my feet and stand on the back of the horse – 'look lively' he said. There was a real panic and firmness in his voice. Unusual, I thought. Having lived with my dad living with my mum for twelve years I thought I had heard everything, but no, this was different. I tried to reach up to the top of the wall but I was a half-body short. My dad twisted, grabbed my ankles and hoisted me high above his head. I grabbed the top of the wall and pulled myself up just as he and the horse took a few steps away. I sat straddling the wall very out of breath – partly exertion, partly fear and partly out of excitement that I would now be able to turn around and look at all the action going on in the field.

It was the first time I could really take in what was happening. I realised I hadn't been able to see anything as we bumped up and down as we had been crossing the uneven ground of the field. Now I saw it all. It was carnage! This is what happens when polite society comes up against reality. It was raw power.

I wondered how we had got to this point. Men and women had developed a system to live what they call a 'superior existence' to creatures and animals. That suggested a control of other things and creatures, then it became 'polite' but it reached a point where it counted for little in the real world. Was 'polite' in fact 'patronising'? It was a word that I would have to look up and check. I remember it being used at the town hall meeting but I wasn't entirely sure what it meant. Someone said it about the mayor during the meeting, but I hadn't had a chance to look it up yet, I'd been so busy. It seemed relevant though. Whatever it meant, I knew that if people weren't careful, polite society could 'polite itself' out of existence.

I thought of Nick and Sam and Johnny. That was a spectacle. But here, now, less than a week later, there were 30 men being chomped on by five creatures with more creatures arriving at the scene. Now it was a picnic in a field.

For years people had lived in fear of the Overshot woods. The woods were on the fringes of the big forest that lay beyond it – Fan O'Gorn Forest. The story goes that people and creatures dwelt in the forest. People would go in the forest and never be seen again. There were also stories of people who had stumbled out of the forest looking stunned and lost. Whatever the truth, people were right to be fearful. It had a history. It had stories.

'Get back in the garden,' my dad shouted from the horse below. 'And get back inside and lock all the doors.'

I felt pretty safe sitting on top of the wall. The creature-carnage was going on about 100 yards away from me. I took one last glance. I saw a tractor towing the canvas caravan fast across the field. My dad was right. It looked useless, the tractor was zigging and zagging across the field bouncing on the uneven ground. I could see men bouncing around inside being thrown against the canvas walls. I said 'I could see' on purpose. Although I couldn't actually 'see' them getting thrown around, I knew there were men inside because two men were thrown out of the back of the trailer. The first was in fact 'angry-man'.

He bounced a few times and landed in a motionless heap. I wondered if he was playing dead. The second man who had fallen out of the moving caravan (I think it was bait-man) was holding a long stick like a spear, but it wasn't a spear because it didn't have a spike on the end. (I think he had stolen the stick from stick-man). It looked pretty useless if you asked me. I was interested because he was the man who had criticised my dad. I was curious – would he die a horrible death? As he climbed to his feet with the long stick in his hand a creature came trotting up to him. He jabbed a stick at the creature a few times. On the fourth or fifth jab the creature grabbed the stick in its mouth and yanked it sideways and out of his grasp. In doing so, it swung around and knocked angry-man off his feet as he raced back to the canvas trailer van. I've only seen something like that once before – in a circus. When clowns were playing window cleaners using a ladder. I never knew at the time but it was clowns imitating creatures.

'Get back in the house now!"

(It was my dad shouting still.) He looked angry. So I took one last look at the battlefield scene and tried to commit everything to memory. Perhaps I'll paint a picture. 'Picnic in the Woods' or 'Picnic in the Fields' – I didn't know which sounded better? I could paint both and they could hang in the town hall alongside the Picnic in the Garden (about Johnny, Nick and Sam during that scary afternoon in the garden). The pictures might even hang there for a hundred years!

And with that thought I slipped down the other side of the garden wall. I raced down the garden as fast as I could – partly because, I have to confess, I was a bit scared not knowing where the creatures were. In some ways it was more scary because I didn't know what was happening or where. They could cross the remaining part of the field very quickly, jump the wall and chase me down the garden. I estimated that I had about nine seconds, so as I ran I counted. I raced down to the end of the garden and the conservatory with its doubled-glass reinforced windows. I did it in eight seconds, although I wondered whether my counting might not be perfect, I might have raced through the seconds too quickly. But I ran also because I might be able to get a good view of the field from the upstairs window. It might help my memory for the painting.

As soon as I got inside the house my mum hugged me fiercely, then held me really firmly by the shoulders (it was the one thing that hurt that morning, but I knew that I shouldn't complain – I still had my head attached).

'Where's your father?' she shouted.

'He rode away.'

She didn't say anything.

'I think he'll be okay. The horse is bigger and I'm sure more tasty than him.'

'Where did he go?'

'I don't know,' I replied, honestly. I felt it was a bit unfair of her to ask – not a minute before my father was having a go at me, now my mum was. What is a boy to do? It was as if everything was my fault. I rolled my eyes a little.

My mum let me go. 'Go to your room and stay there.'

'Okay, good idea,' I said, glad that I would be able to see what was going on.

I passed my little sister on the way at the bottom of the stairs. She looked startled and nervous and excited. From the upstairs window I could see it all. With all the action in the field framed by the large wooden window frame, it was indeed a picture worthy of the town hall. There was no sound, a silent picture of death. But I could imagine the screaming. I reckon I could paint it pretty well.

'Is it carnage?' my little sister said, appearing at my side.

'Total.'

'Was it scary?'

I sighed and thought. I had to tell the truth. I had nothing to gain from saying otherwise. She was too young.

'Yes, a scary morning indeed,' I muttered.

'But they'll be back, won't they?' my sister said, looking both scared and excited. 'They'll have a taste for man-flesh now.'

I nodded. It was true.

I was exhausted. I watched the end of the show then sauntered downstairs and sat at the kitchen table. I was starving. I had hardly eaten anything for breakfast that morning because I had been so nervous and excited.

I looked at the kitchen table in front of me. It was clear. There was nothing on it. Not even the dinner mats.

'Where's lunch?' I asked my mum. 'I'm really hungry.'

She looked at me kind of bewildered.

I checked my watch. I was right. 'It's nearly 12 o'clock, mum. I've have a really busy and scary morning.'

She didn't respond.

'I'm really hungry. I'll eat anything,' I said, before adding, 'But no Shire sprouts.'

DOZ
DAVID O ZEUS

I'm Not Matt Damon

– I – Home Sweet Home

His name was Duncan Sheldrake. It always had been. And it always would be – for as long as he lived on planet earth.

'A pint of bitter shandy, two bitters and a large red, please,' Duncan sighed at the barmaid as he rummaged through his purse of coins, hoping to lessen some of its bulk. As a late forty-something and with distant Scottish ancestry as his only claim to fame, there were few pleasures in a life dominated by a job that paid the bills only. This evening was a collection of some of them – a few drinks, the company of a few old and trusted friends in a nice, old, warm, busy (but not crowded) Oxford pub, the Turf Tavern, and a widescreen television hanging on the hall nearby showing the rugby (Six Nations in fact – England against Ireland). Duncan collected the drinks and a few packets of crisps on the tray, paid the bar-lady, returned her smile as he thanked her and returned to the pub table to join his friends.

He had been lucky with the choice of the table, he had planned to arrive early and secure a decent view of the television, but he had been late. Frustrated, he hung around the door looking around him when the bar manager changed the television channel to the rugby and its pre-match studio discussion. This alerted (and distressed) a few female students sitting on the optimum table and they quickly drained their drinks, grabbed their stuff and left. He slipped into their place and moments later his brother and three other drinking companions arrived. All boded well for an excellent afternoon of chat and rugby.

Along with his young brother David, the group comprised Rodney (an old school friend), Jamie (a visiting 20 year old nephew – to another brother based overseas) and Rebecca, an old friend and former housemate. For the first hour Duncan and Rebecca caught up on the news leaving David and Jamie to catch up on family news. Then the rugby began and all eyes turned to the television screen.

The Six Nations tournament was a fixture in rugby when the four home nations (England, Wales, Ireland and Scotland) joined France and Italy in an annual tournament taking place in February and March. It was particularly important this year because the tournament was seven months away from the Rugby World Cup. It was the last opportunity for the national teams to test their mettle, tactics and players before the real deal in November.

The pub meet was also a good opportunity to catch up on the lives and plans of the old and young faces. David was changing jobs. He had heard two days earlier that an interview for a post in the University had been successful so he was transferring from one rubbish administrative position to another. The good thing was it was a somewhat less rubbish position than his current one. The move would allow David to spend a bit more time on his carpentry – his first love. He had enjoyed it at school and kept it up as a hobby over the years but, feeling that time was running out for him, he was trying to manoeuvre himself into a situation where his commissions for bespoke pieces of furniture (chest of drawers, tables, ornamentally carved household items) would generate enough income for him to downsize and earn a simple living. The ornamentally carved household items were proving particularly popular with mid-life professionals with a bit of disposal income. He currently had commissions for: a bookcase carved to evoke a magical forest, a wooden mobile phone case and wallet, and a mythical creature-inspired hat stand.

Rebecca was visiting from Cornwall to where she had decamped five years earlier to become a life counsellor. Jamie was visiting from Australia as part of his year off – travelling around Europe and considering career options. He had been born in the UK but had emigrated as a four year old with his mum and dad (Duncan's brother). A lover of Mother Nature (oceans in particular), Jamie was considering a future in marine biology. With a blond mop of hair, he was the youngest person at the table and, Duncan reflected with envy, was at a time of his life when options were limitless.

As for Duncan himself, he was planning to return to Italy. He had become fluent in the language having studied and worked in the country in his twenties and early thirties. He intended to continue his blogging and writing about the arts and start video-blogging and podcasting his book and film reviews from an Anglo-Italian perspective.

As for the rugby – within the first seven minutes, Ireland had swung the ball wide after thirteen phases of play and, finding an overlap, Jacob Stockdale had run it in for a try. Jonny Sexton had converted it. Thirty-four minutes in, the men in green were awarded a penalty at the halfway line. Having kicked for touched, the Irish employed a most-trusted move – the catch and drive. The hooker threw to the second row forward, who caught the ball, the scrum members bound and drove fifteen yards to the try-line and carried the ball over. After a simple conversion the score was seventeen points to three. (A penalty kick apiece had added to the scoreboard.) Ireland had dominated play and held sixty-two per cent of possession in the first half, but, as commentator David Coleman had famously said, it was a game of two halves. Anything could happen in the second half especially as the game opened up in the last twenty minutes as players tired, gaps opened up and mistakes were made.

Duncan readily acknowledged that Ireland had been the better team, but he had hopes for an improved second half performance from England. Having listened for a few minutes to the expert assessments from retired international players, Duncan rose to his feet to answer a call of nature. As he edged his way through the throng of rugby fans towards the lavatories, he caught sight of a running banner across the bottom of the screen 'breaking news: massive disaster in Canada – atmospheric interference expected, see BBC News channel for details'. It was similar to a banner that had run across the bottom of the screen as Ireland had been lining up for the line-out that had led to their second try. That first banner had read 'Canada explosion disaster' or something similar. No one was going to switch channels, the pub was full of rugby fans and it was game on between the top two seeds in the Six Nations tournament.

As he turned away from the screen, Duncan managed to catch the eye of another old friend, the pub manager. Given the nod by the manager, Duncan slipped behind the bar and disappeared through the door to the staff lavatory in the cellar – a quiet and welcome alternative to the urinals no doubt currently heaving with beery rugby fans.

– II – Whiteness, Brightness

Whiteness, brightness was the first sense Duncan had, almost before opening his eyes. The whiteness – and it was a clean, pristine whiteness – pierced his eyelids bathing his senses in a curious warmth. He breathed ever so slowly as he opened his eyes feeling completely and totally calm. The whiteness was coming from the ceiling. It was smooth, soft, like snow. But there was no chill. The temperature was perfectly attuned to his feeling. He felt both exhausted and revived. As if he had he run a marathon the day before then had slept a king. He breathed in. The air was crisp, dry, but tasted pure to the point of being almost artificial.

He didn't know where he was or what he had been doing. His mind was blank, almost as if it had been wiped clean. Clean – in a good way. Wiped fresh, perhaps. Of course, he knew who he was. He moved to rub his eyes and became aware of what he was wearing – a white gown made of the softest of fabrics. As he rubbed his eyes he noticed the sheer brilliant clarity of his sight. Everything was in the sharpest of detail. Odd, he thought. He had been wearing glasses since his teens and although he was by no means poorly sighted, he had become accustomed to a slight blurriness in short and middle-distance. As he rubbed his eyes, and then his temples, his fingers touched what felt like a penny attached to either side of his head. He tried to gently pick one away, but found that it was firmly attached to (or was it embedded in?) his skull. He raised himself up onto his elbows to look around and found that under his gown he was wearing what seemed to be a delicate chain mail fabric running the length of his whole body. Christ, have I been in an accident? A car crash? He racked his brains for any memory of getting into a vehicle, but, no, nothing. Propped up on his elbows he looked around him. He was in a medium-sized room. It was, of course, all white. There was very little furniture. Was this a hospital? It looked futuristic in its simplicity. There were no wall hangings, no windows, nothing to give anything away.

As he pulled himself up on the simple cot-like bed and swung his legs over the side he suddenly became aware of the chain mail skin tighten and flex across his back. Lying on the bed he had not felt it.

Aware that he should feel remarkably disconcerted, he was overwhelmed by a sense of peace. He felt safe. Unthreatened. Perhaps I've been drugged, I'm on some sort of medicine, he thought. He rose carefully to his feet and found that he could stand without any difficulty. The chain mail mesh on his back seemed to be supporting his movements.

The soft, white wall to his right was suddenly gently imbued with life. Standing, he turned and slowly walked towards to the wall. To his surprise he thought he could discern a figure in the far distance walking towards him. Was the wall in fact a screen? And was somebody approaching him? Or was it some form of large television or projection screen? He took half a dozen paces towards the figure and stopped a few paces from the wall or screen (or was it a gauze?). He watched. Yes, it was indeed a figure walking towards him. The figure of a young, poised man in a long, white, medical coat stopped in front of him. The man looked similar to Duncan in build and appearance. Almost Duncan's younger self. But fitter, perhaps.

They stood looking at each other for ten seconds. Duncan said nothing. He was waiting for the figure to speak. The figure seemed in no rush.

Then the figure smiled, warmly, displaying a real sense of compassion, even thankfulness.

'Hello Matthew,' the figure said in soft English accent.

'Hello,' Duncan replied cautiously.

'How are you?

'And you are...?' asked Duncan.

The figure smiled and nodded, no doubt expecting the question.

'Where am I?' said Duncan not waiting for a reply to his first question. 'Am I in hospital?'

'Yes, of sorts. You have been in an accident and have experienced a great deal of trauma, but you are well, fit, and, I'm pleased to see, functioning.'

''Functioning'? You're a doctor?'

'Yes, of sorts.'

'Of sorts, again?'

'We have been wondering how to address you when you regained consciousness. We want to be completely honest with you, but we have to manage the rate of that honesty.'

'Has something happened to my family? Friends?'

The figure smiled, and sighed.

'Yes, I am afraid they are no longer with us.'

'The accident?'

'Yes.'

'Where am I?'

Then Duncan twigged something about the figure. It was not a gauze screen hanging between him and the figure. And it wasn't quite a television screen. It was a form of projection, and, he realised, the figure wasn't real.

'Are you Artificial Intelligence? I'm not talking to a real person am I?'

'No, I'm not a real person and, yes, I am a form of Artificial Intelligence.'

'What's going on?'

'Take a seat. Let me introduce you to a few things.'

'Where am I?' said Duncan firmly making clear that that was going to be the first question.

'Here,' said the figure raising his arm to the left whereupon the whole wall to Duncan's right melted away into blackness. Although it wasn't just blackness, it was punctuated with millions of pinpricks of light – stars.'

'Take a seat and let's begin.'

Duncan sat in the armchair looking at the figure receding away in the distance. They had talked for a few hours and shared everything the 'AI life form' thought Duncan could absorb in that time. Duncan gazed out into 'space' or the wall displaying 'space'; his head spinning. He was looking forward to lying down and falling asleep. Hopefully he would wake up in a better place.

The figure had called him 'Matthew' a handful of times in his presentation. Initially Duncan had instinctively wanted to correct him, but then he felt it prudent to let the figure (or 'Doc' as had been agreed) call him what he wanted. Until Duncan knew more, being addressed as 'Matthew' would do.

Duncan had learnt that planet earth had been made unfit for human habitation (in fact pretty much unfit for all life) after a comet impact. The comet had broken up high in the atmosphere and smashed into the earth with the power of three billion times the force of the Hiroshima bomb. Earth as a simple planetary entity would survive, but all life had been extinguished except for Duncan whose remains had been pulled 'from the rocky rubble', and repaired and rebuilt. Odd words, Duncan had thought, but it was the first briefing after all. Details could wait.

Duncan asked about how the comet had been missed by space scientists. Who or what was the Artificial Intelligence life form now known as 'Doc'? Who created it? Had AI been responsible for his recovery? Doc's report had intimated that there was a non-human element to his rescue. Did that mean extraterrestrial involvement? Or was it part of a human escape plan and somehow only he had survived? How damaged had he been? How had they repaired him?

Duncan was absorbing all this information but after a few hours or so he was tiring and it all seemed too fanciful. He decided to withhold what he knew in case this was all some horrible dream. Was he in a coma and hallucinating? Could one be self-aware in such circumstances? Was he was on some sort of psychedelic trip? There were holes in the story. He detected Doc was limiting the information he shared for this reason.

The first briefing was intense. Doc had covered the basics, his answers: his information was limited because, quite frankly, the destruction had wiped out almost all earthly information. From what Doc's masters could glean, it had been clear the earth was going to be hit and so earth's scientists had sent up a rapid data transfer to satellites in the hope information could be saved – information storied quite literally in the space-cloud or 'nebula' as they called it. The sketchy details were that the comet had been missed by scientists initially and when it was only weeks away did it become clear that it would strike the earth. The devastation would be on such a scale that it was impractical to alert the populace – they were doomed anyway. Billions would die within the first few hours and the rest would die within a few weeks through starvation, disease, injury, burns. Every manner of death would be represented in the Armageddon.

Yes, Doc was Artificial Intelligence and had been presented to Duncan in a form that could be mistaken as a family relation to allow for sympathetic communication of the catastrophe and to develop trust. No, humans were not behind the technology of Duncan's (or "Matthew's" as Doc kept calling him) survival, which meant that, yes, it was an alien life form that was behind his survival and the creation of Doc. By this point in the presentation Duncan was indeed beginning to switch off. He wanted to curl up, sleep, and wake up again with the world as it had been and with the rugby playing on the television.

He learned that the chain mail mesh was an exoskeleton that was assisting him in his recovery and the use of his limbs.

It would be removed in due course. Artificial Intelligence had been used to scour the records of the earth's media to build up the environment that was conducive to a speedy recovery on regaining consciousness. Entertainment films with space and disaster scenarios that 'Matthew' was familiar with were used to create the hospital-like room to facilitate the sharing of information and lessen the shock (if that were possible). More briefings by Doc would follow once Duncan had rested.

The subsequent briefings covered how Duncan had been pulled from the rubble. His remains had been transferred to a spacecraft and he was now far away from the earth's solar system. During many 'earth-years' Duncan had been rebuilt from scratch using a combination of unearthly physical and memory-rebuild technologies. The finding of some of his remains had been a fortunate. Drones had searched a targeted area and found the remains encased in a protective casing of resin buried deep in a basement-like shrine in a city of alleged human learning.

– III – Matt

Duncan sat in the armchair opposite Doc (himself standing behind or 'projected in' the wall). During the course of their meetings Duncan had become increasingly quiet and reflective. He had asked for images of the scenes from earth's former landscapes to be projected on the walls as he mulled things over and in the vain hope that he would one day wake up. Occasionally Duncan asked to be shown the view out the spacecraft's 'window' and was shown a Star-Trek-like image of moving through space. He had asked for an image of the earth as it now was, but was shown another patch of sky, they had travelled so far from earth it could not be seen optically.

They had left a probe to monitor the earth, but transmission of updated images took time.

'Where are we going, Doc?' Duncan asked.

'Home,' Doc replied.

'Home?'

'To your new home, Matthew.'

'Why do you keep calling me Matthew?'

'It would be a pleasure and honour to call you 'Matt'?'

'Why is everything a pleasure and honour with you?'

'Because we know how much you meant to your people. Your leadership and insight.'

'You don't know who I am. You have no idea.'

Doc smiled.

'You were chosen.'

'By whom?' Duncan asked exasperated.

'Your people.'

'You were, are, a storyteller, a leader, Matt. Your people followed you. That is why we respect and revere you as the chosen one. That is why it is right that it should be you to seed a new home. To be the leader in the new world.'

'Nobody knew me. I'm not a leader, Doc.'

'You were, Matt. Everybody knew Matt. Matt Damon.'

'Matt Damon?' Duncan muttered, confused. 'What? Matt Damon?'

'Yes,' Doc said, smiling warmly.

'I'm not Matt Damon,' said Duncan, not knowing what to think.

'We looked for you and rebuilt you. You are as close to Matt Damon as you ever were. I'd like to think better, but I am not sure that is possible.'

'I'm not Matt Damon. Matt Damon died on planet earth forty thousand earth-years ago. I look nothing like Matt Damon.'

And with that the wall showing the 'live' image of space travel dissolved into whiteness and from the whiteness emerged the image of a white room with a chair and a bed and a man sitting hunched on the bed. The man was dressed in white cotton covering a chain mail-like exoskeleton mesh. As Duncan adjusted himself on the bed, so did the man adjust himself. Duncan rose to his feet, so did the man. Duncan, his heart pounding, his jaw dropped in confusion and wonder, took a dozen steps towards the figure who moved directly towards him. In a moment Duncan stood directly before the man projected (or reflected) on the wall. Before him he saw Matt, Matt Damon.

'Matt Damon,' Duncan whispered. His confused expression mirrored by Matt Damon standing opposite him.

'You see, Matt,' said Doc. 'You really are Matt Damon.'

I was watching rugby in a pub with my brother, David, my nephew Jamie, and my friends Rodney and Rebecca. It was half-time. Ireland were winning.'

'And the comet struck first in a landmass you called Canada, but it had broken high in the outer atmosphere and large pieces were showered all over your planet earth.'

'I'm not Matt Damon, Doc, you've made a mistake. I don't believe you. This is wrong.'

'We have the evidence. We have seen many of the stories you told, but unfortunately, others were lost; we have recovered and rebuilt what we can. We can show you Matt Damon.'

'I know what Matt Damon looks like and it's not....,' Duncan's voice faded as he waved at the image of Matt Damon in front of him, 'this' he added without a sliver of conviction. 'Why me? Why was I chosen?'

'You fought for justice in times of conflict, often even when there was corruption in your own ranks. You pointed it out. You addressed it. You fought in wars but always maintained the highest integrity. You were familiar with space travel and travelled to your nearest planet and another in a near galaxy, endured great adversity including loneliness, but triumphed. You have genius for mathematics. You understood the law of your peoples and fought for those who were persecuted. You have a love and respect for your fellow animals demonstrated by your nurturing of them. You put your pursuit of love for a woman companion above the plans that a 'god' entity had for you.'

'All fucking movies,' Duncan whispered in despair, his head in his hands.

'Who were you to choose?' he asked aloud. 'Why not choose a scientist?'

'But the scientist nominated you.'

'The scientist?'

'The one who directed the distress call to us.'

'Who the hell was that?'

'We don't know his name. He uploaded as much information to your satellites and then altered the settings on your satellites to send out an SOS on different wavelengths to deep space. It reached us and we answered the call.'

'What did he say?'

'It was very brief. We only have a video message.'

Duncan was stunned. Video message? Doc read Duncan's expression. The wall mirror dissolved into the broken, close up, pixelated image of an agitated man speaking directly into a webcam. He looked exhausted, broken and sad.

'This is...' his words dropped and his voice broke. 'This is planet earth. I am limiting this message to as few words as possible..... It will be converted to all mathematical languages known to us in the hope someone (you) can decipher it. What I am doing has not been authorised, but I am uploading what I can – DNA, history, sciences, law, culture and sport – to the hard drive banks of our JPL-X-2 satellites in the hope you – anybody or anything – can retrieve the data and bear witness to life on earth. All life on earth. We have had gods but they have deserted us. They will die with us. I wish I could offer you a man to bear witness in the flesh. A man who could tell the stories of our peoples and our times. A man of greatness. We have a story to share, we hope you can understand. We hope someone will find these records and perhaps create a Garden of Eden somewhere.'

A surge of hopefulness surged in Duncan. Perhaps he could convince Doc that the scientist was the person they should have cloned. The scientist then lent forward and adjusted the webcam itself before sitting back in his chair. Using the keyboard the scientist pulled out the zoom to reveal a wide-angle image of his room. To Duncan's despair the scientist was wearing a Jason Bourne t-shirt and was sitting in front of a The Martian poster.

'I was watching the rugby,' muttered Duncan despairingly to himself.

'No, Matt, you weren't playing that day. You had retired having lifted its greatest prize.'

Duncan looked at Doc, sighed and let his head fall into his hands again before a thought hit him.

'In your records, Doc, Duncan Sheldrake – he was based in Oxford at the time of the impact. Find me all the Duncan Sheldrakes in Oxford.'

Doc paused (no doubt the AI was searching records).

'I've checked there are no Duncan Sheldrakes in Oxford.'

'All records of population for Oxford have beeen lost?'

'No. There are just no records of a Duncan Sheldrake. But our records are incomplete.'

'No, it's not right. I'm not who you think I am. I'm a fake.'

'In some ways, yes. You are reconstructed. You're DNA, memories, our technology, but as you once said – "I always thought it would be better to be a fake somebody, than a real nobody".'

WTF?

'You predicted this, Matt. But you are not a fake (at least no more than you were during your time on planet earth) regardless of what you might think now. You are as real as they come.'

'It doesn't make any sense. Why? Why do I deserve to go? Why…?'

' "Why not any of these guys?"?' asked Doc.

Duncan nodded.

'Again, you've asked that before – during one of your conflicts. "They all fought just as hard as you, you were chosen." And you triumphed as a result. That is why you must be the one to seed your new home.'

'Matt Damon? The seed of humanity?'

Doc smiled and nodded.

'You should have gone with the scientist,' Duncan muttered.

'The messenger did his job – we harvested as much data as we could from the satellites and other data streams.'

'Do you have any other video about the incident?'

Doc paused.

'Only recordings of the impact itself.'

Duncan started.

'Recorded from satellites,' continued Doc.

Duncan stared hard at Doc before rising to his feet and walking to the wall.

'Play it,' Duncan whispered.

'You might find it distressing.'

'Play it, Doc.'

Doc turned to wall. The video in question flickered into life. The image was from a satellite in a high orbit. Almost all the earth was displayed in all its glory. Half the earth bathed in the light of the sun, the rest in darkness. It always reminded Duncan of a beautiful marble, one that he used to play with as a child on the carpeted sitting room of a neighbour in Eboracum Road. Now here it was suspended in blackness. Remarkably beautiful, tranquil, a force for good. Both vulnerable and safe in the vastness of space.

Then the left edge of the screen brightened a little, after which a flaming spot of light appeared headed straight for the delicate marble, behind it another tumbling ball of light, then another. A whole string of pearls heading straight for the earth in absolute silence. They were large, perhaps half the size of a large country.

The impact was huge. And devastating. Gargantuan amounts of debris were thrown up well beyond the thin film of the atmosphere as other parts of the comet struck the earth hard in different parts of the globe, hammering it relentlessly. Debris, the size of continents, was being thrown up into space.

'This is the image from a satellite that had been tasked to orbit your star, the sun, that the scientists had re-tasked to watch the impact.'

The image switched to a long view of the earth. He watched as, once again, a string of luminous pearls moved slowly from the left of screen straight for the blue and white marble suspended in the blackness. The impacts threw up more materials into space then shrouded the earth in a murky grey shroud that slowly enveloped it.

The video ended.

The wall dissolved into white, then dissolved back again into the blackness of moving space. Duncan stood motionless. Doc slowly turned and walked away into the distance.

– IV – Blue and Orange

Duncan was unsure how much time had passed. But what was time anymore? He had fallen asleep after the video replay. When he woke he stared at the ceiling of the room. The wall was slowly changing between images of the earth – forests, waterfalls, green landscapes. He knew it was Doc's attempt at soothing him, but it just seemed sad and inappropriate now that such natural wonders did not exist. Doc failed to appear in the projection wall and he knew that that too was intentional. Duncan was being given time to mull things over, wallow in reflection. The images on the video wall changed to night-time shots of similar earth images and in time he fell asleep again.

He woke and felt refreshed. A sunrise was displayed on the wall.

He rose from his bed, showered and walked over to Doc's wall and waited.

Moments later Doc's figure appeared in the distance and approached.

'Morning, Matt.'

'Hello Doc, I'm ready.'

Doc tilted his head in a quizzical look suggesting he knew what Duncan was saying but wanted confirmation.

'Let's move on to the next stage. I want to meet your masters. Take me to your leader.'

'As I said, we are trying to introduce the changes to you gradually, to limit any distress.'

'I'm ready, let's get this over with. Tell them Matt Damon is summoning them.'

Doc remained motionless, reluctant, confused.

'Doc, tell them Matt Damon is waiting.'

Doc nodded, turned and walked off into the white oblivion.

Duncan sat on his bed and waited.

Approximately twenty (earth) minutes later, the shade of the room changed and a door materialised in the third wall. The door opened in glided two forms at least twelve feet tall.

Duncan rose to his feet and stood before them.

The alien beings were quite beautiful. Tall, thin, pale, almost translucent. The figures had facial features just discernible in their heads, but Duncan wondered whether he was seeing eyes, nose and a mouth or whether he was just looking for patterns, like seeing images in the clouds.

He had no way to describe them other than saying one had a bluish tinge to their translucent glow, the other had a orange tinge to its translucent glow.

'I hope you are rested,' said Blue.

'Yes, thank you,' muttered Duncan captivated by the sight before him. 'You speak my language?'

'Not quite,' Blue replied, touching an ornamental necklace about its neck. 'This device converts our language to yours and emits sound waves.'

'How do you normally communicate?'

'Put simply, we can communicate by light, sound, whatever pleases us.'

'It is an honour to meet you, Matt.'

'For forty thousand earth-years have we waited to meet Matt Damon.'

'Well, thank you,' muttered Duncan, before asking, 'Where are we?'

'On our vessel, travelling to a quadrant in the Andromeda galaxy.'

'And what is there?'

'We have so much to share with you. But we have time,' said Orange in a calm, delicate, beautifully-spoken tone.

'To a new home,' said Blue equally beautifully. 'You will seed the new planet. We will help you.'

'Are there others? Is it just me?'

'Just you from your original DNA and reconstituted profile, but we have the DNA from the human form and other earth life forms.'

'Did anybody else survive?'

'No.'

'How can you be sure? Much time has passed. Maybe earth has recovered.'

Blue turned to the wall screen behind Duncan who turned to follow his gaze. The image changed from space to an image of a dirty, broken pebble suspended in blackness. It had no colour, just a rocky brown piece of gravel with a large hole gauged out of its roughly spherical shape.

'This is the most recent image we have from our probe,' said Orange, 'her' tone unchanged. 'You can see it is now just a piece of rock. The series of impacts not only displaced much of the water and evaporated the atmosphere, but it knocked the earth off its orbit giving it a modest wobble. This disrupted the orbit of the earth's moon. Thirty thousand years after the impact from the comet, the wobble of your planet and the wobble of its moon's orbit meant they met in their own collision causing the irregularity you now see. The remaining atmosphere boiled off and the seas evaporated. Your planet is now, as you see, the most barren in your solar system.'

Duncan looked at the piece of unrecognisable rock. He struggled to feel anything. It was true, it was barren, featureless. He tried to think of all the history, all the stories that had been contained on its surface for millions of years. All now lost. No trace left to speak of, almost as if it never existed.

'Every planet has its time,' said Orange.

'What's the name of the new planet?' asked Duncan, his mouth dry.

'For now, it only has a number. But we were thinking of New Bourne, but the planet is for you to name.'

'Bourne?' Duncan pondered. 'How about Eden?

'The Garden of Eden? From one of your stories?' asked Orange.

'Um, the garden, perhaps not,' sighed Duncan. 'Connotations.'

'The Wood? The Wood of Eden?

Duncan shook his head.

'The Wood of Holly? A place of which you were once master?' asked Blue. 'And a place that was the envy of your world. A place from which the brightest and best sought to impart their insight and wisdom to the huddled, desperate masses?'

– V – Space and Time

Duncan was learning that time worked differently in space. With the help of Doc, he had operated on the earth cycle of 24 hours. Blue and Orange had told him that the chosen destination had a 27 earth-hour day. He had had a series of meetings with Blue and Orange to discuss all manner of things about the new home. They had shared with Duncan their names but they were difficult to enunciate so they all agreed he would continue to call them by their most prominent colour (to his eye) – Blue and Orange. He learned much about their way of life. Light was at the very heart of their existence. They absorbed it, harnessed it, used it to communicate and learn. Their science was based on being one with light.

On their second meeting Blue and Orange had taken Duncan for a tour of the vessel. Exiting his hospital-like room he had stepped out into a corridor the walls of which were walled by light and soft colours. Depending on his view and focus the walls too were translucent. He could look through them to see other corridors and gangways and rooms and halls and atriums. His furthest focus seemed to give an impression of the ship itself. It seemed as if the vessel was spherical, like an asteroid.

Blue was advising him on how time should be measured on the new planetary home. The 'year' would be shorter, there was more than one moon, so there were a variety of ways of organising the passage of time. Names for 'months', moons and days of the week were up for debate. Duncan had initially been inclined to name many things after earth, but after reflection he was wary of mythologising his previous home. He should mythologise the new world – the nature, the space, his new friends perhaps. Perhaps his choice of names would be neutral or perhaps suggest a source of inspiration while not being beholden to it.

And so it was that Duncan spent many hundreds of days travelling around the spacecraft. Duncan and Blue soon fell into a routine of wandering about the spacecraft talking. Sometimes they sat gazing out into the empty expanse from seats on a viewing deck. Many, many hours were lost either in conversation or deep silence. They talked about everything. At times the magnitude of Duncan's task was overwhelming, other times he was grateful for the support and even looking forward to the challenge. Whatever the conversation Blue always seemed to know the moment when he should walk away leaving Duncan to his thoughts. They became fast friends.

'How far away are we from earth?' Duncan asked early in their meetings.

'A million of your light years.'

'Are there others? Other civilisations?'

'Yes, many, Matt.'

'You've helped others?'

Blue nodded.

'Call me Duncan, please.'

Blue looked at him. His colours swirling.

'Duncan is my new name. I think I want to live as 'Duncan'.'

Duncan interpreted Blue's colour as a polite smile but, as far as he could discern, he suspected the alien was disappointed. He decided he wouldn't press his case too hard, they had saved him after all.

Duncan walked ahead. Blue moved beside him. The 'Acenes' did not walk. They did not float. 'Glide' was the closest Duncan could say they did, but then words seemed to fail on this occasion. They seemed to inhabit space rather than move through it. He was embarrassed at his primitiveness in comparison to the being that was taking an interest in him. Not to mention what they were expecting of him. It was all too much. It obviously showed.

'Why do you worry about the past?' Blue asked. 'It is of no consequence. It cannot be changed. It cannot be challenged. It has passed beyond your control.'

'Why have you given me a past then? Why do I have memories?' Duncan replied.

'To roam. To explore the forming mind. Memories are a landscape on which you build. Respect the landscape, but do not be imprisoned by it. Let it inform you, not threaten, confine or subjugate you.'

Duncan turned and looked out at the black panoply of stars.

'Think of memories as a solar wind,' Blue continued. 'Carrying you forward. The source might burn brightly – all stars burn brightly – but memories are a fuel to burn. A fuel to expend on a journey to a destination often far away from the source.'

'But Blue, I can't help thinking of everything I have known, everything my species has known. All life on earth has gone. I am the sole representative. I am the only vessel of their existence. Their sole witness. How can I....'

But Blue interrupted him.

'Concern yourself with the future and in order to do that you must start in the present. We only left a trace of your primitive existence to help you understand where you are going.'

Duncan looked unconvinced.

'Do not twist your mind into falsehoods. For whom? For what purpose? For show? Who is watching? You have lived, Matt,' said Blue, before correcting himself. 'I'm sorry, 'Duncan'. You have lived perhaps more than any of your kind. You have everything you need, so don't indulge in the past. Indulge in the future.'

And with that, Blue would move away into the spacecraft leaving Duncan to his thoughts.

At times Duncan felt overwhelmed by his predicament. The news of the lost earth, the acknowledgement of his rescue, the struggle to accept the situation as it was presented to him by Blue. Everything was new. In his previous existence he would reflect on ideas drawn from the accumulated wisdom and reflection of many others who had put pen to paper over many thousands of earth-years. As he struggled, it gradually dawned on him that the difficulty he was experiencing was borne of values and understanding that were themselves born on a tiny speck of dust floating in the coldest blackness in a fleeting moment in a timeless universe.

In due course a dot of insight revealed itself deep inside him. In yet more time, it grew and became a pearl. He realised that he needed to listen. Listen without prejudice. Listen in a manner that he had never listened before – not only to Blue, but to himself – and then develop the skill of self-reflection.

His task was made somewhat easier by the circumstances in which he had found himself – travelling beyond the speed of light in outer-space without the prospect of a conversation with another human being.

His was a wholly new situation.

What did trouble Duncan was the dread of responsibility.

'What should I do on this new planet?' he would ask Blue. 'Should what I do on the new planet reflect the experience of life on earth?'

'No, remember the past now is nothing. Don't busy yourself with what is no more.'

Such comments would be met by blank looks from Duncan.

'Although you know much from your previous work on earth (such as your success at surviving on other planets), you are not alone. We will help you,' Blue said. 'We shall provide some shelter and a small community of, once again, impressionable people. But they will need guidance.'

Duncan looked transfixed at Blue's swirling features as he considered the proposal. Being called upon to not only start a new life was one thing, but start a new civilisation altogether? That was a tall order. He would need all the help he could get.

'What else do I need to consider?' he asked Blue.

'You have worry in your eyes. Do not worry. You know much already,' said Blue.

'Um, start at the beginning anyway.' said Duncan, 'Just in case I wasn't paying attention on set.'

Blue's colours swirled in what Duncan now knew was the equivalent of 'does not compute'.

'I just want to make sure you have got it right,' muttered Duncan.

'We could have implanted much new information, but we wanted you to have some memories of your life on former planet earth.'

'Can you read my thoughts?' asked Duncan.

'They are too primitive, I'm afraid,' replied Blue.

'You don't know what is going on in my head?' Duncan checked.

Blue shimmered in the negative. Duncan took a breath and sighed deeply.

'Blue, I thank you for everything you have done. But I don't believe I am the person you think I am.'

'Belief, Matt, Duncan, is a description. Nothing more.'

Duncan shook his head.

'You will find a way. You are, after all, the finest of your kind,' the alien said.

'Perhaps on earth millennia ago,' reflected Duncan.

'Living is accepting a destiny,' Blue protested (as much as an Acenes can). 'All human life has now been lived. The only earth-hours of human life left are yours. Your responsibility is to use those earth-hours to reach a destination. You accomplished much in other primitive circumstances, among other simple, primitive peoples.'

'It was all fiction,' muttered Duncan, deep down glad that if there were to be a history written of life on planet earth, it would be him who wrote it.

'Everything is fiction,' replied Blue as he readied himself for departure from that earth-day's conversation. 'Everything is story. It is all about the story you tell. You are the master storyteller. You can tell the story of darkness. Or you can tell the story of light.'

– VI – Time for Reflection

Earth-days and earth-days would pass. Duncan would reflect and reflect some more. He was unsure how much time passed. He could not describe it as 'months' because months did not exist now. Even on earth the concept of a 'month' did not exist now. The moon had been destroyed and now drifted about the solar system in fragments. The earth's orbit had changed. How was time to be measured? It seemed odd to measure time in such a way – the origin and means of measurement had been shattered into pieces many thousands of earth-years before. And it wasn't 'years' either, because earth-years didn't exist. So, if time didn't exist by earth's measure, did it exist at all? It was all so complicated.

Questions to Blue continued. Sometimes Blue would smile (or what Duncan interpreted as a smile) and slip away. Duncan knew that Blue would have an answer (or perhaps many answers), but the point was that it was up to Duncan to figure it out. Whenever it became tough, Blue tried to reassure Duncan that he had the strength.

'As you once said, Matt: "*You know, sometimes all you need is 20 seconds of insane courage. Just, literally, 20 seconds of just, embarrassing bravery. And I promise you, something great will come of it.*"'

The quote meant nothing to Duncan, though obviously something to Blue judging by the subsequent swirls of colour.

Sometimes Blue's words did strike a chord and, as the journey through the stars continued, Duncan found himself gravitating to a particular way of thinking.

'Existence is only time,' Blue once said, many earth-months into the journey. 'Time is about investment. *You* decide what you want to invest in.'

'How do I decide what to invest in?' Duncan would whisper.

'When your end-of-time comes, you will know if you have made sound investments – only *you* can describe. It is *your* time after all.'

'Time is about the moment of death?'

Blue smiled.

'Life is one unique moment in which to invest.'

As the earth-hours, earth-days, earth-months passed, Duncan reflected on conversations with Blue, his memories, his choices, and he learned there was always one thing ever-present – mortality. There would indeed be a 'last day'. If there could be a last day for a planet (or even the universe) there would certainly be a last day for him. In fact, it was the only question asked by Duncan to which Blue would give a definitive 'yes'.

Which led Duncan to reflect further. Thinking of the many billions of people whose days had been bound to a floating, blue marble, he wished he could ask their departed souls had they been satisfied with their investment? If there was an answer, would evidence of that answer (or even evidence of their 'investment') remain?

'There was no evidence in my case, the planet was destroyed.'

'But there was Matt Damon,' Blue protested in swirls.

Duncan looked at Blue.

'*You.*'

Duncan looked bemused.

'All the life forms that ever existed on planet earth were ultimately investing in Matt Damon,' Blue continued, 'whether they knew it or not. *You*, Matt Damon, are your solar system's crowning achievement. I mean, 'Duncan'.'

Duncan's self-reflection and learning continued. For how long, he did not know. He would have to re-think Time's nature, its measure. It would need a lot of reflection. But he had time. Ironically.

Still the Acenes would pose questions only to then slip away. I suppose to 'ask a question' invites reflection, pondered Duncan. To 'ask a question *of* us' is to issue a challenge, it invites action. Maybe that is the role of a god – to ask and to ask *of* – that's all. And to help us along the way, we are gifted time.

And was Blue that Higher Authority – God? Surely, any god would know that Duncan wasn't Matt Damon. Unless of course, Blue *did* know that Duncan wasn't Matt Damon and this was part of a plan – an exercise in identity. Was that what the mission to a new home was all about? Choosing who 'we' wanted to be? Did Duncan deep down want to be Matt Damon and the Acenes had picked up on that when rebuilding him? Had everybody on planet earth wanted, deep down, to be Matt Damon?

Sitting quietly in a quiet corner of the vessel he would spend his time staring out at space through the translucent walls. Over time it was the act of gazing into nothingness and 'the everything' of space that emptied him, cleansed him – almost as if space itself was designed to induce reflection.

His thoughts turned to what life might indeed to be like on the new planet. He had seen images of the new home and it bore a striking resemblance to earth, but fresher, brighter, if that were possible. The new planet was, like him, a clean slate. Perhaps he did have a role to play. To give human life another million years. But what was the best way to start a life? Laws, customs and practices? Belief-systems? Or none? But some rules by which to live by, surely? Rugby, perhaps? An excellent team game, roles for everyone. Physical, but fair.

The questions and conundrums were confusing, but simultaneously liberating. It was a challenge indeed. Duncan knew that however long and hard he looked at the vast vistas of matter and energy and in any direction, he would never see his old world again. He realised that what distinguished one sensation from another was Time. It was an allowance. A facilitator. Blue and Orange were gifting him time to figure all these things out.

– VII – Arrival

As they descended to the planet, he felt the gravity take his body. The approach from space had given him a hint of what was to come. Once again one of the walls of the spacecraft had acted as a window onto the (new) world. The planetary surface was very similar to the former earth, though more lush. Duncan struggled to process his thoughts and feelings as the craft moved high over the never-ending expanse of forests dappled as they were with a multitude of colours. His eyes drank in the spectacle of the planet below him.

The calmness Duncan felt had settled over him much, much earlier. He had no idea how long he had spent gazing out across the darkness of space on his way to this new home. He had long dispensed with earth's units of time. His calmness was not based on enlightenment; he had not answered any of the questions he had asked both himself and Blue, but he felt quietly confident that he had identified what he described as 'earthbound dogma'. Just as he had dispensed with earth-time, he had also dispensed with many earth-practices; he was even beginning to refer to them as 'rocky pebble practices'. An early conclusion was that he would not have 'laws' – even the idea of 'law' – on the new planet. After all, law was a human invention. His conversations with Blue about rocky pebble laws had evolved into something else as they journeyed further and further away from his first home. Duncan had learnt that the universe itself didn't have laws. Laws were fixed, harsh, unforgiving, foreign and again, 'fiction'. It was better to think of the universe as having (in rocky pebble parlance) 'behaviour' or even 'habits'. It was a strange evolution of thinking for Duncan. It took time to adjust.

Additionally, Duncan had concluded, there would not be 'constants', as such, in the new world. They too were an earthbound fiction. If the speed of light and even gravity were not constant (as he had learnt from Blue), why should anything else be?

Duncan had also spent, what he described as his own, 'space-time' reflecting on the nature and influence of memory. Memory too evolves, he noted. Memory was not a constant, so perhaps the hold on him of the memory of earth should be limited too. He had used his space-time to reflect on the extinction of humanity and how it could be seen (in rocky pebble terms) as a failure. But why was extinction a 'failure'? Where had the desire for extended life, immortality (in one unchanging form), come from? Continuance or survival in one physical form was not a given in the universe. In order to survive, one must evolve. Observing the blackness and the stars and the momentous change of the universe he had learnt that everything was about evolution. If there was anything that could be said about the universe, it was a creature of change – creation.

He reflected on the life cycles of the former earth – just as a plant's cells, when it died, left behind a structure to enable water to travel, leading to rebirth and growth, so did exploding stars create the elements and gaseous clouds from which more stars and planets (and plants) were formed. Perhaps death itself was another rocky pebble fiction. Death should not be perceived as an end-point in a linear narrative, but rather a curve in a vast spiral of life.

So, by the time Duncan was gliding over his new home, he knew that he would not bring the notion of death to the new world, but an understanding of a life spiral. Earthbound humanity had therefore been part of this spiral – a point of a few hundred thousand earth-years of the modern human brain (and only a few hundred years of modern scientific thinking). He was not beholden to their fleeting conclusions; it was foolish to think so. In fact he had asked Blue whether he should even describe himself as 'human'? Perhaps a new term was required. But Blue, as ever, had shimmered (a smile, perhaps?) and glided away.

The task of laying the groundwork for a life-form on a new planet had often led Duncan to analyse how earthbound humanity had developed its sense of meaning. He had instinctively found himself trying to ascertain the origin of 'meaning' by reducing moments in humanity's development to small historical occurrences. Sitting for much of his space-time absorbing the apparent timelessness and unfathomable scale of the universe through the translucent wall of Blue's ship, Duncan could not reconcile the quest for meaning in such fleeting earthbound moments. Similarly, he could not discern value in the rocky pebble pursuit of reducing things to their constituent parts. Analysis of molecules, atoms and quarks could not describe the role, behaviour or experience of a human, animal or plant.

As the spacecraft had approached the new home's solar system, Duncan shared his primitive observations with Blue explaining that the 'whole' and not the sum of all parts would be the formative influence on the new planet. When Duncan asked whether the skies on the new planet would be clear and that the stars and galaxies visible, Blue, once again, just shimmered and glided away.

The craft slowed as it reached the edge of a forest and approached the bluest of seas. The view below him was truly an Eden, uncorrupted, untarnished, unspoilt. Before it reached the sea the craft turned and circled over a mouth of a river before settling on a large clearing surrounded by the grandest of trees.

Having landed he could feel the effort it took for the blood to be pumped around his body and to his brain. His body would get used to it. The door of the craft lowered and Duncan walked down the ramp alone looking at the new physical world laid out before him. Orange, Blue, Green and Yellow followed at a respectful distance.

It was a feast for all the senses. A gentle cool wind brushed across his face and body. He felt his hair lift and move as the air embraced it. The hair on his arms pinged upright before swooning at the touch of the breeze. His eyes were hit by more colours than he had ever known. Having spent so much time in the controlled lighting environment of the ship, his eyes were unprepared for the fairground of changing shades of light as he turned his head this way and that. And sounds – the whistle of wind through trees, the hum of insect life and the occasional squawk from unseen creatures.

Duncan stepped on to the soft grass. Seeing the soft form of green vegetation moist with dew under his foot, he removed his shoes and sunk his feet into the lush grass. Its green body was stronger than anything he could remember on earth. In fact he could hardly recall doing such a thing back on the original planet. The chilly, wet softness of the grass enveloping his feet he took as a planetary kiss of welcome. Life in all its richness had been breathed upon the surface of this planetary world. His wonder dissolved any sadness of the barren, rocky pebble floating around a once-familiar sun an unfathomable distance away.

He could hear the gentle rush of water from the river just out of sight behind the trees. He was desperate to taste it. Real water, fresh, clean. They couldn't have been a few hundred yards from the sea. He couldn't have chosen a better location for the first site of the new civilisation. Gathered neatly around an open clearing were a handful of simple, but beautifully engineered housing structures provided by Blue and his crew. Paths led away from the clearing into the wood where he could see additional cabins on stilts.

The sky was a rich blue, although with a slightly different aspect to it. A very discreet swirl of colour shimmered right across the sky. Even the sky was alive. Even though it was 'day', stars could still be discerned. Three of the four moons of this new home were visible. One, christened 'Emerald', was moving discernibly. Another, Sapphire, seemed disconcertingly large in the sky.

It was wondrous. He heard some soft gentle steps behind him. He turned and looked. It was the partner Blue and his friends had created for him. Another human recreated in her prime to Duncan's requirements using all the technology and records of the planet earth. She was to be Duncan's partner and the mother of the new people – the Wood of Holly's very own Eve. She took his hand and, looking as beautiful as he could ever have hoped, took in the sight of her new home.

Duncan turned and gazed in gratitude at his rescuers. They were not just the rescuers of him but of life itself.

He looked at Raquel dressed in a fur outfit beside him.

How did I get here, he whispered to himself.

He was touched and moved deeply. He needed to thank Green, Orange, Yellow, but most of all Blue. But how should he express such profound gratitude?

'I'm......, I'm....,' but the words failed him. Duncan wished he could communicate as they did, by thought, with colour. Words were too, too weak, far too primitive. What words could they hear that would express his gratitude not only for himself, but for all of his kind.

'I....I....'

Then it dawned. He looked at them all. And smiled.

'I *am*...Matt. Damon,' he said slowly, straightening his back, raising his head, pushing out his chest and nodding slowly. 'Matt. Damon. Indeed.'

Orange, Blue, Turquoise, Yellow and Green glowed and shimmered. The light rose up inside them, dissolved and swirled.

It pointed at his friends, each in turn.

'Matt Damon thanks you,' he said, nodding solemnly.

The whirls of colour within their translucent forms turned into a storm, before gently clearing and dissolving into their own true colour – serenity after a storm.

'And so it has come to pass,' Blue said, 'Matt Damon has landed. Long and gracious life to the Damonites on Bourne,' and, with that, Blue and his alien colleagues, bowed.

The Elephant of Marrakech

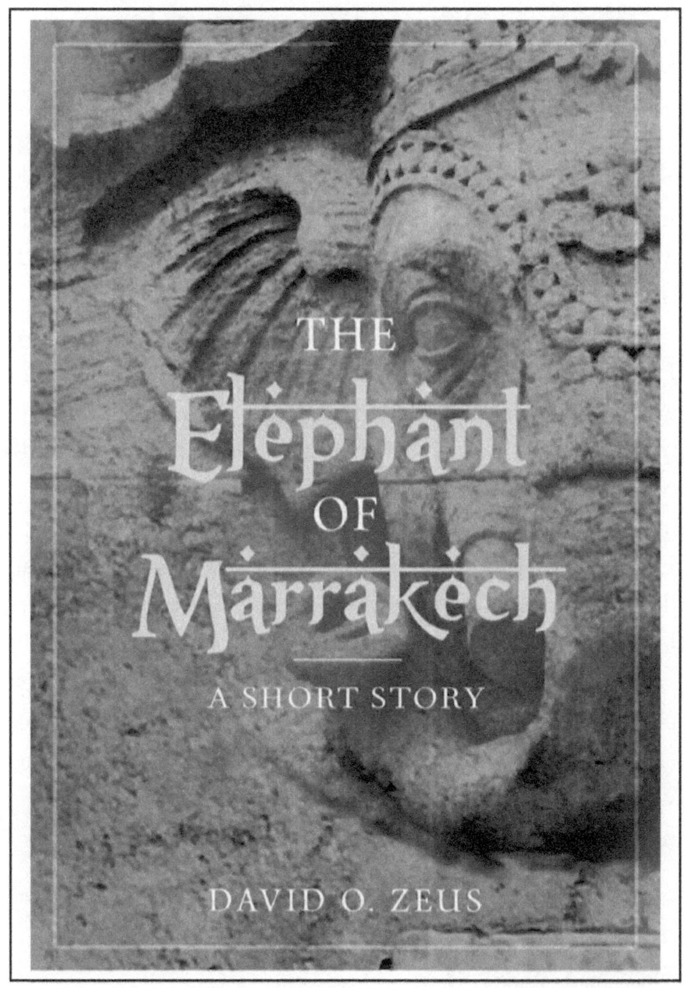

– I – Marrakech

As Fred disembarked the aircraft and strolled into the airport building he felt his body sigh in thanks. He was back in Marrakech, Morocco's second city. He had last been in the city seven years earlier. Now, on his return, he could close the circle. Throw the monkey from his back. Shake the heaviness from his heart. He was not a businessman, an assassin, a lover, a mover or a shaker. He was a holiday-maker here to set things right. To finish that unfinished business.

Fred's first visit to Marrakech had been relatively spontaneous and without any expectations. He had joined a tour group and travelled around the country for two weeks. His second trip, however, had a clear objective. To the outsider it consisted of a ten-day walking holiday in the Atlas Mountains followed by a few days in Marrakech itself, but to the insider (him alone) there was a serious matter to be resolved that had been bugging him since that final night of his first visit to Marrakech. He wasn't denying the walking holiday was a cover for something else because no-one asked. (If anyone had asked, he would, of course, deny it.) There was method in his holiday planning. He was here to find the elephant and do what he should have done on that final night in Marrakech seven summers before.

– II – The First Booking

There was, of course, a time 'before the elephant'.

'The *holiday*,' Fred's junior office colleague had said with a big, fat beautiful smile, too quickly for his liking. Surely the dilemma required more thought? The question had been: 'Do I work during my two weeks of holiday leave and make significant progress on my house redecoration, or just escape overseas and have a holiday?'

He ignored her first reply. His question had been rhetorical, he wasn't inviting a reply from Mel. Maybe in a world of over-sharing social media the youth of today did not understand the rhetorical question. Fred was deliberating privately. He was not inviting a response.

He continued to reflect (out loud):

'A break would be good, I could just relax, but then I would return and wouldn't have made any progress with the house.'

'The holiday,' his colleague Mel repeated, but more firmly this time and with a giggle and a bigger smile made fatter with the endearing exuberance of youth.

He paused. A holiday was the easy way out. His reflection continued.

'The thing is, I might get bored after a few days, so I would need to keep busy with stuff, I think.'

'*Definitely* the holiday,' his colleague repeated with emphasis.

He determined to reach a decision at the end of that working day when Mel had left the office (therefore denying her any credit for the decision). And so, at thirty-seven years of age, he found himself sitting in the reception of a travel agent. (He noted: a travel agent for the 'traveller' not the 'holiday-maker'.)

Looking around at the advertisements for flights and tours around the world, he feared he might be making a mistake. How did they make their money unless they whacked on a large commission? Shouldn't he be hunting for something online and patching together his own itinerary?

His number flashed up on the screen and, having been directed to a man (much younger than him), he got straight to the point.

'I have two weeks of holiday leave which I am obliged to take before the beginning of October otherwise I lose it. I have been encouraged to take a break overseas by others,' (he had thought that by referring to 'others' it might mean the agent would also take pity and give him a good deal).

'Is there anywhere I can go for two weeks that is part-relaxing, part-stimulating,' he asked. Before the travel agent had a chance to reply, he further explained that not having the time to muster friends or family as travelling companions (they were all getting married, washing bibs or stuck in career-development-mode) he would be holidaying on his own on this particular occasion.

Wanting the travel agent to take him seriously, he intimated that he wanted to walk out the door that day with flights and holiday booked to depart two weeks later. The agent pulled out a brochure and showed him tours to Bhutan, Cambodia, China. The images of ancient structures on misty mountaintops suddenly piqued his interest – they were all places he had wanted to visit. Um, but only for two weeks? I would want to spend a bit more time there, he thought, but warming to the idea of guided tours to exotic places he felt inclined to save the long-haul destinations to a time when he had more than two weeks at his disposal.

'There is this one – Morocco,' said the agent handing over a summary of the two-week break. 'I've done it. It's very good.'

Fred looked at the itinerary. The tour group would meet in Casablanca, then travel to the oldest Imperial City, Fes, from where there was a day trip to Meknes and the nearby Roman ruins of Volubis. A long drive across the Middle Atlas (and then High Atlas) mountains to Erg Chebbi followed. After camping on the western edge of the Sahara in the dunes of Merzouga for a few days the tour group moved on to Todra Gorge and its famous oasis. After a four hour drive through the Valley of 1000 Kasbahs the group would spend the night near Ouarzazate and visits the hilltop village fortified by numerous Kasbahs, Ait Benhaddou. The penultimate stop in the coastal city of Essouira would 'replenish the soul' according to the tour write-up, before the final night in Marrakech and the return flight home.

It looked good, but it was the two nights in the Sahara that had caught his eye. Lying on warm sand in the silence of the desert and looking up at the Milky Way through unpolluted skies was something he had always wanted to do. Apparently the sound of nothing was worth listening to.

The travel agent did his best to sell him the merits of visiting the various cities, ruins, Bedouin camps, Kasbahs and resorts, but he was already sold on the idea.

'It ends in Marrakech an ideal place for sightseeing and shopping.'

The client looked hard at the travel agent, a man ten years younger than himself.

'Who goes on these things?' Fred asked (without uttering the words: *not a bunch of losers, I hope?*).

The agent read his thoughts.

'A great mix. Sometimes couples, students, a mix of male and females. They're not the old fuddy-duddy types who tend to go on cruises. These tours are for the more active type, besides the 'comfort' level is limited.'

Fred nodded and listened. He was ready to sign up, hoping his pensive expression might induce the agent to do a good deal. After all, he was giving him business.

'I've done this tour,' the agent volunteered again as if that was an endorsement.

On receipt of a blank gaze, the agent tapped away on his computer and ran through the list of those already signed up. 'For the September tour there are single travellers in their twenties and thirties from all over the world – South America, Japan, Australia. A couple in their late-fifties from Canada, one late-sixties individual from Australia. A couples of mid-thirties ladies from Scotland. Two single male Canadians in their forties. And more.'

As a lone traveller in a decent sized group, Fred reflected, he could get lost in the crowd. It might be nice to have beers and lemonade in the shade with fellow travellers after a day walking around the sights. Encouraged by the sound that he was mid-range and mid-level, and keen to deliver on his promise of being decisive, he thought, okay, what the hell.

'Sign me up'.

Back in the office, he casually broke the news to his colleague, Mel.

'Ooo, who knows who you might meet,' Mel said but this time with a twinkle in her eye.

'A business angel, you mean?' he said, someone who would come into business with me?'

'Yeah…,' his colleague giggled, eyes wide. 'That would be good.'

He didn't want a complicated holiday – no romantic drama. He had heard stories of group holidays; no, he would be careful to avoid hullabaloo, though deep down he feared that he might find his gaze drifting towards a group member only to subsequently find himself adjusting his pace to walk beside her as they wandered around Roman ruins. No, it was not something he wanted. He didn't want to be preoccupied with seating arrangements at mealtimes or expend energy trying to not look grumpy or bored at any given time. He wanted none of that. It was a holiday. He would engage in conversation as and when necessary. Look bored as and when he wanted. No hard work. An opportunity to recharge in the sunshine and sand of the Sahara. After all what was the point of a holiday if one were constantly distracted?

– III – The Return Trip

So it was, that, seven years earlier, Morocco had chosen him. However, on this occasion, he had chosen Morocco, or more specifically, Marrakech. It had not been a dead cert. Although he had reflected on returning to the city in the years since his first trip, he had delayed his return in order to explore other parts of the world. After all, there were elephants to be found in Cambodia, Nepal and China. Weren't there? Well, yes, he had discovered, but not quite like the elephant of Marrakech.

So earlier that summer (and when he had been reflecting on holiday options), he was cycling to work in Oxonville when he paused at a junction waiting for the traffic lights to change. He heard the squeak of a window above him being opened. He looked up to see the figure of a young woman move away from the window. Yet, it was not the sight of the woman that stopped him in his cycle lane, but the sight of a carved elephant ornament on the brickwork high above his head and looking wholly out of place. He had never noticed it before. Indeed there might be other places that had elephants yet to be explored, but the decision had been made. On this second occasion there was no need for any smiley work colleague to cajole him into a decision; a decision had been made. Marrakech was calling him.

That very lunchtime he logged on to the website of the same travel company years before and booked his trip to Morocco. Not the same holiday, but a walking tour in the Atlas Mountains, a tour that both started and ended in Marrakech. What had been unfinished business for years would finally be addressed.

As he waited for his bag at Marrakech airport's luggage carousel, he saw emerge from the carousel flap for his London flight a travel bag emblazoned with the tour company logo on the side, Thyme Travel. A bag identical to the one he had been sent by the tour company ahead of the trip. He had chosen not to use the tour company bag (too big with a poor strap design) preferring his trusty canvas travel bag that had accompanied him across five continents. Nevertheless, he wondered whether its owner would be on his tour. While keeping a beady eye out for the owner he was then surprised to see an identical Thyme Travel tour bag emerge through the plastic curtain strips and tumble onto the conveyor belt. Then another, then more and more began to circle the carousel. He realised he was probably looking at the luggage belonging to the other group members. And all coming from the UK.

Now a relatively seasoned traveller on such group tours, he knew that a good mix of nationalities and ages helped the feeling of being removed from his usual world. In fact, the mix was a formative factor in selecting the tour, but more recently tour companies had not shared the gender, age and nationalities of group members for data protection reasons. This had not troubled him so much on this occasion because his motivation was the elephant of Marrakech. Nevertheless, he knew that the airport would be the first opportunity for him to assess the group and the possible success of the trip.

Picking his bag and moving through customs he soon found his way to two tour staff collecting people off the flights. He learnt that the flight from the UK was unloading travellers for two separate walking tours. In a group of nearly twenty, there was one attractive lady who might have been competition for Mia and Jessica seven years earlier. But as the travellers were being divided into smaller groups in the airport terminal he realised that the young attractive lady was going to be in the other group. Might they travel back to the hotel today and have a few days together in Marrakech first? No, everybody was split and the two tours went their different ways. He wouldn't see her again. Jessica and Mia were safe. The search for the elephant was on.

– IV – Mia and Jessica

The first holiday had started in Casablanca. Fred had arrived alone at the airport but, quite by chance, he bumped into two Scottish ladies and the three of them made their way to the hotel. At the hotel he was introduced to the tour members who had already landed; the remainder were due to land later that night or the following morning. The travel agent had been right and by all accounts it had started well, it was a mixed group. He met the two Canadian forty-somethings, the retired Canadian couple, the Japanese student, the young English student couple and finally, the Australian girl, Jessica. Late-twenties, with gentle curves and with skin lightly touched by the Australian sun, Jessica (with hair in a bob) was a blonde.

Jessica was also travelling on her own and so, having been advised to stock up on provisions (including water), he had casually suggested to her that he had spotted a supermarket fifty yards from the hotel and why didn't they wander down together that evening to purchase supplies? She accepted (readily, he thought). Ten minutes wandering around the market laid a firm foundation for…something. Quite what, he did not know. If he had learnt anything in his thirty-seven years, it was that life was largely the anticipation of things that would not come to pass. Nevertheless, as they compared provisions, juggled currency calculations, swapped a few background details, the prospects were good by the time they had returned to the hotel. Perhaps these two weeks were going to be a fine break, he thought, as he bade her good night. A nice distraction. A foreign country.

Anyway, that was his feeling until breakfast the following day.

Sitting at the hotel breakfast table, with blonde Jessica beside him, the tour leader introduced a few new arrivals to the group, including more Canadians, Australians and finally the young Argentine, Mia. Late-twenties, with gentle curves and with skin lightly touched by the South American sun, Mia (with long dark hair) was a brunette.

Truth be told, as a type (and given the choice), Fred leaned towards brunettes. Over his breakfast pastry and coffee he felt that this exotic distraction might not be the ideal addition to the tour having met Jessica the previous day. Now, goddamnit, he was spoilt for choice about which one (blonde or brunette) he was not going to reflect upon as they journeyed around deserts and kasbahs for two weeks. Listening to Mia's Latino sparkle he wondered whether he should spend the energy of the two weeks denying an interest in both. Did that mean the available energy had to be equally divided between ignoring both or would it require twice the energy thus making the holiday twice as draining? Damn, what a holiday this was promising to be.

Alternatively, he could bite the bullet and succumb to exploring the field of play with one of them. But if so, which one?

With these profound concerns turning over in his mind as he stuffed his face with breakfast croissants, he noted, with some relief, that time was on his side. There were two weeks in which to survey the landscape by which time an answer (or winner) would emerge. Choices shouldn't be rushed.

– V – Dilemma

The holiday started with a four hour train journey from Casablanca to Fes. For Fred, when travelling by train or automobile in the UK, there was always a destination, a cause in mind. But travel-without-cause leaves only landscape and time. As the train hours slipped past, so did Fred's life in the UK recede.

Arriving in Fes, Morocco's oldest city and former capital, the group was escorted from the hotel to a viewpoint from which they could survey old Fes (Fes el Bali) before following the local guide through the cramped and bustling medina itself. As he walked, he soaked up the detail and history of the 9,400 narrow lanes of the medina lined by local tradesmen and shopkeepers. His slow walk was only interrupted to make way for boys pushing carts of food produce or mules laden with clanking metal goods. Such was the throng of people going about their business that, if one wasn't careful, one could soon become separated from the group and (but for the sudden appearance of young men weaving their way through on mopeds) be truly lost in a world unchanged since the Middle Ages.

With so much going on there was little time for conversation. It was just a matter of inhaling the aromas and bathing in the warmth of the North African sun. He smiled as he witnessed the formation of source material for anecdotes that would be pulled out and delivered over a dinner table in Canada or Australia. He acknowledged that he might even make it as a bit-part player into stories that might last for decades only to disappear as the generations passed.

In spite of the hubbub there were shared snatches of conversation between group members as each one learned a little about another as they walked deeper into the medina. In time, his home world loosened its grip on his mind. Its powers melted and fell away to the stone floor allowing a profound peace to descend upon him.

Fred's promises to himself back in the UK and at the Casablanca breakfast table also started to slip. He berated himself for dropping back to watch the forms of Jessica and Mia move their way through the crowds. Perhaps in time one swaying form would catch his eye more than the other? Jessica wore figure-hugging trousers and a loose lace top that appeared to be semi-transparent (or was that his imagination?). Her warm Australian features nestled lightly under her blonde bob. There was a warmth in her eyes and a calm rhythm in her gait. Her accent was gentle and there was a shyness in her manner, a shyness borne of modesty rather than insecurity. She was an early career, white collar professional from the west coast of Australia. The outdoor life was evident in her slim, toned forearms and manicured hands. Just as he found himself weakening – and weaving a web into which he might trap her – he caught himself. This was a holiday. There was to be no drama. With that thought, he turned his attention to the spices and leathers stalls and the jarring sight of a severed camel head hanging on a hook.

By the time he gave in to the inclination to return his gaze to the travellers moving ahead of him he was grateful that

Jessica's form had melted into the crowd a little further ahead. He wouldn't have to fight the pull of her form swaying down the avenue. Unfortunately, the devil within pinched him and he sought out the form of Mia. She too was walking ahead of him but not as far as Jessica. Mia was a keen amateur photographer so she was always dropping back to pause, frame a picture, focus and snap. He didn't have a camera with him so employed the traveller's meander. The meander required a slight acceleration to overtake group members, but within moments he was walking behind Mia. She wore sandals, a long flowing black skirt under which, he imagined, the air cooled her limbs. Mia's skin was not so much the golden hue of Jessica's, but the darker, richer Argentinian shade. Like Jessica, Mia too wore a cool white top but with long sleeves to her wrists around which numerous bangles hung. As she prepared her photographs she would flick her long dark hair out of the way and, once the photo had been taken, jabber her thanks to the locals. She played to the gallery. And the gallery loved her.

He was unsure which he preferred – the easy beach temperament of Oz or the crackling Latina fire. It was further complicated by shapes – the firmer Australian behind (tightened up by surfing or beach volleyball) or the rounder form to be found swaying on the dance floors of Latin America.

Enough!, he told himself shaking his head in self-disgust, he was on holiday. There was a fine (but dirty) line between lingering and leering. He picked up his pace and weaved his own way through the tour group and the locals to the front of the group and the tour guide. No harm in learning a bit about the local culture, he thought in the vain hope it would take his mind off curves and lines. He chatted with the tour guide and learnt a little about the history of the souk. His thoughts then turned to the whereabouts of a decent rug seller. He was always minded to pick up a memento of his travels. A souvenir transcended time. In years gone by, he had picked up posters of Gaudi's work in Barcelona, lamps from Damascus and had framed his own photographs of the Giza pyramids and Petra.

As he chatted away, a thought flashed across his mind. His own backside was now available for view by both Jessica and Mia (with camera). He was wearing light cotton trousers and a white safari shirt and baseball cap. With a background in sports and a gym practitioner, he suspected the shirt fell pleasingly off his shoulders and his hill-running lent a firmness to his own buttocks. Were thoughts now being fleshed out in Jessica's and Mia's minds of the gym-honed behind and cool look of the Englishman?

The group walked and paused before ending up in a dining room sitting on cushions around a low table on which a salad lunch was laid before them. As a younger man he might have influenced the seating arrangements to suit him but, as an older man, he now struggled to decide beside whom he should sit. It's a holiday, he thought. Let's just relax and let it go.

The afternoon continued with the tour of leather tanneries and a pottery shop. As the group swirled back and forth looking at the leather goods and pottery, he made a point of sharing a few remarks on the goods and asking for opinions from both Jessica and Mia. (Men underestimate the potential of shopping trips to impress the ladies.) He followed through and bought a few items to show it was not just mindless banter. In fact, he concluded, there was no harm in establishing a consultation routine for the various shopping stops of the two week tour. Time would tell.

He played hard to get. It worked. They didn't get him. They were also playing hard to get (again, successfully). Walking through the twisting, turning avenues of the old city of Fes, they finally ended up in a rug merchants. He consulted extensively with both women to the point that he cornered himself into blowing his souvenir budget on a carpet weave.

– VI – Mia

The following day the group travelled out to Meknes, a smaller neighbour of Fes, for tours of more souqs and spice stalls. Little alliances were forming between individuals and couples, and couples and couples. For the time being at least he wanted to remain a free agent and so was happy to wander by himself to find what seemed to be a reliable eating establishment for lunch. On finding one, he ordered a stomach-friendly dish of salad and chicken. In the heat of the middle of the day, he sat under an awning relishing an ice-cream only to see Mia sashaying along the edge of the restaurant awnings alone taking advantage of the shade. She had seen him and did not alter course and was therefore arguably intending to join him. He made it easy for her and waved the ice-cream, voiced his appreciation of it and pointed her towards the refrigerated cart and seller not far away. She accepted the invitation, placed her bag on the chair beside him and went and bought herself an ice-cream. They spent the last 20 minutes of the lunch break licking the melted cream from their (own) fingers, talking about the tour leader, the highlights and group bonding.

Maybe Mia was the one after all, he thought. Jessica had disappeared with one of the elderly Australian travellers. If Jessica saw Mia and him together, she might step back and the anxiety of choice would not be visited upon him.

Having taken a few baby steps at lunchtime, matters returned to normal for the tour of the Roman ruins at Volubis. The Roman ruins were a fine example of the imperial empire at its might. In the terrible heat of the afternoon there were regular attempts to stop and seek shelter in the shade of the ruins of broken columns and arches. Spread over a large expanse of sand, the ancient structures allowed the group to break up and re-form as the tour continued. Thus was he able to play cool in the blistering heat. Wandering slowly behind the group broken up by the wind, but held together by desert, he watched the contenders move. The shared ice-cream with Mia had done its job and their interaction was continued in the shade, but he reminded himself it was still a holiday.

The evening was spent in a pleasant restaurant in Fes. He chatted at length to one of the Canadians about life and accountancy in San Francisco, but as the evening broke up and the group moved to a rooftop bar, a small collection of the travellers chatted about the day. Beside him sat Mia. A corner had been turned.

– VII – Jessica

The following day the tour group boarded a 16-seater van for the air-conditioned trip through the Atlas Mountains. Through a peculiar unspoken process, Fred was pleased to find himself on a single seat by the door (or later, beside the English tour guide, Sarah, at the front of the vehicle). He was content to watch the empty vistas of the desert roll by, interrupted only by nomadic shepherds and their herds of sheep. The drive through the Atlas Mountains transported them into another world and a different time. The Roman influences were left behind and the pre-history of the Sahara beckoned. They stopped at a border town Erfoud and transferred to Land Rovers for the race to the auberge (lodge) at Erg Chebbi, on the western fringe of the Sahara desert, before the sinking of the setting sun.

On the first night the tour group camped out in Berber tents in the dunes one hundred metres from the auberge. The coldness of the night and a meal cooked on a fire under the stars bonded the group yet further. After the following day's camel ride into the (fifty metre high) dunes of Merzouga, the second night was spent deeper in the desert. A hearty meal was cooked and conversation crackled around the large campfire as tour members moved back and forth refilling their plates. With the only light available from the stars and the flickering fire, the group conversation became a whisper, then mutterings between smaller groups, then hushed words between pairs as the tired travellers rested first on their elbows, then their backs to take in the majesty of the Milky Way in all its brilliance above them.

Without any planning he found himself lying next to Jessica on the edge of the group. The fire died down further and the cold of the desert crept into the camp and the voices dropped yet further. When he had exhausted all his knowledge of the constellations above them and fudged further references to unseen constellations, Fred moved on to the subject of her life in Australia. He had to stop himself from apologising for letting their bonding slip after the first day's supermarket trip saying he had thought it polite to spend time with other members of the group. As they talked about their lives on different sides of the planet, a calmness and warmth crept in between them. There was something powerful about the simplicity of that shared moment. In truth, he found himself imagining a lifetime of lying by her side and talking into the night.

Back in the UK his evening would be flooded by artificial light – computers, smartphones, tablets, television live, television on demand. Coupled with all the business of the day (shopping, bills, correspondence), not to mention the news (political, economic, social, personal), his existence was at best a test of endurance, at worst overwhelming. If it wasn't a personal crisis, it was a national crisis. Everything was a crisis.

If it wasn't a crisis, it was a conflict. But here, in the dunes of Merzouga, there was just sand and stars. And company.

It was 'visceral company' – not a term used back home, he thought. He couldn't shake the feeling that, if through some global catastrophe the modern world were swept away leaving only sand dunes and constellations, then everything would be okay. Western life was a noisy search for answers. But answers are found in silence, Fred concluded. With Jessica by his side, all he could hear was her breathing. But when it was accompanied by the silence of the desert and watched over by starlight, her presence became his world.

How could he have not seen it? He was being foolish, thinking of Mia as a contender. She was merely a distraction. A distraction you might expect of a young 29 year old South American would have on a 37 year old man. No, Jessica was the one he should focus on. The fact of her 27 years was an irrelevance.

The fire died, more blankets were requested and the night ended with him facing Jessica murmuring into the night under several Berber blankets. Were it not for their sleeping bags cocooning them and limiting movement, he wondered what might have happened as the coldness reached under the blankets and their bodies sought other warmth. No matter, he thought, they would soon be in hotels with soft linen. And if not, no matter, he was on holiday after all.

– VIII – Return to the Atlas Mountains

There were no nights under the stars on Fred's second visit to Morocco. It was all about hiking – for that he was grateful. As the tour group was driven into the High Atlas mountains, the silences were not lost to ruminations on romance. Nor was the silence the result of language barriers, it could all be attributable to British reserve. There was not one hint that beautiful creatures from the southern hemisphere even existed.

As the group drove through the sandy, parched landscapes, Fred relived the scenes and scenarios of Mia and Jessica. He had mixed feelings. He was both secretly pleased but also disappointed that on this second trip he was not to be distracted. He would not find himself wanting to walk behind one group member more than another (which, he concluded, was a good thing because this was a walking holiday packed full of five hour hikes across dusty plains). His first holiday had included Roman ruins, deserts, long drives through mountains, oases, rock formations, Kasbahs, souks and cities. But on his second holiday there was a lack of such variety giving him time to think. It was clear to him that he needed to right the wrongs of his first trip when he returned to Marrakech.

– IX – Jessica Consolidates

On the day following the night in the dunes (of the first trip) the group rose early, boarded their camels and headed back to the auberge at Erg Chebbi. Mia's noisy cheerfulness was not lost on Fred nor were her regular efforts to trundle up close to him and point out sights in the empty landscape. But his thoughts were with Jessica and the night before. Was Mia playing for his attention having spent the night on the other side of the group wondering what was going on in the darkness twenty feet away? Fred did not know, but he did now know where his heart was.

At the auberge the group loaded up four-wheel drive vehicles and raced back to firm ground whereupon they boarded the 16-seater van for a five hour journey to Todra Valley and its gorge. He did not want to make clear his intentions to Jessica just yet. It was still week one of the holiday. Besides it was respectful to Mia. Content in his decision, he relaxed in the front seat of the van beside the tour guide and watched the Moroccan landscape roll by.

Todra Gorge itself rose an impressive 300 feet high above the settlement of Tinehar at its base – home to hotels and small businesses. Having unpacked at the hotel in late afternoon, the tour group was escorted to the entrance of the gorge – looking more like a long crack in the cliff than anything else. They walked into the gorge along a quarter-mile paved walkway beside which ran a stream. The babbling water, the shade and the late hour cooled the stroll. Like Volubis the group members drifted apart as they made their own way deeper into the gorge, pausing to take photos, mixing with the locals and waving away children bearing gifts of bangles and scarves. Fred hung back enjoying the coolness and taking time to videotape a few moments for posterity.

In his viewfinder he zoomed in on Jessica as she strolled a few dozen yards ahead of him (keeping a sufficiently wide angle of the gorge to justify the lingering shot). He watched as she walked past stalls and locals including a few young men standing chatting by the stream. Suddenly, in full view of his recording, he watched as a young, slim man took two steps towards the blonde Australian visitor and reached out to grab her head in an attempt to pull her into a kiss.

Jessica immediately pulled away and walked on picking up her pace, but not before Fred had broken into a jog towards her. He was by her side in seconds and, in full view of the local men, slipped his arm around her waist in a she's-with-me-kinda-way. With a she's-with-me-kinda-glare at the local men, they walked on. Jessica did not flinch at the gesture and the arm now about her waist.

Fortuitously, there were similar small groups of men dotted at intervals on the pathway further in the gorge. Fred's arm remained around Jessica's waist for a hundred yards at strolling pace only to be removed in a demonstration of non-presumptiveness, but was immediately returned around her waist at any sign of a threat of attention (including from bangle-laden children).

His mind did momentarily flash to Mia, but a quick glance around them suggested she had been swallowed up by the gorge's grandeur and was not even a witness.

The following day the group was led on a tour of the palmery surrounding the settlement at the base of the gorge. An oasis, in fact. They walked through abandoned ruins of sand-brick houses and along the edges of the palm tree-shaded fields. Fred moved back and forth between group members and, taking the opportunity, offered Jessica a welcome home-stay if she ever wished to visit the UK. They were a third of the way through the trip. The matter was settled.

– X – Mia Rallies

The next stop on the tour schedule was Dades Valley, known as the Valley of 1,000 Kasbahs. Now travelling across the southern part of the Morocco, the group halted for the night at the desert city of Ouarzazate. The tour group leader, Sarah, announced that as the day cooled she would lead a group across the wadi (the dry river bed) to the fortified village of Ait Benhaddou. An hour before sun down, and refreshed by a rest and a shower at their hotel, the group followed their leader across the wadi towards the imposing fortification. Rising high above the plain, framed by the Atlas mountains, the brown mud collection of Kasbahs behind the forty foot high walls clinging to the side of a hill looked like a place untouched for two thousand years.

Tour members were left alone to climb to the summit of Ait Benhaddou. As they did so, many stopped to take photographs of the scenes and wadi below. It was at one overlook that Fred was joined by the Canadians, the Scottish friends and Mia. With Mia's birthday imminent, the Argentine referred to her worries of turning thirty. The Scottish and Canadians made reassuring noises that satisfied Mia – in part because the noises noted that her birthday would not be forgotten and would be celebrated by the group before the tour ended. Playfully, Mia quietly started to hum happy birthday to herself as she focused her camera lens on the muddy brown landscape turned orange by the sinking sun. Scottish Anne hummed along with Mia and as a matter of politeness Fred joined in. A conclusion of the hummed verse did not bring about the conclusion of the rendition, for Mia now started to sing the words to the song. Wanting to bring a quietness to the Kasbah, Fred quietly began to whisper-sing the words of happy birthday to hurry it along to its end. He hoped Anne would join him in his rendition, but he soon found that she had disappeared from their side along with the Canadians. This left him alone on the barricade of a Kasbah whisper-singing happy birthday to Mia who suddenly stopped her humming and turned to watch him sing.

With the solitude, the sinking sun, the still air (now touched by the coolness of the coming night), he suddenly became conscious of the intimate nature of the moment – something that appeared not to be lost on Mia also for her gaze remained fixed on him. His whispered rendition softened to a breathless whisper.

Wholly unintentionally, he was drawn into the moment and was unsure whether he should congratulate himself for master-minding the quiet moment with a beautiful South American woman. The moment seemed to have worked for

Mia as well, because, at the very least, she had shut up. As the last breathy 'happy birthday to Mia' passed his lips it became clear (like an approaching locomotive) that this was one of those moments a man should take advantage of. As Mia stepped forward he felt a surge of panic deep inside him. He knew that in any other situation he would act, but there were gremlins in his thought process. Mia planted a soft, slow kiss on his cheek. Whether she whispered a 'thank you' before the kiss or afterwards, he was unsure. His head was spinning. The gremlins had been identified – they were working on behalf of that other one, the blonde, er, Jessica.

To act on his instinct would be washing away the Dunes of Merzouga and the arm about the waist at Todra Gorge. He wasn't ready. If he had known that the Kasbah kiss was to appear, he could have given it some thought. But no, nobody and nothing had prepared him. If he had more time, he might have acted but, as he steadied himself (and his head spun), he heard the voices of Canadians and English students by his side and the sounds of camera shutters.

The tour of the village concluded as the sky turned a darker blue, nevertheless the Kasbah kiss of Ait Benhaddou hung over the night. A 'moment' had been shared and, as he strolled back across the dry wadi to the hotel, he concluded that Mia was where the excitement lay. He surprised himself. He had clarity. It was probably a good thing he had not reacted immediately, but both he and Mia had turned a corner (again). It was a long-time coming, but he knew the score. The ground had been laid. She would be the one. He would not pass on the next moment. Perhaps he could show a little thoughtfulness. Perhaps the choice of birthday gift would seal the deal.

– XI – The Square of Death

There were two more places to visit in the second week – Essaouira and Marrakech. Time was pressing and matters would need to be concluded soon. Fred did not wish to reveal his intentions in front of others so once again he took the opportunity to sit at the front of the van and rest easy on the way to Essaouira. The grand reveal could wait. Besides, there was no rush. The group started whispering about a gift for the tour leader which led to whispers of birthday gifts for Mia and another birthday celebrant, the Canadian, Victor. Whispers concluded with the agreement that tour members would present birthday gifts at the end of tour dinner in Djemaa el Fna square in Marrakech.

Being guided around the souk in Essaouira later that day Fred paid attention to what items Mia was ogling and haggling for with the local shopkeepers. Seeing her haggle for, then walk away from a pair of ruby red stone earrings, he nipped back later and purchased them on the spot.

Feeling happy with himself he thought it would indeed seal the deal on the final night, but in the intervening time there were moments when he disconcertingly swung towards Jessica. Fortunately, Mia's constant references to her thirtieth birthday kept him on track. Marrakech and the end of the tour would provide the final answer. Jumping on the public bus to Marrakech he was pleasantly surprised to find Mia joining him by his side. Little did the brunette know that her birthday earrings were tucked away in his bag ahead of the final night in Marrakech. Tucked in his bag also was the only other gift he had for a tour member, the other birthday celebrant, Victor – a contrivance to make it not look too generous for the South American beauty.

Having arrived in Marrakech late-morning, the group booked into a hotel before jumping into taxis to the main tourist attraction – Djemaa el Fna Square. After a short orientation tour by the group leader, members were left to explore and shop in the adjacent souk with instructions to return to the square for the final night's celebratory dinner. The group soon drifted apart as they hunted bargains.

Deep in the souk Fred bumped into Jessica and within moments they were walking along together. Once again, a calming sense of 'company' descended upon him. A sensation not felt since the night in the desert. They stopped for a drink at a little cafe. Aware that the presentation of birthday gifts was scheduled for that evening he mentioned, with a tut, sigh and roll of his eyes, his purchase of earrings for Mia. They left the cafe and continued shopping. He forgot about Mia. If she did flit into his consciousness, it was with the gladness of having a break from the brunette's chatter.

Jessica and Fred stopped to browse items together comparing notes on what they should take home to the UK and Australia.

'For your wife, sir?' asked a store manager at a scarf stall holding up a number of scarves.

Fred didn't baulk. In fact, it felt nice.

He also noted that Jessica didn't do either of two things that might be expected in the circumstances. She didn't deny that she was his wife and, secondly, she didn't flinch at the suggestion. In fact, she turned to Fred raising her eyebrows in an expectant way much like a wife might do when expecting her husband to buy her a gift. Fred played along. So, there they were – a man and a woman standing alone in a heaving souk neither flinching at the mention of being the other's spouse.

'What do you think, darling?' he asked her in all seriousness.

'Um, I like that one too,' she replied pointing to another, more expensive-looking, scarf.

Realising he was obliged to act, but within a budget (and thinking he might be bounced into buying two if he didn't act quickly), he haggled, nodded and bought the desired scarf.

'Wrapped up or...?' said the store manager nodding towards Jessica.

Fred took the scarf and wrapped it around Jessica's shoulders.

'Beautiful, no?' said the seller.

Fred nodded and smiled, muttering quietly, 'Of course'.

Fred and Jessica meandered through the stalls and past shop fronts selling all manner of goods. His sense of peace in Jessica's companionship deepened, but there was also a sense of relief – he had neutralized the purchase of earrings for Mia. Yet, this only confused him. Why would he want to neutralise the purchase of the earrings? He did not know. What he did know was that he would not swap that hour in the souk for anything. Or anybody.

Bumping into other group members coming to the end of their own shopping trips, Fred and Jessica joined them in heading back to the hotel to freshen up, rest and prepare for the final night's festivities. Walking into Djemaa el Fna square at night was different to the square in day. It had an unworldly quality that pulled in many thousands of locals and tourists alike. Now illuminated by ten thousand electric light bulbs strung up on wires along the avenues of eateries, half the square was laid out with tables. The square hummed with chefs and waiters as they prepared to feed the chattering visitors. Smoke from the open-air barbecues, carrying aromas of meat and spices, drifted across the square while the eating establishments sent out young waiters to entice cautious travellers to their tables. Potential diners meandered slowly up and down the aisles unsure whether a full table was a recommendation or if an empty table would be the place for a splendid discovery.

The choice of table was not an issue for Fred's tour group. Their tour guide, Sarah, had already booked the table in advance. As the group coalesced around the long table, such were Fred's conflicted feelings for both Jessica and Mia that he made a conscious effort not to try and manufacture a seating arrangement. He weaved his way to the middle of table and sat first, letting the group members find their own place, thus leaving his own destiny in the lap of the gods. Within moments the table was seated.

Mia had sat opposite him.

Turning to his left he found Jessica had sat beside him.

The evening started with the exchange gifts. First to the tour leader, Sarah, then to the birthday boy, Victor, then the birthday girl, Mia. She loved the earrings. 'How thoughtful!' She seemed genuinely touched that Fred had remembered them from the shop in Essaouira. She put on her earrings and through the course of the evening made much of her gift and the gift-giver, Fred, sitting opposite. He said nothing; nor did Jessica who sat wrapped in the scarf he had bought her a few hours earlier.

He recalled the Kasbah kiss of Ait Benhaddou, yet he carried within him the dunes of Merzouga. Expertly navigating and surfing the table conversation, he tried to define their differences. Mia forced herself into his present. Jessica enticed thoughts of the future. Mia was coital, Jessica was post-coital. The difference in the wearing of gifts was not lost on him. Mia's gift had been presented, accepted and celebrated in public; Jessica's gift had been wrapped around her shoulders in the privacy of an intimate moment.

Was there a choice of dishes on offer that evening? Was this a life choice?

Decisions, decisions. What did I do to deserve this, he thought, as he smiled and chatted away as everyone remained none the wiser.

Sitting there in the Djemaa el Fna square, he felt he had learned nothing. In fact, he had regressed as a knowledgeable man. Two weeks had passed and he was no further on. Not only was he back to square one, he was literally camped out in square one. He was not surprised to learn that Djemaa el Fna translated as 'the place of death' (the place where Sultans had displayed the heads of their enemies).

Fortunately, planning was not left to him alone. Tour members were talking of a final expedition – a trip to a nightclub bar. That would be the place where his destiny would be revealed. He had three hours at least. He would forfeit all responsibility for what was to follow given the chance.

The meal went along pleasantly. He was careful to share attentiveness with the blonde beside him and the brunette opposite, all the while trying to ascertain which choice he would regret the most. Would regret evolve over time? Eighteen months later what would be his wish? Three years later? Seven? Ten years? With a degree of anticipation and dread he joined the group as they rose from the benches. The tour leader Sarah was not joining them.

'Just head down Mohammad V avenue until you see the elephant. Turn right and the club is fifty yards down on your right,' she said.

Using the illuminated Koutoubia Mosque's minaret rising high in the night sky as a way to orientate themselves, the group slowly strolled towards the exit from the place of death and, very possibly he feared, to the place of hell. For within

180 minutes a decision would be made by him or for him. Everybody was going to the club.

'Look for the elephant,' someone cried as they headed down the wide avenue.

– XII – The Elephant

'Where's the elephant?' Fred asked the man in some exasperation pointing towards the wall seven years later. He was the third local man Fred had stumbled across who appeared to be able to understand English and hopefully the first who would be able to help.

'What?' the old man replied looking startled.

'It was right here, I think,' Fred said, pointing again to a corner of a side street running off the wide Mohammad V Avenue. 'The elephant.'

The local man still looked bewildered. The Englishman could not find it. Fred had been walking up the avenue and diving in and out of side streets for an hour and a half.

'What elephant?' replied another man in broken English. 'No elephant in Marrakech.'

Patiently, very patiently, Fred described the elephant for the man, but to no avail.

Alarmed at meeting such an agitated pale stranger accosting locals about the whereabouts of an animal, the local man hurried off.

For seven years Fred had been passing an elephant carved onto an old building in his hometown without noticing it. He wasn't going to continue to neglect his destiny now that he was back in Marrakech. It had not occurred to him that he would not be able to find the elephant with relative ease. Having landed in the city ten days earlier, he had made a point not to reacquaint himself with the nightclub until his return to the city after the week in the Atlas mountains. He wanted his head to be in a space where he could devote himself to the task in hand.

The last evening of that second trip had begun so well. There had been nothing to be alarmed about. Being the last night of the tour he had once again found himself in the city's central square, Djemaa el Fna, for a farewell dinner with his hiking group. Having returned from the dusty mountains earlier in the day he soon suspected that their hotel was possibly the very same Marrakech hotel as his first trip. Perhaps this second holiday was matching up quite nicely to the first? A symmetry was emerging. Maybe things would be easier than he thought. Perhaps he hadn't been neglectful all those years before, it was merely a precursor for the revelation this time around. This time he was ready.

Once again the tour group – this time the hikers – sat around a long table on the square, the smoke and smells buffeted by the hum of the nightlife swirling around them. Fred had been transported back in time. Not just seven years, but twenty seven, seventy years, seven hundred years. The square was a place that existed apart from time. Fred watched the throng of locals and visitors wondering how many of them had travelled back to the square to remedy mistakes in their youth (or even in previous lives). He nodded and smiled as his co-hikers reflected on the adventures in the mountains during the week and shared plans for other walks in other parts of the world, but Fred's mind was elsewhere. All he could think about was bringing closure to the dilemma of the blonde and the brunette.

The conversation turned to plans after the meal. A bar? A walk? More shopping? Fred let the hikers announce their own plans and when asked of his own, he said he would have a slow wander back to the hotel.

'Shopping? No present-buying?' Fred was asked.

'No, I've bought all my presents,' he replied. (He was only thinking of two – a scarf and a pair of earrings.)

'I'll see you back at the hotel or tomorrow morning…,' he said waving his friends off.

Fred stood in the middle of the square watching as his hiker-friends were swallowed up in smoke and the light of ten thousand light bulbs. As they receded, so did seven years. The two nights had indeed become one. Only in Marrakech. Once satisfied he was alone, he turned and walked to the darker corner of the square towards the Mohammad V Avenue to catch up with other, older friends.

Finding the club the first time had been easy – and all because of the elephant on the corner. It was as clear as day – at night. The group, including Mia and Jessica, all turned off the avenue on the corner adorned by the unmistakable presence of the elephant, walked fifty yards down the side street to a discreet establishment ablaze with light before climbing the dozen steps into the club. And, boy, what club.

Some buildings, some places, are built and decorated in the hope a 'space' will be created. But very rarely there are spaces that are 'captured' – spaces around which walls are built, painted, adorned with decorations and carefully illuminated. They are spaces that cannot be created by man alone. This club was just such a space. It breathed all by itself.

Balls of light (orange, blues, yellows, greens, reds) were artfully suspended about the club's walls, ceilings, pillars and booths. Working with the shadows, they created a wondrous environment. A long drinks bar stretched down one side deep into the sacred place which opened out into an open floor area giving room for people to move, talk and dance. The sound was a quiet whisper of voices, cushioned by music created on centuries-old musical instruments. Around the open floor were couches and booths all inviting people to rest and reflect. Sometimes the space invited its guests to share quietly, other times it invited them to move. It asked no questions, it gave no answers. Fred was captivated. He chatted. He laughed. He danced. In such a place there was room for everyone and everything. There was space and time for both earrings and scarves, for both the Kasbah Kiss of Ait Benhaddou and the Dunes of Merzouga. The club accommodated everything and all time. In such a place no choices were demanded…so none were made.

And so it was that, seven years later, Fred stood alone and bereft, staring at a dirty-plastered blank wall on a street corner. A mobile telephone sales kiosk had been positioned close to the wall and dominated the corner leading off to (what he was convinced was) the side avenue in question. The ornamental carving of the elephant's head (about the size of a child's bicycle) had indeed been unmistakable. With its trunk curled about its head, its features had been partly hidden seven years earlier by vegetation hanging over from a garden on the other side of the wall. He couldn't in all honesty remember what the elephant 'carving' had been made of – brass, cement, granite, marble? Once upon a time locals might have used it as a water fountain. Whatever its origin, it had seemed eternal.

For years he had been thinking about the moment when the carving would guide him once again to the club. Many hours had been spent in rueful reflection on that last evening in the company of Jessica and Mia – in a place both guarded and signposted by the elephant. On his return to Marrakech what had he been expecting to find there? Mia and Jessica? Still there chatting to him, dancing with him, all the while looking deep and searchingly into his eyes? Competing for an answer to their own questions?

But here he was. He was ready now. He was back and ready to choose this time. Which one, he didn't know. The scarf? The earrings? The Dunes of Merzouga or the Kasbah Kiss of Ait Benhaddou would be placed in their rightful order.

All he needed was the elephant, but where was it? Did he need to mutter some spell for it to appear? 'Abracadabra'? 'Open Sesame'? Elephants have long memories for goodness sake, but this one had forgotten him after only seven years.

Fred spent many hours walking up and down the Mohammad V Avenue searching for that ornamental animal carving. Ever, ever so slowly the truth dawned – he had confused the elephant with a signpost. A signpost pointing the way. It wasn't. It had been a gateway. And gateways to sacred spaces exist only for the briefest of moments before they dissolve in the wake of Father Time's onward march. Signposts can be made wood, brass, concrete, marble or granite and can often be revisited, but gateways to other worlds are ethereal, personal and fleeting.

Fred tired as the darkest part of the night finally claimed his hopes and revealed to him the fruitlessness of his return visit to Marrakech. A few hours before the rising of the sun, he trudged back to his hotel, alone. Not only was there nothing to show from his second trip, there was nothing to show from his first trip either. Nothing. No earrings, no scarf. Nothing.

DAVID O ZEUS

Book of Giants
(Journal 9)

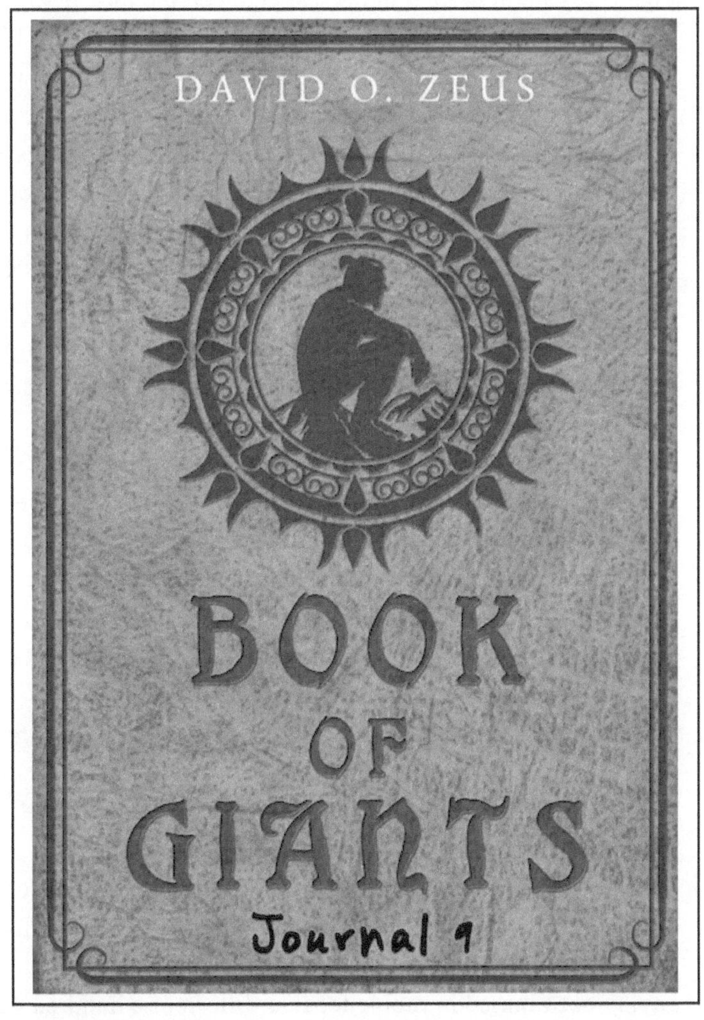

– I – Introductions

This is my ninth journal in the last eighteen months. It's ironic, I started them so that I could transfer the entries to my blogs and social media accounts when I got the chance, but now I'm permanently old school – writing stuff in notebooks with a pen! Incredible. That said, I'm sort of enjoying it. The blogs and social media are not coming back, I know that now. For the first month or so I thought they must come back. I couldn't imagine a world when they couldn't come back. Then, for a bunch of months, I wasn't so sure. Then, after six months, I thought the Internet and phones and everything wouldn't be coming back, but deep down inside I was hedging my bets. I was thinking maybe I was being pessimistic. Now, I know with an absolute certainty that we will never see them again. So here I am writing in journals, diaries, notebooks. I used to have two hundred followers on my blog, three thousand on Instagram and eleven hundred on Twitter. Now I just have anyone who picks up my journals. (Er, which is none.) I used to monitor the blog followers and cheer when someone signed up. But now I'm beginning to think that no one will read these words. They will be lost and probably destroyed as a building falls around me.

It's crazy. I'm in a constant state of panic that I will lose my previous volumes. When I am not panicking it is only because I am thinking I have normalised my panic (or paranoia) to such an extent that I don't notice it. But if, just if, they do survive (damaged, burnt, covered in blood or whatever) having been buried in rubble for five, fifteen or a hundred years and you are reading this and have read the other volumes (great

– they've survived!), forgive this repetition. If they don't and you only pick up this one (Journal 9), I'll give a brief summary of where we are. Please take care of it. It's the only witness to me, my very existence now. I confess there is a romantic in me that says maybe these journals will become a bit of the record of this time in the planet's history. (I say the 'planet's history' and not 'human history' because I think this is pretty much the end of human history.)

One other note that I always add: if you do come across the other journals, I think volumes 1.3 and 2.4 and 4.6 are the most informative. Journal 7.7 also has a lot about the major turning point in the story of this city – when I felt it was seriously lost. Finally I now instinctively know that these words (in fact, nothing) will be backed up in the cloud, ever. When I first started making these journal entries I used to forget that there was only one copy. I suppose that is why I am so paranoid. There is no cloud. Or rather there are, but they are just the old school, white floating ones (but even they are pretty rare now – clouds are mostly grey or black). I feel like I'm living in an ancient time. Sometimes I wish I could conjure up some of those ancient people (when everything was in black and white :)). They could give me so many tips about surviving. But I'm learning. I'm becoming a bit of an animal, in fact. I don't mean in an uncivilised way. I mean in a way that means I can survive. It's a tough world I now realise and you have to be tough to survive. Tough and skilled. I shudder at the thought of what people were like back in the day. We had become so soft. In fact, sometimes I wondered how I survived in the old world at all.

Back to the standard introduction – I wish I could photocopy this and stick it in the beginning of each journal, but it's not possible. Electricity would be nice, let alone access to a working copier.

I started Journal 1 within five days of the Internet going down. I was having thoughts and ideas and a few funny things happened to me that would have been great for the blog, so I grabbed a little notebook and started making notes. Anyway, here we are on Journal 9 eighteen months later.

If you are reading this in a hundred years time, I don't know how this ends and I don't know what you guys will call this period in history. The time of giants, maybe. We call them 'Orgs', inspired by the Orcs in *Lord of the Rings*, I suppose (note to self: I must try and find a copy of the Tolkien trilogy), and maybe the Borg (*Star Trek*, if you don't know); although, Randall called them something different. (I'll talk about Randall later.)

The Orgs are the top predator now, preying on the billions of humans – although it would be far fewer now. Not that the Orgs have been responsible for killing all 90% (a guess) of the humans who had disappeared. Many people have starved, others have died from medical neglect and disease, untreated conditions and illnesses, injuries caused (directly or indirectly) by the Orgs themselves. Hospitals don't exist now. Not really. You do find some people with medical expertise, but they don't blow a trumpet about it. Can't blame them. It's not safe.

In summary, it was the solar flare I suppose that kicked it all off. They said it was coming – plasma discharge formations were seen in the sky before and after. When the solar flare proper happened (and the coronal mass ejections) it created all sorts of havoc. Communications died, the Internet went down (never to return), there were fires, confusion, a freaky tingling in the air. Conventional television and radio all went down (everything was digital, you see). They managed to get some analogue broadcasting back up, but all the tech (phones, cameras, email) that generated content was digital, so it never really lasted. So we are back to word of mouth and the printed (or handwritten) word passed from hand to hand. Then there were the massive electrical storms and fires. It all got very weird. (It still is weird. But 'weird' now is normal.)

I have mixed feelings. There is a part of me that feels that I should be grateful for living in a dramatic time, like a soldier.

With all the sources of news and information down, I cannot tell you where the giants came from – though obviously from the underworld or whatever. The solar flare disrupted so much stuff (including the magnetic sphere apparently) that everything went to pot. Who the hell knows. But it's our reality now. Myth has become reality. I suppose these are indeed the giants of the bible, the trolls of Scandinavia, the *fee fi fo fum* of England. But then again, I can't be sure.

I personally didn't see any giants for months, so they were a sort of mythical creature. When I did see one, boy, did I know it was the end of the world. There was no chance we would defeat them. No chance at all. The military were pretty useless, the solar flare and coronal mass ejections saw to that. Besides, to have a working military, not only do you have to have working military technology (guns, planes, satellites and shit), but you have to have infrastructure (to move stuff – ammo and fuel) around. The giants saw to some of the infrastructure, railways gone, roads and airports in pieces. And you have to have the people to do it. If people are not fed, nursed, or their towns and homes are getting attacked, then you have a demotivated military as the months go on. The only possibility of humans surviving is if a small number of us get smart and stay smart. And then maybe we could live in harmony with the Orgs. Perhaps in time they will return underground. Or perhaps we will. I've heard that there are all sorts of ancient tunnel systems dating back thousands of years. Definitely in Europe.

Apparently you can get from Scotland to Italy by going underground. I do wonder if there was a time when we used to escape from the giants on a regular basis. There are stories in ancient books, but the mainstream pooh-poohed them. But the mainstream are all dead now so haven't learned anything (and wasted everybody else's time in the process).

I'm not sure I am one of the real smart ones. Good enough to survive long term. I'm staying in the city (what's left of it) for now. Lots of people thought it would be safer in the city so they flocked to the conurbations of high-rises to compete with the sizes of the Orgs – some must be sixty feet tall. There are rumours of others even bigger, but I am going to hazard a guess they are a myth.

– II – The Current Situation – Place and People

I've moved around a bit. I now give a helluva lot of thought to where I'm going to stay. It feels as if I've tried them all – underground, ground level residential, ground level city, high rise city, suburbs. I haven't gone out into the country, it's too difficult, unpredictable. My current place is downtown, halfway up a high rise residential building surrounded on three sides by buildings of the same height or taller. I've been moving between spaces (I call them 'nest holes' – there's no other description really) for the last four months. The current requirements are: residential, above the fourteenth floor, below the twentieth; ideally a corner apartment (allowing me to see 270 degrees around my nest hole) with a partially broken (at least 40% broken) facade, i.e. walls that are at least 40% open to the elements; no electricity, but hopefully running water. Then a bunch of simple things: the ability to hang curtains or drapes from the ceiling (this is harder to do than you think – you need to tie the drapes (curtains, screens) to something) and at least one (ideally small) room in the apartment without any windows. Also, one entrance secured with a wooden door.

Depending on the time or place you are reading this, you might think some of the above is strange, but anybody living in these times would know. As I've said, as far as I can say right now (and anything might change) you have to be near supplies and by that I mean shops and stores that you can reach without breaking cover (crossing streets and squares). Places you can reach within a 200 second sprint and shops with large stores of tinned foods to keep you going without concern. It is also good to find stores with basements – partly because it is safer when collecting goods, but also because they are hidden from other raiders, survivors. The forty foot high piles of rubble heaped at the bottom of smashed high-rises and skyscrapers help. In fact, the best store I had was perfectly hidden by the debris of a collapsed skyscraper on 17th street.

It has to be downtown because you need to be near supplies. There is no point in hauling loads of supplies to your nest hole which you have to vacate five days later. No, it has become clear that you have to strike the right balance between being mobile and secure. (See Journals 2 to 6 for details on life in other situations.) That said, I think I might want to move away from the city now. I have a sense things are going to get bad soon.

It's not as if there is any advice coming from anywhere out there. There is no government (at least not one I know of) and there is no way to predict what might happen. The future is unknown. Perhaps in time groups will gather together and communities form, but it isn't really happening yet.

There was a time when other people were the enemy, but there are fewer now and those remaining are far more savvy. It makes sense to keep a low profile and cooperate as and when we come across each other. Large groups attract the giants, I'm guessing it is the smell, odour of people. It's always best to keep any odours weak. That's why I try to wash twice a week. Running water is rare though. Now often contaminated with diseases, blood and fluids from decomposing human remains.

Some Orgs used to be based in the city, now they are out of town and just raid now and again. They spend their nights out in the country then just trundle into town when it takes their fancy (like a trip to the mall) or if there is a survivor-related disturbance. They work alone, but sometimes you might find a couple foraging in the same area.

I realised it far too late, but they probably see tower blocks as supermarket shelves wandering around picking fruit out of the flats to eat. I know no different now, so can't change my ways.

– III – This Week

It's been a big week. If I can say that – I've lost track of the days of the week and the dates. It's a long, painful story. Computers, phones and electronic devices batteries have all died. There are generators, but anybody who is anybody knows to keep them off. It acts like a neon come-get-me sign. The orgs come running. I try to keep a rough track of time in my journals, but I have been unwell a few times and got disorientated. I've lost so many days and I just don't know where we are. I think it's mid-September. The summer I think has passed, but the trouble is, what with all the solar activity and disruption, the leftover pollution from volcanic ash, forest fires and, I suspect (but don't know) the nuclear detonations, the climate has been a bit haywire and unpredictable. But mid-September is my best guess. Give or take four weeks, I would guess. I have lost track of time of the day. My wristwatch packed up a month ago and all the watches in the stores are all dying. I can't replace the battery in my own watch, I don't have the tools. Apparently there are old world watches that don't need batteries, they could be wound up on a daily basis. It's a fantastic idea. When I do venture out I try and find apartments that belonged to old people in the hope that I'll find one tucked in a drawer somewhere. Trouble is, it's not as if I could wind it to the correct time. I don't know the time! And it is not as if I need to schedule my time to match somebody else's. I could only guess, but it would be useful. I could keep track of how long I've been out away from my nest hole, how long I've been asleep. Maybe I'll meet someone who has a watch of their own and we can schedule a meeting or enact some sort of plan.

So, what happened today. The summer has departed and the winter is approaching. In the summer the days start early and the first thing you do is roll out from under the blankets and look out to the plains in the west. It's important – if (or when) you can see an Org coming (even from miles away), you have time to take evasive measures. But with the onset of winter, daylight arrives later and then there's the fog – the fog and mist. So, after the events of last night (described below), I was on edge, I couldn't sleep and rose just as it was getting light. Looking out of the window I could probably see only thirty yards. It was all whiteness. A cloud suspended within the city; whiteness from block to block. After staring into the depths of the haze I saw a shadow form in its midst. A shadow not only moving within the mist, but creating mini-swirls as vortexes were formed from the movement of a physical body within it. The soft blackness of the shadows rose, I estimated, to a hundred feet in height inside the whiteness.

I think I know what had sparked it. This is why you have to be so careful. The evening before was a nightmare. I had fallen asleep in the late afternoon in my nest hole. Suddenly (if there can be a 'sudden' when asleep) I was aware of light. For a moment I thought it must be the sun – the day was beginning. But I knew the opening of the apartment to the skies did not face east. Secondly, the mornings have a smell and warmth about them. But this time there was no morning aroma. The sun had not warmed the asphalt, the grass in the nearby parks and the air itself that flowed around the blocks. It was still the cold night air.

I opened my eyes to see the ceiling light on. The bulb blaring light. I had not seen electrically-generated light for over a year. I sort of didn't understand it. It wasn't making sense. I then snapped awake and panicked. I threw off the blankets, jumped to my feet and raced in circles thinking how do I address the problem. Memories of my old life kicked in and I started spinning around looking for a light switch. As I hit it and the light died, I found myself panicking further. There was still some illumination in a hallway around the corner. But there was a bigger problem. I was forced to choose. Do I give up this nest hole altogether right now or do I try and rescue the situation?

It was worth the risk. I raced to the front door, kicked down the furniture stuff blocking the entrance securely, threw open the door and raced down the corridor – in light! The corridor was illuminated, for Christ's sake! My head was thumping. True fear, I had learnt much earlier, has a sound – a thunderous roar in one's head. It got louder as I heard elevators moving up and down in their shafts.

I knew it must be in the basement and threw myself into the stairwell and started jumping down flights of stairs, as many as I could at a time. Fourteen storeys – it took forever. The more I raced down the sicker I felt – the lights had been on for too long!

I landed in the basement. I sort of knew my way around a bit. Before I move into any new place I do a *recce* – partly to assess the lay of the land, partly to survey the possible escape routes, partly to assess any threats. Stupidly, for the last few places I had stopped checking the electrical generators and circuit power grids. I had assumed their days were over. I was moving so fast I was slamming my body into walls as I cornered at speed. Fortunately, bizarrely, the lights were still (obviously) switched on so I was making quite good time. I arrived at the basement power control room. Locked doors had long been a thing of the past – too many survivors had been scavenging and raiding. The cabinets housing all the gear with levers switches and dials were behind metal cabinet doors that were themselves lying hanging aimlessly on their hinges. Perhaps if I paused and tried to read the labels and signs I might have seen what I really need to switch, break, turn, but I just started hitting, switching and pulling everything.

Normally, on any normal day or night, when I move around there is just the noise of me moving around. If I stop moving, any noise stops. Not this time though. Just as I started hammering and turning anything on the electrical panels in front of me, there was crashing and banging of another sort as another bloke, about my age, crashed into the basement room just as I had done ten seconds earlier. He was carrying a small water fire extinguisher and started on the panels in front of him spraying water into any exposed electrical circuit, broken lever or dial. We didn't say a word to each other or even acknowledge the other's presence. We had never met before yet we were allies in destroying the electrical panels in front of us. I had suspected there would be others in the building, but I wasn't keen to find out for sure and nor, obviously, was he. Life was just too tricky. Survivors knew that.

After much hammering, water spraying, kicking and punching (along with a load of sparks, crackles and mini-explosions from the cabinets themselves), the lights in the room flickered and died. The hum of the electrical cabinets gave way to a blackness of soundlessness. The silence was only broken by our heavy breathing. As my eyes adjusted I discerned the mildest of illumination coming from the wrists of my co-vandal. Looking at them I recognised them to be bicyclist illumination ankle and wrists straps. Nice idea, I thought. In the panic I had forgotten to grab my small wind-up torch.

'I reckon four minutes,' he said.

I nodded, panting and exhausted after my flurry of activity.

'Not bad,' he said, not convinced. 'I guess it is another four hours until dawn.'

I nodded trying to bring my breathing under control. It was also odd to hear another person's voice. I had, of course, seen people at a distance as they scrambled over the rubble looking for stores and supplies, but I was now of the view it was safer to keep a low profile. I wondered whether others were of the same mindset – they probably were, having survived for so long.

'Trouble is,' I said, 'it would have powered up the other buildings on the block.'

He sighed, his chest sank and his head dropped. He was skinny like me. Lack of food, foot-travel only and sheer terror will do that to you. He raised his eyes to mine.

'If it did, they might serve as a distraction? Maybe.'

I nodded slowly.

'How long have you been here,' I asked.

'Don't know. I think about fifty days. You?'

'Maybe seventy, eighty. I lose track.'

He nodded. 'We came from the outskirts. We couldn't get the supplies anymore.'

I nodded.

'This is a good place,' I muttered. 'Or it was.'

'Who could it be? You think someone is trying to reclaim the city? Make it habitable?'

I shook my head. 'No, can't see it. Crazy.'

We paused in silence and thought. The implications, the implications.

'Maybe they are trying to generate power for some other purpose and power just flowed to the city,' I continued. 'Could be some automated system; or AI re-configuring and trying to reset?'

'After all this time?'

'AI could be based a thousand miles away. Who knows what's happening.'

He nodded. Nobody knew what was going on. It was probably a mistake by some wannabe do-gooder, naive hero that had landed the city in trouble.

'You here with others?'

He nodded again and was about to say something, then stopped. We knew it was best left to keep quiet.

'Anyway,' he nodded towards the door, 'you can find your way?'

'Yep,' I replied knowing what he was asking. 'I'll go first.'

I took a few steps away towards the door, just as I was about to disappear in the blackness and be lost from the light rising from his wrists, I turned.

'Good luck.'

Quiet words, but well meant. He knew it. Existing was a daily workout of trial and error. If we had had both come this far, we had both done well. We had both a proven track record. But it could be gone in an instant.

'You too', he said, with the exact same thoughts in mind.

And with that I stepped away in the blackness never to see him again. I suspect he was dead five hours later, judging by events the following morning.

Feeling my way up from the basement in the blackness took a minute or so. As soon as I was in the stairwell I had the bannister rail to guide me. Of course, in the darkness there was no signage to be seen and, when counting the steps as one climbs fourteen storeys, a person can lose track. For this reason I had notched markings in the metal bannister informing me of what floor I was on. That way, if I had ever needed to make an urgent entrance or a fast exit, I could do it with the brush of a hand. I had made a point of marking the bannisters to all twenty-four floors of the apartment building. That way, if anybody figured out what the markings were and they stopped on the fourteenth floor, then they might guess someone was there. That was something I could do without. As I climbed the stairs towards by nest hole and reflected on the drama of the night, I found it somewhat reassuring to have met someone that had been thinking the same way I had for almost a year. I had no idea which floor he was living on. If he had gone first, he might have feared I would have followed the light on his wrist.

I reached my nest hole, entered and replaced the 'stuff' to reinforce the door. I walked over to the open wall opening and pulled back the light drape and looked west across the city towards the plains. Nothing, as far as I could see. I looked east as best I could. I couldn't see the sun. It was all dark. All dark save for a dozen skyscrapers and office buildings on my block. One of the buildings fell dark as I was watching, no doubt as a result of a similar panic by its residents. Must have been seventeen minutes illuminated, I guessed. We'll all see what it is like in the morning.

– IV – Morning

The morning was exactly as I feared. If it was September, it brought the mist. I remembered the previous year (it seems a world away now) when I appreciated the mist. I thought it hid us from them. But one learns. There are no easy fixes. This morning after a few hours of rest I was up at the break of dawn and sat perched on a stool looking westwards through the gap in the skyscrapers out at the plains. I packed my few belongings and left them by the door. I also had a rope (secured to a radiator) bundled up ready to throw out the window. It wouldn't get me far, but it might help me drop a few storeys. I once had a parachute ready but I saw a friend try using one without any luck.

I had a quick dry flannel wash and rubbed some grass in my armpits and on any exposed flesh. I think it works, confusing the Orgs just enough. I also have a bag of soil to use as camouflage. I think their sense of smell is better than their sight, but it at least it means they don't see a blob of white hiding behind the curtains.

The Org didn't come from the plains; its profile would have been visible above the mist that clung to the ground. No, the Org was already in the city. And hunting. If it had been a mindless wander then I would have heard something. It was the swirling of the mist a few blocks away that gave it away. With the sunlight cutting through the mist at angles I could see an object moving. And then ever so slowly it appeared. First, a dark shadow appeared to form in the swirling mist, then the swirling accelerated and the shadow took a form. Soon the Org was discernible. I could hear it too. Like a child walking across a kitchen floor covered with breakfast cereal, it was trying to move quietly, no doubt trying not to alert its prey. It stepped across piles of rubble and placed each foot gently though still crushing the broken cement blocks from fallen high rises that littered the roadways.

Just before it finally broke out of the mist, I saw it pause, turn, and hold still. I think it was sniffing through the broken facades of buildings. I saw the shadow raise an arm and brush away the facades of the residential high rise, tearing away its outer wall like sweeping away cobwebs hanging over bookshelves.

I stepped back into the room. I suspected the Org would continue down the block towards me. Although the facade of my building had already been partially pulled away, there was a danger the Org would swipe away and bring the whole facade down. I raced back to the windowless study room, but within moments my instinct was telling me it wouldn't be safe. I was on the fourteenth floor. It would take me a few minutes to get out of there. Suddenly there was a god almighty crash of masonry and concrete. The Org had just scraped across the front of the building next door. The whole building shuddered, my whole body shook. It had been a couple months since I had been so close to a giant. At that time I had followed my instinct and it had saved me. My mind made up, I darted out of the windowless room and headed to the hall to pick up my bag.

Movement out of the corner of my eye distracted me – it was the curtains blowing and swirling in the gusts of wind prompted by the movements of the giant outside. As the ragged fabric parted I saw the Org outside the building. It had its back to me, sniffing the high rise opposite. I knew it would turn in a minute and I couldn't guarantee it would not get a whiff from me. Time to be creative. I abandoned the thought of the retrieving my escape-bag and, with only my shoulder-bag strapped across my upper body, I darted into the adjacent room, grabbed the rope, threw it out the window. Gripping the end of the forty foot rope, I hurled myself out. My plan (or rather hope) was to swing out from the building then, on the backswing, to aim for a window into which I could throw myself. That way I would descend about four storeys in a matter of seconds. I would then have to get creative about descending the next one hundred feet to the ground debris level.

My timing was impeccable. As I sailed through the mist and came swinging back towards a window, I heard the crash and then felt the rope give way. The Org had brushed away my part of the building. The fourteenth floor on which the rope had been secured was collapsing into the floor below and so I dropped two more storeys further than intended. I landed flat against the side three feet from a window opening. I pulled myself in just as the Org swept many of the above floors into the street below. For a brief moment (and because I had seen similar things happen to others so many times), I felt I was seconds away from death. But I had escaped. Whether the giant had detected my odour or that of others I couldn't say. I kept hold of my end of the rope as the other end fell past the window along with much of the fourteenth floor. My heart sank at the thought of my escape-bag (containing most of my worldly belongings) somewhere in all the falling masonry and brick.

I dived under a dining table for a dozen seconds as the crashing tailed off. Dust and crushed concrete swirled around me. Possibly an excellent moment to escape I thought. Dashing back to the window to see if I could discern the shadow of the Org moving around, I saw nothing but swirling grey mist and dust. I also saw a male and female scramble out of the window four storeys below me directly on to the pile of building debris now six storeys high.

I decided not to risk descending through the internal stairs. The debris pile was near enough – the other end of the rope was buried in it somewhere. So, as quick as I could I secured my end of the rope to a pillar, climbed out and, throwing my shoulder bag over the wire, used it as a handgrip in a makeshift zip wire to descend the forty feet to the top of the new debris pile. Landing ahead of the male and female I could see they were struggling, but time was not on our side. The swirling grey mist and dust hid us no more. The black shadow of the Org appeared in the mist high above us.

I was faced with a dilemma. For eighteen months it had been every man for himself. And there were no heroics needed here. It was an outmoded mode of thinking.

I turned again to the couple behind and below me. The young man (not my friend from the previous night) was pushing his female companion (his girlfriend?) up through the debris. I decided to help, I am ashamed to say, because she was pretty. It is the sign of the times. I was unsure I would have helped if she wasn't pretty or just plain-looking. But it was instinctive. I had been alone for a year and the possibility of companionship was attractive. She had a soft pale skin, no doubt from a life lived hidden underground, and a vulnerability that had endured much. Usually endurance weathers a person's soul, but occasionally the same hardship can deepen it. Her scraggly, brown hair was cropped roughly at a neck. She was slim but there was an athleticism and strength in her limbs and movements. Those who had survived were of a certain type. They were the type in the days before the giants that would have gone untested and relatively unnoticed. The Orgs had brought Darwinism into the cities. No doubt there was a Darwinian purge going on across all the lands. The narcissist had long been cleansed from the city and the surrounding lands; people cared not for them in the race for survival. The bullies and so called alpha males had also gone. The bullies had been turned on early in the first six months. It had soon become clear that those seeking to cause disruption and control others by fear served no purpose in these new times; they were surrounded and ruthlessly dispatched. Ironically, they were a weak link. The criminal was an extension of the bully and so they had also gone; easily identified, people saw no role for them.

Those alpha-types (and wannabe alpha-types and heroes) had either tried to challenge the Org and been ripped from their complacency or been ignored by the 'true survivors'. I lost count of those who had graduated from wannabe hero to death. It was those who had the fittest combination of mind and spirit who had prospered. In the early days the body had been weakened – lack of food, constant anxiety and daily exertion had seen to that. But a true survivor's body had subsequently been strengthened through the very act of survival. In the time of giants the meek would indeed inherit the earth.

This true survivor was the quiet, thoughtful, resilient mammal who was forever alert to the danger, never complacent and ready to adapt and evolve. Wholly pragmatic. It was a fallacy put forward in fiction that surviving groups were microcosms of the time before an apocalypse where all sorts of character-types remained and formed into smaller community groups reflecting society at large. No, the character types had died off (or been killed off) one by one in the previous eighteen months. Those who had defined themselves as saviours of a corrupt society and trumpeted their virtue had also not lasted. In fact, those who self-proclaimed their virtue were the first to fall. Either their message had fallen on deaf ears or the pretenders among their ranks deserted them. They were left alone. Such an ideology could not survive in the age of the Org. It was everyone for him or her self.

Of course, many worthy people were lost too, but it made me realise that at times of great anguish and catastrophe humanity's gene pool was cleansed, renewed.

I pulled the young woman up to me. Her companion remained below, out of reach. I was conflicted. There was an immediate threat. Should I help guide the woman up cross the debris to the safety of the building or should I stay longer reaching down to her companion and, in so doing, put myself at greater risk? As the shadow in the dust and fog moved above us, I paused evaluating the risk.

Suddenly there was a deafening crack above me. I straightened up, stepped back and watched as the swirling mist of shadow and light above us took a different, darker form and in a sudden whirl of death the young man disappeared in a flash as the giant took him. I admired his honour for helping his companion, but pitied his foolishness – there is a thin line between the two. I made a mental note: beware of altruism, beware of selflessness.

My dilemma resolved, I turned and clambered away up the debris pile grabbing the young woman, her eyes locked, almost emotionless, on the clouds of dirt and thunder above. The moment I touched her she knew the score and for a fleeting moment looked into my eyes before we raced up to an opening in a building on the other side of the debris pile. An opening that must have been two storeys high, but in the city now, you would never know. As we made our way a couple of differently-pitched screams suggested the Org had found others; it bought my new companion and I a bit of time.

We knew we were not safe and raced through the broken building without saying a word to each other. Probably a former office building, judging by the wheeled chairs and wiring hanging down from the ceiling, the place had an air of despair about it. Everything was covered in the dirty whiteness of decay. The people who had lived and spent forty per cent of their lives in these spaces weren't coming back. They were dead too. The memories of the work, the business that had gone on in this space for decades had turned to dust. It was almost as if the owners had not only left and been forgotten, but never existed. And if meaning is measured and validated in 'existence', their brief lives had had no meaning. Little had they known it, no doubt.

With my new companion we reached the far side the building away from the noise outside, descended one storey then stepped out on to the debris and crossed the street. In situations such as this I would always try and keep one block between the Org and me. My companion moved swiftly and, though shell-shocked, seemed resolute. She was indeed a survivor.

We entered another building, found a stairwell, then a basement car-park. We would wait until dark and then decide our next moves. We found a spot hidden away in some rubble that was blocking the garage's exit except for a small gap. This gap allowed us another escape route but it was also a way to monitor what was happening outside on the street. We sat opposite each other saying nothing. I checked my shoulder bag for supplies – I always carried food for 48 hours. I watched as she did the same and spotted similar food supplies in her bag.

'Rest,' I said. 'We'll discuss options at darkness.'

– V – Rest

I dozed until mid-afternoon, all the time listening to the Org move around the district – sometimes heading towards us, sometimes away. I had time to reflect. Three dead today at least. Their bodies would never be found. I remembered the days when I would witness three hundred die. Now death could be counted on one hand. Nothing reminds me more of the falling population than the small numbers now killed during an Org raid. There just aren't the people around.

It had been so different. In the early days there were periods when I was ill. I suppose my body was adjusting to the bugs, the lack of food, the cold – I had food poisoning, developed migraines because of lack of sleep and stress, caught the flu – in fact, everything. Being exposed to lots of people who were also picking up bugs and developing illnesses didn't help. In hindsight I was grateful for the blur of sickness – the reality of the world falls away and clarity is all that's left when you're shivering and despairing in the darkness. I think illness is life's way of not only saying slow down, but also 'shut the hell up and listen'. So, whenever I was ill in the early days, I became aware that I had an instinctive nervousness around crowds. I always felt that I should put distance between them and me. I therefore made the effort to live as independently as possible.

It must have been in the second month of the 'new epoch' when, suffering with flu, I was curled up in the darkest, furthest corner of a basement car-park in downtown. The basement must have been home to a thousand people. I assumed (perhaps we all assumed) there was safety in numbers. We were doing the right thing. But as I shivered and sweated, I wanted all those people to disappear. All I could think about was the hum of their chatter and gallons of sweaty breath being pumped out. Even though we were aware of the danger (that Orgs would detect the odour of such a large group of people), the then so-called 'leaders' (alpha-types, arguably) were adamant the room was secure and the only option.

On day three (if that was what it was) of my flu, it was too much. I crawled out of the underground basement car park and dragged myself across the street, down one block and into a basement service room in a department store. I curled up and sweated for days. Two or three days later I heard the tell-tale signs of an approaching giant followed by almighty booms and crashes.

I crawled out knowing deep down what had happened, I returned to the previous basement hiding place to find the whole building demolished and in its place a massive crater several storeys deep as if several Orgs had spent a day digging for treasure.

I promised myself I would never stay with a group again. And that's how I've survived, I'm sure of it. That, and of course, a generous helping of a quickly-developed aptitude for this kind of survival and a stubborn willingness to adapt. Every time I had moved from the suburbs to the city or from a basement to a high rise there had been a degree of calculation. But there had been occasions when I had been forced to move. Those were times of panic. On leaving each nest hole (I must have been through nearly forty) I thought I had surrendered the best option available to me. I wouldn't know where to go.

In the early days when I was forced out, I was caught off guard. I was back to nothing. But now, eighteen months later, I was indifferent to such sudden shocks. It was routine. Disappointing, sure, but I knew I would find something. I just needed to rest and the answer would emerge. What was different now was that the answer was not in the expectation of a 'rescue' or things getting better. For the first year I thought any nest hole arrangement was in the context of biding my time and waiting for the cavalry to arrive. I now realised that I had been brought up on too many movies. That was all fiction, I was living a real life in a broken world. Whatever had happened was global. I had to jettison all understanding of the world from the micro (clean water by tap or bottle; a means to call for help, whether from a neighbour or a police force) to the macro (a nation's state and borders; the expectation of four seasons) and establish a way of looking at existence as a wholly blank canvas. A wholly new world order in which the homo sapiens was not the top predator. Quite the opposite. The next 100 years, 500 years, one thousand years would probably see humankind as a scavenger. The time for countering the rise of the giants had passed, now it was all about survival.

I was now thinking of a different future. The options I had discounted in the past – moving out of the city, moving further afield, even to the coast – were now possibilities. Earlier in the year I had met an old guy who spoke about an ancient underground cave network unused by giants running the breadth of the continent. He had said, these kind of things had happened before. Collapses of civilisations were not new. Humans had survived. It was cyclical.

I asked him where the nearest entrance to the network was. He just pointed out the windows to the west. Look for the man-made hills that hid an entrance or were within one hundred paces of an entrance. He seemed a wise soul. I was sorry when we parted. Randall was someone I would have ignored in the old world. In fact, the old world order would have dismissed and ridiculed him. Now he was a wise, old soul indeed. I recorded much of what he told me in Journal 5, I think (a volume sitting in the dust and debris of the collapsed building, my former nest hole). I kicked myself for not packing it in my daypack. I thought it was too precious to carry around with me. It even had maps. I think of Randall now and wondered if he made it out.

I also needed Journal 7 for the options and plans I had compiled a year into the new epoch. The journal didn't keep a record of contacts or people who could be of help. The concept of an 'address book' does not exist now. People are rarely found in the place you first contacted them and even if they didn't move, the city streets were buried under changing mountains of debris. Besides any 'contacts' were almost certainly dead and there was no phone system (the mobile network had been one of the first things to fail along with the electricity grid). I couldn't say for sure if any network came back (or even exists now) because my phone battery died and it was almost impossible to find somewhere to charge it. In those early days we were all looting batteries from shops in the hope that the new batteries had a bit of juice just in case the phone network came back online. On reflection I suppose it was only then (failure of the network and electricity grid) that it seemed to become a legitimate catastrophe. We didn't see it coming. I still think it bizarre. So, yes, note to self: I need to try and find Journal 5 and 7 at least. I need my plans.

I could hardly recall the old world now. It has slipped into the recesses of a museum of dream-like worlds. I almost gasp as I recollect that world – it was so naive. I suppose all utopias are. The ruling collective were simple and narcissistic. The only positive thing about the new epoch is that the smug collective has been wiped from the face of the earth.

Regrets? I think I should have made the more of the time I spent with Randall and his son, Carl. I suppose that is what civilisations go through – unsettling destruction followed by a period of downtime when humans adjust, try to re-organise. These days it has just been about survival, but I am thinking that now that I have survival skills I should think about progressing to the next stage – a form of organised and collective survival. But one can only do that with the help, skills and understanding of others – like Randall and Carl.

I'm going to rest now. Ironically, hearing the thunder of collapsing buildings and Orgs digging through the rubble is reassuring, it is the silence that is the most unsettling. I also know that the rubble helps hide entrances to basements and subways. So, with the gentle thunder in the background, I will rest.

– VI – Evening

It was getting dark. With her arms wrapped around her, my new companion was asleep nestled in a bundle of dirty, but dry, tarpaulin that absorbed the shock of the hard edges of the broken masonry mattress. We needed a few supplies before it got too dark, but I let her sleep. Time-permitting we could then look for somewhere more suitable to prepare food – something that could be prepared (warmed) quickly producing as little odour as possible.

I crept up the debris pile filling the entrance to the basement car park. There was a small opening through the rubble through which I could see the failing light of the day. There had been no indication that the basement was currently in use though it was almost certainly a refuge that had been used before. The small entrance was not accidental, it had been maintained. Masonry had been moved to prop up the entrance's sides to prevent it collapsing into a larger and more obvious hole. Plywood sheeting was also propped up nearby as if it had been used as a means to obscure the entrance from outside. My guess was that it had been used in previous months, but the user (or users) had been forced to move on, or had died in an Org raid, or were decomposing in a heap deeper in the basement having been injured, having caught an infection, or who knows, having been murdered by another survivor. I don't think there is much to worry about though with regards to there being violent individuals lurking in the darkness. I think we have reached a time beyond murder as something to be feared – survivors are now of a kind.

I squeezed through the opening and climbed to the top of the pile in the middle of the street outside. I could still hear the Org perhaps four blocks away. In the olden days they could disappear for days, weeks, partly because they would have had their fill and pickings were plentiful wherever they went. Nowadays there were fewer around and so they lingered more. It was always a dilemma in the quiet times, to make a dash for it and head west as Randall had suggested, but when you are outside the city you were exposed. You cannot hide on the open plain and, with the climate being what it was, if you managed to avoid the Orgs, the cold and wet and toxic clouds would get you. If you reached the mountains, you had done well, but no one knew the dangers that lurked there.

As luck would have it, the partially collapsed residential building next door had brought down with it a larder of supplies (no doubt stored in the early days) – tinned food and, packs of pasta littered the lower levels of the debris pile. It would save me a trip to some of my own stores – the nearest were in the direction of the Org, the others (in other directions) further away. Wherever I stayed I had always made a point of having knowledge of a storage site within two kilometres in all four directions.

As I climbed down the debris pile I heard some rustling. I was careful – there were sometimes wild animals also scavenging for food – but I soon saw a thirty-something man bending over a pile of debris and, rather than removing stones and broken bricks, he was adding to the pile. I approached. He heard me coming, looked up, seemed unconcerned and continued with his business muttering quietly to himself. I stopped and watched. I realised he was burying someone. I waited until he had finished his little prayer then approached.

I didn't recognise him. I used to think there would be a time when I would recognise everybody in my neighbourhood, there being so few of us, but he was a stranger. Again, I noticed the thin, pale, gaunt look of the man. I wondered what he had been in the old world – an accountant, bureaucrat, barista, small-business owner? I suppose I didn't look much better. I couldn't recall when I last looked in a mirror.

I didn't enquire about his loss. A sudden death was not news anymore. He might as well have been doing some gardening when I disturbed him. We shook hands.

'There's a supermarket two blocks down,' he said nodding in the direction of the Org.

'I know it,' I replied looking in the direction he had nodded before turning back to him. 'You heard anything of interest?'

He shook his head. By 'interest' I meant anything of the outside world – beyond the half dozen blocks. He looked despondent.

'Thinking of heading west though.'

'The Gunnison caves?'

He looked up, suddenly interested. 'Are they real?'

'I've heard about them,' I said, without much conviction, 'from, what I think was, a trusted source.'

He nodded. It was always good to have stories corroborated from different sources.

'The power surge last night?'

'My guess was it was an anomaly,' I replied. 'Probably malfunctioning AI, nothing to do with any coordinated revival. Cannot see how anybody would think it would help. I don't think there is the planning out there.'

'The signs about a gathering – night of the full moon. You've seen them?'

'No,' I said, shaking my head. This was a surprise. 'I know there were attempts to re-organise in the early days, but after the Coors Field purge, I assumed they had died a death.'

The Coors Field purge was a night (in fact two nights) of horrors near the first anniversary of the passing of the old world. Probably ninety per cent of the then population perished directly in (or as a result of) the events occurring in those forty-eight hours.

'Post-Coors Field?' I asked.

He nodded.

'They are old, but I think people do see them, so maybe there are some efforts to make contact, share information.'

I looked up at the moon just visible above the broken skyline of the once formidable city. I estimated that it was probably ten days before the moon was full.

'We need all the help we can get.'

I nodded. Glad to hear that I wasn't the only one who was running short of ideas.

'I met a guy,' I said, 'Randall, who knew all about the cave network.'

'Never met him, but I've heard of him.'

'He said the cave network was out west, beyond Black Mountain.'

My new friend nodded, looking unwell at the thought. I could empathise.

'I tried in the spring, but turned back,' I muttered. 'An advance party never made it. They were intercepted. We turned back to the city. We couldn't be sure where the Orgs were. There were too many of us. Now, we are too few. I hoped there would be another visit from someone like Randall, but none.'

He nodded.

'Yeah, someone with a library in his head. It's too late now. We have to wait for the spring,' he said, before adding, 'if we get a spring.'

'Did you ever meet a guy called Robert Bloch?'

He shook his head.

'I met him when I was camped down in Park Avenue maybe ten months ago. I think he was lost in the Coors Field purge. He was a solar scientist. He talked of the possibility of another flare.'

'Would it help?'

'I'd take anything that might throw up a change.'

'So would I,' he said.

I recognised his spirit. Each and every day in the new epoch was like living on a coastline – a place of hardened experience meets an ocean of the unknown. If the Orgs didn't get you, the breaking waves would.

Nevertheless, I recognised the stoicism in his bearing. It was also good to talk. On occasions like this it was good to communicate with others. I always felt comfortable in secure forms of accommodation, but when I was forced out from a hiding hole I wondered if I should take the opportunity to try and reach out to others. But how would we communicate? When I found people within the city, they usually didn't want to talk. People were wary of making contact with the outside world and bringing in unsavoury characters into their circle, but, as I've said, I was now thinking that we had reached a point where all the unsavoury characters had gone. Sure, some might have survived if it had been man versus man, but it was now man versus giant.

I nodded at my friend (everybody I met were friends) in thanks, 'I'll look out for those posters.'

He smiled a tired smile of acknowledgement. I looked down at the heap under the blanket at his feet. He nodded in return. Enough said.

I turned and climbed down and started sifting through the debris for the tinned food. I heard him mutter a few more prayers then disappear over the top of the debris pile and into the oncoming night.

– VII – Hall of Records

I thought of the bereaved man's loss. I too had buried people. As the months had passed, the graves became more rudimentary. I had started with burying people (including Graham, Matt) in gardens, parks, then I laid others (Rosana, Luciana) in basements. Now we were at a point that a blanket and a few stones amidst street debris and rubbish were enough. But it wasn't all bad – the odour of decomposing friends masked the presence of the living for a while. As for my own family, I couldn't say where they were resting. I had long assumed they had passed.

His reference to a library triggered a memory. In the early days (and a time before I met Randall) I had once bedded down in a library. In that time of innocence and ignorance (bliss) I had used the time to read all sorts of books to distract me from the disintegrating world outside. I read novels and history books. Admittedly I had tried to read a few books about solar activity, solar minimums and maximums and solar flares, in the hope of learning something about the trouble we had found ourselves in, but they were too dense and, by that stage, out of date. I read history books as a matter of general interest and to reminisce about a world that was now lost and certain to be forgotten, certainly irrelevant. Ah, the golden times of wars of men against men – a time when diplomacy was an option, a time when surrender followed by peace was a possibility. But the books soon depressed me. They used to say history should be read for it always repeats itself – but I didn't fancy it now, there was no chance of history repeating itself. We were in new territory.

When in the library I also took the opportunity to acquire maps of the area and read a few cookery books to not only help keep me alive, but also to provide some variety in my diet. At the time I had had to leave the library nest hole in a rush, but I now made a mental note to return to the library and do some research on the existence of Randall's caves and mounds. Perhaps I might be able to return to the history books to find references to the Org phenomenon. But where would such books be filed? Under history? Or under myth and legends section? Or, dare I say, the 'conspiracy' section? The complacency of the old world made me sick at times. A part of me was glad it had gone the way it had, but if Randall had been right and this had happened before, there should be some material on the subject. The Internet had once superseded the book; now it didn't exist, but I recalled there had been a transitional phase – searchable DVD encyclopedias. In my library days I had come across simple guides to generate a small voltage of electrical power with acid and car batteries. I might be able to play the DVDs (assuming I could find them) on a laptop (assuming I could find one – with a DVD player). In the early days I had also hidden a few solar battery panels at one of my storage points in the hope the skies could brighten one day. Having learnt the hard way I never stored such materials on a roof in the hope enough sun could penetrate the toxic haze. I never knew if the building would be there the following day. But maybe the time was right to return to my library.

And as for the future. I would need to think. In the long term, do I remain in the city? Or plan for a trip to find the mounds, caves and tunnels? It would need careful consideration (assuming circumstances didn't force my hand). I would speak to my new companion and see if she had any news. If her plans matched mine and she seemed 'together in the head' (a help rather a hindrance) then maybe we would spend time together. Besides, there was the 'companionship thing'. A bit of physical comfort might not go amiss. But I was wary. The number of times I had seen one of a pair (or a group) lose their lives as they tried to 'save' another. A companion is 'baggage' as much as a blessing and, in today's world, the difference mattered.

In the short term, I would be spending time in the city. I would try and rescue some of my old journals, after all they might be the only record of the birth of this new epoch. I would also return to the library and conduct further research. I feared the digital realm (and digital history) would soon be unreachable and the physical, paper-based world was being torn down, crumbling to dust or burning up. Diaries like mine might be the only record not only of this time, but, I increasingly thought, of *all* time. It was true that the acceleration by social media to a narcissistic, polarised world had lessened society's likelihood of surviving the trauma in the first place. What had been designed to bring people together had in fact driven them apart – to such an extent that survival was now on the scale of the individual.

Nevertheless, I should make an effort to record and reflect on the former world so that, should men's time came again, the surviving peoples might learn from the previous mistakes. But where should I leave these journals? Perhaps in the very same library, in its buried basement. If people in the future were to go looking for information, they would probably try and find a library, a repository of information and records. But would people from the future be able to read these words? Surely I can't be alone in doing this? Perhaps an opportunity to safely deposit these records and journals will present itself. A place hidden, underground. It would have to be quite impressive so that if one of our descendants discovered the place it would architecturally grand enough to know that it was a place of importance. A cavern, an underground cathedral, a grand hall marked by a mound of earth or rubble that would be impenetrable to the giants or disguised well enough that the

Orgs would miss it (but men wouldn't). Perhaps the mounds, hills that Randall had spoken of have a cache of records of the earlier lost time? Perhaps those records even listed ways to defeat or at least survive in a time of giants? Yes, I need to find a place where all our stories could be stored. And one day, once all is said and done, a hall of records would persist. And all lost knowledge recovered.

Sack Truck

– I – Sack Truck

It was the first weekday after being 'let go'. Even though he was now not welcome in his workplace, he was pleased to have (for the time being at least) his gym membership. He had paid the reduced annual fee through a special deal through his (now former) employer and it had another eight months to run, with luck. He certainly wasn't going to inform the gym himself and he hoped his former employer's Human Resources department would overlook the matter. Access to a rowing machine and weights would allow him to burn off the nervous energy and clear his head, allowing him to think what he might do for the rest of his life. Things were changing though and, at forty-six years of age, he couldn't keep up with the world.

Refreshed from the gym session, he jumped on his bicycle and cycled to the job centre to register as 'unemployed'. Not two minutes down the road, he turned into a quiet old part of town that had a handful of shops and businesses amidst the pretty buildings. It was there that he saw the lorry parked up on the pavement. Sitting by itself, near the rear end of the vehicle was the sack truck. It was the first one he had seen since 'the conversation' seven days earlier. In fact, it was possibly the first one he had seen for months. Who knows, maybe even years? He bore it (nor the idea of it) no ill will, but it was noteworthy that a reference to such a mundane, innocuous, inanimate workplace object could impact a life to such a degree and in such a short space of time.

– II – Buster

His life, such as it was, had changed as the result of the briefest of conversations with a young, new, female work colleague. In the space of sixty seconds, an exchange about the best way by which to transport several piles of boxes two hundred yards from the workplace to an event venue had altered his work prospects forever. The boxes (containing promotional material – flyers, hand-outs) were too heavy to be comfortably carried the distance by one person. Additionally, the route was twisting and hazardous – not ideal for awkward boxes to be carried by two people. To top it all, transportation by vehicle was also not practicable.

'How are we going to do this?' the young lady asked him, her senior colleague.

Prompted by memories of working in warehouses twenty-five years earlier, he had replied: 'Do we have a sack truck?'

Her brow furrowed. She looked confused.

'Sack truck?' she mumbled.

Her confusion prompted a sliver of doubt in him. Had he, in fact, been incorrect? From where had he pulled the term 'sack truck'? From a distant memory of using one? He had in mind the image of a sack truck or what he thought to be commonly known as a 'sack truck'. The device was a two-wheeled, two-handled contraption that allowed the easy-transport of a number of boxes stacked up on top of one other, the lowest box resting on a large lip between wheels. The truck-device would slip its lip under the stacked boxes and, by tipping the truck backwards, the user would lift the load off the floor; the weight resting against a back-support when the object was tipped backwards. It was a shelf on wheels. Why it was called a 'sack truck' therefore, he was unsure. The image of an actual sack on such a truck was unsatisfactory. The sack (of, for instance, potatoes) would presumably collapse off the shelf rendering the vehicle ineffective. Why wasn't it called a box truck? Or if indeed the truck had been used to transport sacks, it would have been sensible to have a 'container' of three sides, even four? Like a square bucket? But if this were so, why was it not called a 'bucket truck'? (As long as it was clear the wheeled contraption was not intended to transport buckets.)

Working through these thoughts rapidly, he dispensed with using logic and opted for instinct. Whether that 'instinct' was based in his gut or an obscure part of his brain, he did not know. This was probably the mistake – to remove his response(s) from the thought-processing, logic-based part of his brain. Or rather, it most certainly was the mistake. Nevertheless, it provided him with sense of confidence that, yes, he felt sure the correct term was indeed 'sack truck'.

'Why is it called a sack truck?' she asked again. 'What's it for?'

Knowing that an answer along the lines of 'it is used for transporting sacks' would not be sufficient for the young woman (whose university degree in the arts and humanities would almost certainly preclude her from accepting a job working in a warehouse) when the items to be transported were indeed boxes and not sacks, he sought an alternative answer. Unfortunately, he was still using the instinctive, non-logical part of his brain (or gut). Therefore he couldn't in that very moment account for the words that passed his lips and travelled rapidly (at the speed of sound) towards her pink pert ears perched either side of a wholly innocent expression of innocence and inquiry.

'For transporting gonads,' he said to her. Out loud.

It was one of those moments when the speaker finds it difficult to establish whether the thought had come first (only to be then expressed inadvertently), or whether the words had emerged from the mouth of their own volition dragging (any) thought behind them. For a moment it was totally unknown to him why he had he conjured up an image of a sack truck carrying a (one assumes, human) scrotum. Presumably the user of the sack truck was the owner of the scrotum. He had no memory of a recent conversation or incident in which his (or anybody else's) scrotum was raised. Besides, the proportions were all wrong. Yet simultaneously, he knew the most obvious contender for the image of a scrotum on a transportation device was from his teenage years reading comics. One such comic was *Viz* with its beloved comic character 'Buster' in the famous comic strip – *Buster Gonad and his Unfeasibly Large Testicles*. And the image worked: Buster walking along the pavement pushing a sack truck on which were placed his unfeasibly large testicles. But in the comic strip Buster had been pushing a wheel-barrow, surely, and not a sack truck?

Sometimes when playing squash, the squash ball would hit the red line. He would check the legitimacy of the shot with his squash partner with the words 'was that down?' prompting a polite exchange of views. Depending on the importance of the point in the game, there was a discussion. Often they would play a 'let' and, in their words, let 'Him upstairs' clarify the matter. Yet, often there was an urge to request the footage of the point be rewound and examined – a result of too much time watching replays of televised sport. He would often wonder what television replays and the Internet were doing to the minds of the younger generation. The expectation that things could be reviewed and checked instantaneously could not be healthy. Couldn't people just get used to the idea that things just happened once? Anyway, he had a similar instinct standing in front of the young woman. Could he please replay the moment and check what he had said?

But no. She was looking confused mixed with a hint of disbelief. Her brow had furrowed, much like a young child hearing that Father Christmas might be a fictional character. Perhaps she doesn't know what gonads are, he thought (then pleaded – with 'Him upstairs'). Please let it be true that secondary education really had dumbed down. (Tertiary education was irrelevant. If a young woman didn't know what gonads were by the time she had left school it was unlikely she would come across the term at university.)

'What are gonads?' he willed her to ask.

A type of onion, was his ready answer; but her question never came.

It was fifty-fifty, as one nanosecond dragged on into another. Why the delay in responding? Was she trying to process why her senior colleague would bring into the conversation the fleshy matter hanging between a man's (his) legs?

– III – Human Resources

The second conversation was the following day. He was sat opposite the head of Human Resources in an office behind a closed door. There was a slight lull in the conversation.

'Why are you smiling?' the Human Resources manager asked.

He wasn't aware that he had been smiling and it was not a smile prompted by the conversation preceding her enquiry. He was smiling because she was, he was ashamed to say, quite attractive. Or should he be ashamed? He couldn't help it. She was a similar age. That is to say, eleven years younger than him. Though he would never say that out loud. She had a slim and nicely-defined leg resting on another shapely leg. Her business skirt suit clung and hung just right whether she sat still or adjusted herself in her seat. A white blouse was open at the neck showing a warm glow to her skin. Her soft, round face was perfectly framed by a bob of blond hair. Her eyes were slightly larger than average and nestled nicely above cheekbones cushioned by a hint of puppy fat. Her mouth had a slight crooked quality to it that was endearing. As he had listened to her talking during the previous ten minutes he had felt himself drifting away from the content of the conversation and soaking in her womanly qualities (like bathing in warm milk). Again he tried to place the attractiveness and he was once again taken back to his youth. She had a similar quality to Felicity Kendall in the 1970s sitcom, *The Good Life*. Yes. An endearing sweet nature, but was he permitted to entertain such a thought? Surely as a ten year old he could not be condemned for having been bewitched by the charms of Felicity playing her character, Barbara Good. As his present reaction was in part attributable to the memory of experience of a ten year old, then it was surely entirely valid?

'Why are you smiling?' she asked for a second time.

He knew immediately it was a tricky question. He couldn't say he was deriving any amusement from the content of the conversation up to that point. It would not be appropriate, that he knew. He wasn't stupid (although he could hazard a guess that an observer would beg to differ). No. It needed thought. He had not mentioned any reference to *Viz* and the thought processes (or lack of them) the previous day. It was doubtful she had ever heard of *Viz* or any of the characters – Nobby's Pile, Johnny Fartpants, the Fat Slags, Cockney Wanker, Terry Fuckwit and, of course, Buster Gonad. Some women would have come across it in their youth and a select few were no doubt fans, but they would be in a very small minority. *Viz* was very much a boys' comic. A comic the boys' mothers would not understand or really appreciate. Too sophisticated in a teenage boy's sort of way. He had a sister and her teenage magazine material had been *Just Seventeen* and *Tracy*. He had often wondered about the millions spent and man-hours wasted on research trying to determine if men and women were in fact the same. They weren't. It was wholly different reading experience. All any researcher had to do was read the comics.

He did think he could start a conversation about Buster or Johnny or Nobby or Terry, but even in his head he didn't know where it would go.

He then thought he saw a thought flash across her face, the thought being: am I really going to have to ask the question a third time?

No, he wouldn't embarrass her and him. He snapped back to the present.

'Because I think you're attractive,' he said.

He sat very still. In fact, they both sat very still.

'Cute?' he murmured. 'Think Barbara Good.'

This is unusual, he thought. He wouldn't expect pretty much the same thing to happen to him two days in a row. He didn't have a request in his head to replay it. The ball was very clearly in. (Or was it out?)

– IV – The Doctor(s)

He hadn't given much thought to the gender of the doctor. He was formally registered with a male doctor of broadly the same age and had been expecting to see him right up to the moment he arrived at the GP's door. Being informed that his own doctor was away and that he was therefore seeing 'Dr Francis' had rung no alarm bells. As he sat down in front of the lady-doctor he started to kick himself repeatedly. He shouldn't have let himself feel encouraged at the thought of seeing a doctor so soon after the conversation with Human Resources even if he (or rather she) had a specialisation in psychological disorders. Sitting there listening to the lady-doctor he realised how much he had wanted to see a male doctor. After all, with a male doctor he could wrap it all up in ten minutes and a doctor's note could be written. Five minutes on Buster and five minutes on Felicity Kendall (as Barbara Good) and all would be well. Sure, some embarrassment for a few weeks at work, but the letter would have done its job. Who knows, he might even qualify for a couple of weeks of paid medical leave. Best case scenario, work colleagues might even be supportive on his return and nod in sympathy that senior management had been piling on the work. But he was not there yet, he was sitting opposite Dr Francis who had been weaned on *Just Seventeen*.

Dare he ask to see a male-doctor?

He turned it over in his mind. If the doctor did not know the circumstances of the visit then it might be permissible. She might understand that his medical concerns were of a particular sort that might understandably have the sympathy of a male doctor. Trouble was, she knew the trouble. As the doctor readied herself for the consultation he detected she was about to ask her first question. If he were to do it, *then 'twere well it were done quickly*, but knowing he had been off his game for the previous 48 hours, he dallied and she got her first question in.

'Do you mind if we are joined by students?' she asked.

He was thrown and it showed.

'Doctors in training,' she continued. 'They would just observe.'

Instinctively a cooperative person and knowing that all doctors had to be trained and that he had benefited from trained doctors himself, he shrugged his shoulders and wobbled his head in a manner that could not be construed as a refusal. And so, he watched in slow motion as Dr Francis rose from her chair, walked over to an interior door that she opened and stepped back to allow the passage into the room of two student doctors. One was blond with hair tied back in a pigtail, the other mousy-haired with a light dusting of freckles on her cheeks. He seemed to zone out for a few moments because the next thing he knew he was sitting opposite the three lady doctors all looking at him. His mind went blank, but not blank enough to wonder what the two student doctors would be writing on the A5 pads resting on their laps, pens at the ready. Whatever it was, he could tell they were respectfully attentive.

He paused. Breathed quietly. Collected his thoughts and summoned all his politeness and courage.

'Do you think I could see a man?'

As had been the case recently, it was difficult to judge the passage of time. Not wanting the silence between the four of them to go on for too long, he added: 'not that I think you don't know what you're talking about, but I think a male doctor would understand more.' Then for good measure, he added: 'better'.

– V – The Library

Having had a few stressful days he needed to get out of the house. He was going stir-crazy. He needed space, time, air. So, rather than pace about the house drinking coffee and turning recent events over in his mind until they reached an unacceptably high spin velocity, he headed into town. It didn't relax him – too many people rushing about with concerned looks on their faces. Just looking at their strained features made him tired. It was the modern world after all. Walking about town didn't distract him, didn't relax him. In fact, it reinforced the idea that the world was moving too fast. And so he took a detour to a local park.

The park, its perimeter protected by eight-foot high walls and forty-foot high trees, was quieter and slower, thankfully. Trees and plants and shrubs have less of a rush about them, he concluded. It helped. He found himself walking slower than at any point in the last week. As his step slowed, so did his racing heart and his spinning head. He reflected on the office, his interaction with Human Resources and his little episode at the doctors' surgery. At least being suspended from work meant he had time to compile a legal defence, should it be needed. He had hoped any doctor's note wouldn't get him out of the tight spot he had found himself in, but nothing was certain anymore.

He thought about how the world had reached this point. What was he missing? What was next? What did he need to look out for? It was at that moment that he felt a little ripple of panic deep inside him. He needed to get out of the park. Why would a lone man be walking alone in a park, a public space? What could he be up to, people might ask? The ripple became a wave – *I need to get out of here*. He scoured the park for the nearest exit and took off at a pace that he had been cursing all day.

As he was dashing from the park, he caught sight of a small community library nestled in the trees in the corner of the green space. Many libraries had closed in recent years, so they were a rarity. This was probably staffed by cheap volunteers with shelves full of accumulated wisdom and was a safe space from the raging world. A quiet repository of sanity. Of course, he thought, just what the doctor ordered.

As he raced up the steps and entered the musty confines of the establishment, he realised that he was onto a winner – he could do some research. He could brush up on the law or, even better, he could address the start of his troubles, his reference to

Buster Gonad. He could describe Buster and his influence on popular culture and his own childhood. He could even secure physical evidence supporting the existence of the comic book character in the form of a few *Viz* annuals.

That said (or rather thought), he knew he must be careful not to rush into a course of action he might later regret. Nevertheless, he felt relief for the first time in days.

For twenty minutes he wandered between the library shelves browsing those sections where he might expect to find old annual editions of the *Viz* publication, but they were not to be found. He had hoped to find them in the children's section, but that was pretty sparse. Besides, he didn't want to linger too long in the children's section; you never knew who or what he might encounter – a child perhaps? At which point there would be no limit the trouble he might find himself in.

He searched the boys' section, or rather he searched *for* the boys' section but couldn't find it. There was a "young person's" section, but it was mostly girl-orientated. Anything suggesting inexplicably large testicles seemed to have disappeared off the face of the earth. It soon dawned on him that he might need help. He was becoming increasingly determined to leave the premises having made some progress with his predicament (or rather legal defence). If he did not make progress that day, the world would certainly move on and there was no knowing how it might react to what came out of his mouth by the end of the week.

From a safe vantage point he watched the librarian's desk. There appeared to be three librarians on duty. One old (or 'mature', he corrected himself) female, one young female and one young, pale, slim male. Having had his fill of trying to explain himself to the ladies, he waited until the females had moved away from the desk then approached the young man.

'Hello, excuse me, I looking for any past *Viz* annuals?'

The young, male librarian looked blank.

'The author?'

'*Viz*?' the visitor repeated.

'Who is the target demographic?'

'Children. Well, once upon a time,' he muttered sheepishly. 'Teenagers, I suppose.'

The young librarian tapped away on the keyboard in front of him and scanned the results on the computer.

'Yes, we have some,' he said looking at the screen, 'but they are under lock and key.'

'Lock and key? Ooo, Rare books?'

'Let me get my colleague,' the librarian said.

'Your colleague?'

'Yes,' the librarian said with a confused nod.

'A woman?'

'Liz?' the young, bearded librarian called out to the back office.

A young female librarian woman joined them at the desk.

'You want to see a copy of the publication *Viz*?' she asked, puzzled.

'Yes,' he replied. 'Is that weird?'

'We've removed all *Viz* compilations from our shelves.'

'Why?'

'They're somewhat out of date,' she said with a smile suggesting she knew what she was talking about.

'Oh, I always thought of them as timeless.'

'They can damage young people's minds.'

'Nobby Pile's will do that,' he muttered with smile with a nod and a wink.

The mature, lady librarian now joined them.

'Why do you want to see these *Viz* publications?' the mature librarian asked, her brow furrowed like so many before her.

'Research.'

All three library staff looked unconvinced.

'I might be a victim…..of its workings,' he haltingly whispered.

It was a good word. It did the trick.

Within minutes he found himself in a metal cage built into a windowless room in the library's basement. The young librarian, Liz, showed him to a battered, wooden table in the middle of the cage starkly illuminated by one dust-covered bulb. As he sat waiting looking around at the shelves of dusty books (themselves locked in cages), he was transported back in time – many of them were brightly coloured children's books from the previous millennium. Before long a grim-faced librarian returned and placed five copies of past *Viz* annual editions dating to the 1980s and early 1990s on the table in front of him. In truth, the sight of them brought a small glow to his heart. He gazed upon faded images of old friends dancing about in playgrounds, playing drums, hanging out of trees and urinating into flowerpots. He suddenly noticed that the librarian had not left. She was standing over him.

'I'll be careful,' he said, hoping he would be left alone. 'Do I need to sign something?'

The librarian looked blank.

'A disclaimer or something?' he chuckled, raising his eyebrows and a smile.

It was the first time he had known a chuckle to echo – but the room was quiet and it was a windowless basement room after all. Not a soft furnishing to be seen.

Left alone, he spent an hour or so reliving a world lost to him. It was as if he was canoeing down the Amazon and finding lost civilizations at every turn in the river – lost in the jungle of modernity. Grand and fair places forgotten to the world. Treasure troves of art, culture, characters and adventures. There was *Nobby's Piles* (Nobby parachuting and job-hunting in orchestras and zoos), *The Fat Slags* on regular nights out in the town and *Norman's Knob* (following Norman's adventures rubbing his magic knob and getting into all sorts of trouble – often with the law). There was *Mike Smitt (He's a Patronising Git)* solving the world's problems and, of course, *Buster Gonad and His Unfeasibly Large Testicles*.

He didn't hear the turn of the key in the door, but he suddenly felt the presence of the two young women standing over him – Liz, the librarian, and a young police officer. He felt a sudden stab to the heart. What had he done? But his heart was still lifted by the mirth engendered by seeing Buster caught up a tree while children threw stones at his unfeasibly large testicles (having mistook them for bird nests) and Buster painting one of his own testicles to look like an Easter egg only for it to win a village competition. Similarly, he was still tickled at being reacquainted with old friends: Billy the Fish, the Bottom Inspectors, Roger Mellie (The Man on the Telly), Postman Plod (The Miserable Bastard), Johnny Fartpants and Tubby Tucker. But the events of recent days seemed to be having an effect on him – the close proximity of two females with regulations, codes of conduct, societal expectations and even the law on their side (and nothing on his – or so it felt) made him nervous.

Nevertheless he remained upbeat and polite, smiling generously, hoping it might stir a similar response from them. It didn't. He was solemnly informed by the woman police officer that he had been heard laughing and this had been a cause for concern. He had claimed to be conducting research, yet his demeanour suggested otherwise.

He nodded, thoughtfully, but, still tickled by the adventures of Buster and Co., he thought that lifting the mood was the answer. He jabbed his finger at the open *Viz* comics on the table with a smile and a look of mirth and wonder.

'If you had testicles, you'd understand,' he said to the young ladies.

He immediately checked himself and realised that his judgement might have slipped again. He knew immediately that he should try to be (or at least signal that he was) 'inclusive'. Besides, he could not make any assumptions.

'Do either of you have, or have you ever had, testicles?'

– VI – The Police Station

He wasn't used to sitting in silence with strangers, but he was tired of talking, explaining to others only to be on the receiving end of glares. He was wary now. His appointed solicitor, sitting across the table from him in police interview room one, was scouring the paperwork laid out on the table between them. He had tried to read the paperwork himself but his brain was fried. He concluded that the visit to a police station would have its bonuses. He could have a chat with the duty solicitor about the week's events at no cost to himself, so he would save himself a bob or two. Trouble was, just as you can't choose the gender of the officer who is going to arrest you, you can't chose the gender of the duty solicitor. When asked if he wanted the duty solicitor present during the interview, he had gratefully accepted and added for good measure (a practice which was proving to be contrary to his best interests) that he didn't mind if the solicitor was a man or a woman. It didn't help (and it didn't matter); the solicitor was neither apparently.

The solicitor was reading the police officer's brief account of the incident (up to the point that she had lost consciousness) and the witness statement of the librarian woman on arriving on the scene in the library's basement moments later. He was hoping somewhere in the text of either statement that there would be a clear indication that the hard blow to the policewoman's head was not his fault.

It had all started when he was being escorted from the basement library room (by the policewoman) to the library's main reception. (The librarian, Liz, had gone upstairs ahead to ask the policewoman's colleague to bring the police vehicle around to the entrance.) Having exited the library's basement cage of 'rare and dangerous' books, the policewoman was guiding him towards the stairs leading to the ground floor. Near the bottom of the stairs leading from the basement was a door. An old, heavy door. He had taken a few quick steps forward and opened the door for the police officer. She had stopped and not moved.

'I'm not infantilising you by opening this door,' he had said. 'But it is heavy.'

He thought – can someone look angry in a blank way? Or was that a contradiction in terms?

The officer had remained steadfast and grim-faced.

'I know this kind of door,' he had continued. 'I noticed it when I was led down here by the librarian. The closing mechanism is misconfigured,' he had said pointing at the overhead hinge-like mechanism attaching the top of the door to the doorframe. 'Furthermore, the door is incorrectly hung, which means part of the lower edge of the door is getting stuck on the uneven paving slabs. A nasty combination – a faulty closer, a heavy door and badly hung.'

The police officer had looked blank. He therefore elucidated.

'Let me elucidate,' he said. 'Commonly there are two types of overhead door opener,' he said pointing at her in a manner to stop her talking. (She wasn't.) 'Ironic, I know, when we think of the device, we (or rather you) might think the device *closes* the door, but in fact this is really a device that opens it,' he said pointing again to the mechanism clamped to the top of the door.

She continued to not interrupt him. He had therefore continued.

'Broadly speaking the two types work on the same principle. The first type is a spring within the cylinder that provides force. But a spring by itself would make the movement too violent, so there is a piston filled with air. As the door opens the cylinder fills with air. As it closes the escaping air slows the movement of the door. The device can be calibrated to the weight of the door to achieve the desired resistance. The second type is broadly the same but uses a hydraulic liquid.'

Still silence. Perhaps the policewoman was now indeed curious.

'Interestingly, there are four *styles*: surface mounted (like this one); concealed in the door; concealed in the frame; concealed in the floor. This device,' he had said pointing to the device, 'is an old air type – you can tell by the slight air hiss as the air is expelled under the weight of the closing door. Trouble is, this device is faulty. The valve seals are worn down, I suspect. The probability of a violent action is therefore increased and, as I said, the door needs to be re-hung so that it does not stick on the paving slab,' he said pointing to her feet. 'You see, the pressure builds and pushes the door free suddenly resulting in a sudden violent movement.'

'So, be careful. It could end up crushing your...' (oh, what the hell, he thought) 'testicles...,' he chuckled. '...If you had them.'

He had hoped it would lighten the increasingly sombre mood – perhaps she hadn't understood the joke the first time round.

'Thank you for that explanation,' the police officer said tilting her head. 'I had no idea how doors worked.'

'You misunderstand me…'

'Oh, again, I'm sorry, sir. My fault.'

'You don't have to call me "sir", I'm not your master. This is a faulty door. The Edwards mechanism has been superseded by the Michelpot counter-weight.'

He berated himself for wishing that he could run into a man on days like this.

'Look,' he said, 'there is a sign on the door – *Take Care, Faulty Door*. If it wasn't there, I would have suggested they put up just such a note.'

'You give people suggestions?

'I like to think I'm the helpful type.'

'You must be proud.'

'Oh no, I'm too modest,' he muttered, slightly embarrassed and not quite able to place her tone. Whatever the tone, he suspected that he was the one at fault. He had learned that now.

So, with a barely discernible sigh, he had walked through the door himself. He had failed. He stood on the other side with an arm outstretched still holding the door open. The young woman didn't move. He took a few steps back releasing the door and saying a quiet prayer. The door remained open but it was a matter of time. (For 'time', think seconds.) The door would hold then break, he knew. He stepped away, listening for the shudder. Seeing that he was moving off the young woman police officer stepped forward.

There was a shudder, whoosh, then a bang, then a crumpling sound.

And so it was that he had found himself in a police interview room with the solicitor reviewing a statement from the injured woman and the librarian who had arrived on the scene moments later.

'It's fine. You did nothing wrong,' said the solicitor, eyes rising from the paperwork.

'Really? That's a relief.'

'They can't charge you with anything. They might suggest you do some awareness training.'

'On what? Effective communication of door opening and closing mechanisms?'

The solicitor smiled.

'Health and Safety?' he asked.

The solicitor smiled again.

' "Chivalry in the 21st Century?" (Should be a short course),' he chuckled. 'Or "Women"? (Should be a long one.)'

He chuckled and smiled again. He could feel the relief as his shoulders relaxed.

'Is it online training? Or one of those groups?'

'Possibly a group discussion, classroom based. Therapy-based talking and awareness.'

'I don't fancy a group chat. They are all a bit self-indulgent. I'd end up explaining the door mechanism, then I'd find myself back here,' he said with a roll of the eyes. 'Unless it was with a bunch a blokes.'

He exited the police station and headed straight for the nearest pub. Being mid-afternoon the pub was pretty much empty except for a handful of middle-aged men hunched over their pints. Had they also just emerged from the police station? He shuffled to a perch at the end of the bar and ordered a beer employing the least amount of eye contact with the barmaid as humanly possible. In a pub he was left alone. It was an institution, a safe space, invented by men for men. He hoped it wouldn't go extinct. Over the next few hours he pondered the world, his predicament while staring at the beer bubbles racing to the top of his pint and exploding in a hundred violent, terrorist acts.

In hindsight, had he known he was being filmed as he conducted his research in the library's basement and that his laughter was indicative of antisocial sentiments, he might have been more self-aware. Or was it mindful? What was the opposite of mindfulness? Could it be diagnosed? If so, could it be treated? And if it could be diagnosed, was he entitled to benefits as a result? Or even compensation on the grounds of discrimination if he lost his job?

He struggled to recognise the world. His head spun. But 'spinning' suggested operationally sound. No, the cogs and gears of his mind were slipping. The workings of his mind were not syncing with the outside world. His mental software was out of date and software patches were not being issued. His operating system was not being supported. Was this Alzheimer's? Had his brain's wiring gone askew? There were a few questions though – Who determined that there something was wrong with his brain? Who took the measurements, wrote the textbooks? Who made the law? Most importantly, who could help? A doctor? lawyer? A watchmaker?

He felt conflicted. Should he be resentful of *Viz*? If he hadn't viewed the material in his youth Buster might not have popped into his head through a backdoor. Or should he even be resentful of his youth? Of the very concept of youth? Youth, by its nature, goes out of date. He hadn't asked to experience teenage youth. He hadn't asked to be born. He was, quite literally, a victim of life. Could he sue *Viz* for indoctrinating him? He wondered if women were having similar problems with articles found in *Just Seventeen* and *Tracy*.

– VII – The Job Centre

So, here he was cycling to the job centre seven days from uttering those fateful words to the young female colleague. He pulled up outside the dreary building, jumped off his bike and locked it to a railing. As he walked up the steps of the premises he realised he had not stepped inside such a building for over twenty years. He had been in continuous employment having graduated in the early 1990s. Since that time he had been officially regarded as a net contributor to the State and to society's well-being over all. Now, here he was – less of an asset, more of a burden. Not quite as valuable in the workplace. His contribution questionable. His presence a liability. It was dawning on him that his life was out of his hands, the world moved faster than his brain could develop. He pulled a ticket from the machine at reception giving him a number to wait in line. Keeping an eye on the digital display for his number to flash and call him for interview, he browsed the vacancies on the electronic screens and paper noticeboards. He had no particular job in mind. He was open to ideas. He could apply for similar administrative positions, but they all had their challenges and an employment reference might be difficult to come by. Besides, a role in a quieter, simpler environment appealed. A role in which he could relax. And so his eye drifted away from office environments to work opportunities outside in the fresh air, manual work, small business work, factory and warehouse work, even jobs that involved driving.

He had been thrown in at the deep end. He hadn't considered a career change until it was forced upon him, but maybe it was not all bad. In some ways the events of the last week had been a release. Maybe it was his body, his subconscious, crying out for change. After all, he had always known that he had really wanted to spend his time outdoors. He even had romantic notions of maintaining old steam trains and puffing across the countryside.

After twenty minutes he heard a 'bing' from the digital display behind him. He turned to see his number flashing. He wandered over to the desk six with his CV and notes in hand and sat down across from a young, lady interviewer. As she ran through a list of questions and reviewed his CV he noted his life had come full circle.

'So, why do you want a change?' the woman asked.

'Well, I was sort of let go,' he replied. 'Or rather, I am in the process of being let go, I think.'

'You're in the process of being 'let go'?' the woman enquired.

'Paperwork,' he muttered with a smile, rolling his eyes. 'Takes time.'

She looked at him and waited. Why couldn't she just say 'please explain more'?

'It's been a difficult week. A perfect storm,' he added.

No response.

He took a breath and continued.

'I said something inadvertently to a young woman colleague.'

Pause. Her eyes fixed on his, her eyebrows raised, her posture pert, he thought.

'I referred to oversized male genitals,' he sighed. 'Not mine, I might add. Anyway, I was called in to see Human Resources, but apparently it was my fault that I described the Human Resources lady as "cute", even though she asked me why I was smiling at her. After that, someone thought it was a good idea for me to see a doctor to see what was going on.'

'And what did the doctor think was going on?'

'They were women, three of them, so who the hell knows. I asked to see a man – someone who would understand what I talking about – but none was available.'

The woman took a breath and nodded slowly.

'Then when I was taking time out from all the stress, I decided to head to the library to relax while also doing some research to help my case.'

'Research on employment law?'

'No, oversized male genitals.'

'I see.'

'Testicles, in particular. From boys' comics dating back to my childhood. I was in the library rare books room (a cage in fact), just reading stuff and laughing. Apparently, they thought my interest in the material was suspect. Anyway, I knocked out a policewoman. I say "I" it wasn't me, it was the door that knocked her out.'

'What happened?'

'A door closed on her suddenly. I tried to explain to her the faulty door mechanism...'

'But?'

'But she didn't have it up here,' he said, tapping his right temple.

'Oh, so it wasn't a case of her not being strong enough to open the door?' asked the lady interviewer.

'No, it certainly was not a matter of her physical strength. You'll never hear me saying women aren't the policing presence their male counterparts can be because of their physical capabilities, no, it was because she didn't listen, process in her mind what I was telling her,' he said, tapping his temple again.

'I see,' she sighed, returning to her notes. 'So, you were saying, you've been sacked?'

'It's looking that way. It's not official yet.'

The interviewer returned to the list of job options in front of her.

'Best to avoid office environments then?' she muttered, without looking up.

'If they have women,' he chuckled, then added on reflection: 'So many offices do nowadays. Which can be problematic.'

Suddenly alert to the person sitting opposite him, he added: 'Present company excepted, of course.'

He tried to read the expression on her face. She was giving nothing away.

'You *are* a woman, aren't you?' he asked, suddenly concerned he had put his foot in it.

Nothing.

'Now, at least? Today?'

'Are you familiar with warehouse environments?' she asked, without looking up.

'Yes, of course. I worked in them in my youth.'

She smiled, apparently relieved.

'Are you licensed to drive a forklift truck?'

'No, I'm afraid not,' he replied, shaking his head, but the question brought back warm memories of working in warehouses in his youth – wandering back and forth along the aisles, picking goods off shelves, placing them in a trolley and rolling them off to the packing and dispatch department, all the while lost to the world with his headphones in his ears listening to the radio. Better than being stuck at a keyboard.

Yes, he began to think. A warehouse role might just be the place for me to regroup, acclimatise and think through my options. I'm still young.

He saw her scribble down his reply in the negative on the form in front of her. He sensed she was about to move the conversation along. He needed to act quickly.

'I know how to handle other warehouse machinery,' he hastily added, 'and tools for packing and stacking, and transportation devices…including sack trucks.'

The woman looked up, her brow furrowed in confusion. Or that is how he read her expression. Perhaps she had never worked in a warehouse.

'Sack trucks,' he repeated. 'For transporting gonads.'

A Life's Work

– I– New Jersey

Criminals have families too and, at one hundred years of age, Sonny Brusco's was large. He had four children – two daughters, two sons. His eldest was 69, his youngest nearly sixty. There were the grandchildren and great-grandchildren of which there were nearly twenty. There were two sons-in-law and two daughters-in-law not to mention his own nephews, nieces and cousins and all their off-spring. Though he was a mobster-boss, he wasn't the forgotten, disgraced family member. He was still its head and respected by all with the Brusco name. All of which wasn't bad considering he had been in jail for fifty years. In fact, he had spent more than fifty years in jail, but this last fifty-year stretch was his latest and, presumably, his last. Wheelchair-bound, he was being discharged from Egdon Heath prison near Trenton in New Jersey – partly out of pity for the frail man that he was, but also because it was cheaper for the authorities. Why nurse a geriatric at exorbitant cost when his family could deal with the colostomy bags? It was no trouble for the family because 'family' had been the family business since its establishment, by Sonny, over eighty years earlier.

'Behave now, Sonny, we don't want to see you wheeled back in here,' said the guard, laughing as the old mobster was wheeled out of the prison yard. 'You know the world has changed out there. Be careful. All sorts of new laws. An old-school criminal like you won't survive long.'

'You should be careful, I still have friends,' muttered Sonny.

'Haven't you heard, Sonny? They're all in the cemetery,' the guard laughed. 'You have only your family now and they're all getting on.'

Sonny would have spat on the guard if he felt he could spare, let alone raise, the spittle; he wasn't the brutal gangster he had been. He had known some of the guards' fathers and they had treated him with respect. If they hadn't done so, they would have learnt the hard way – either they or a family member would have felt the hard end of crossing Sonny Brusco. His influence had started to fade in the 1980s, dwindled further in the 1990s and had all been extinguished in the 2000s. Now in the late 2010s, references to him and his influence were only to be found in the local history sections of the library. Even the Internet was light on the works of Sonny Brusco.

When he had been incarcerated, black and white televisions were standard. News bulletins were thirty minutes long. If you missed the news (on any of the three channels) you had to wait until the following day. Most newspapers did have photographs (black and white) but the images were poor and faces quickly forgotten. You had to schedule phone calls in the hope of reaching someone or, as in Sonny's case, speak to gang members in person about jobs to be done. He had spent thousands bribing telecom engineers to keep a handful of lines away from the Feds. He would never admit it to himself or others, but deep down he suspected his business model might have struggled in the latter half of the twentieth century anyway. So much of his business had been founded upon the ability to threaten officials with violence against them or their families. It had been easy. But times had changed. Women now held many public roles and he had never authorised the murder of a woman. Sure, some had got in the way of his gang's business and had had met a messy end, but not by design. How could his business model have coped in the 1990s and beyond? He wasn't sure.

That said, the family business had survived as best it could, but had been greatly diminished. The way to make easy money now was in technology and 'online' – something that was beyond him. His sons had tried to get into it, but they were not cut from the same cloth as their father. Tech criminals were younger, more inclined to work alone and in what he struggled to recall as 'cyber-space'. Those baby-faced criminals didn't even have to meet in person. They were beyond his understanding and beyond his reach. You can't break the legs of an avatar.

The smiles and waves from the guards as Sonny was wheeled out were not tinged with fear. They knew he was a spent force and at best had only a few years of living in peace with his extended family. It was a sorry change from the power he had once wielded when he had first been admitted to the high security wing of the prison. The FBI had finally nailed him on a multitude of racketeering and fraud charges, each piled up on one another. They couldn't get him on murder or even conspiracy to murder even though he had been caught on videotape describing his preferred way to dispose of bodies. A conspiracy of factors – witnesses suddenly disappearing, lost evidence, the inadmissibility of evidence – nearly resulted in Sonny escaping any form of justice, but the leaking of the videotape to the press had made the television news. It had dominated the 30 minute programmes for almost a week; as a result the Attorney General couldn't let the case slide or he would never have had any hope of fulfilling his own political ambitions. And so, Sonny had gone to jail (but not without spoiling the Attorney General's ambitions by way of a couple of broken legs and slipped discs in a car crash in Roehampton).

'Can't say we want to see you back here, Sonny,' the guard called after him as he watched the old man get helped into the people carrier on the road outside the prison by an old man, presumably a relative. 'Now you're out, take time to smell the flowers. Before you know it you'll be pushing up your own daisies.'

The guard chuckled at his own jokes.

'You're a brave man,' muttered his fellow guard to him.

'I'll think we'll be okay. He's had his day. I'm more worried about the Yankees' relief pitcher,' replied the chuckling guard before turning away never to see the old man again.

– II – New York

Father (Sonny) and (second) son, Robbie, drove towards the New Jersey turnpike. Although Robbie had visited his father once every six weeks on average there had been dry periods. Now 61, he could hardly recall his father being on the outside. He did have some hazy memories, but there were so faint that he couldn't be sure that he hadn't invented them. Just because his father had been inside Egdon Heath, a ninety-minute drive from Manhattan, didn't mean that he had missed out on developing a relationship with his father. He had mentally processed the relationship over the decades and become reconciled to the idea of an absent father.

In the last fifty years, Robbie's feelings for Sonny had bounced around all the emotions to be found on the whole boy-father-relationship-spectrum. There had been the anger, the pride, the resentment, the frustration, the love, the shame, the relief. The anger had been born from the deprivation of a normal father-son relationship and the stress it had put on his mother (who had died of lung cancer nearly thirty years earlier). The pride had reared its inconvenient head when Robbie was shown a surprising degree of courtesy in a number of New York 'business circles'. The resentment stemmed from expectations placed on him, first by his father and then by others in those same circles (about the family 'business'). The frustration was a cousin of the resentment. Robbie's life options were limited – he would forever be his father's son. He could not bring himself to move to another part of the country and start over. After all, where would he go? He had not been skilled or hard-working enough to make it on his own terms and on his own name (certainly not to the degree that would have kept him in the manner to which he was accustomed).

The love was to be found in the quiet moments. The shame was a counterweight to the pride – some doors to social circles were closed because of who he was. Then there were the questions that he was obliged to answer from his own children as they were growing up and learning about the exploits of their grandfather.

Robbie had driven the route from the prison to his sister's home in Manhattan countless times over the decades and here he was doing it for the final time. It was an unusual (or rather, unheard of) experience – the first time in over fifty years that they had been alone together in a confined space. His father's release from prison meant many rituals were to be canned because this time his father was in the back of the vehicle.

It had been agreed that Robbie would be the only one to meet dad at the prison. A low-key, surprise welcome back party was scheduled to take place in his sister's grand apartment on the Upper East side. A family reunion outside the gates of Egdon Heath prison would have been too much of a spectacle. Besides, it might have found itself in the newspapers, though drawing up in his car outside the prison gates at seven o'clock that morning and seeing nothing but a few paper bags blowing around on an empty road, Robbie chided himself for having thought there would be any media interest. Sonny's work was buried deep in another century as far as the press was concerned. The key had first turned in Sonny's cell's door at a time when both *Star Wars* and *Jaws* were over five years away from pre-production. When Sonny was jailed, Jimmy Connors was a seventeen year old tennis prodigy and yet to play in a Grand Slam tournament and nobody had heard of a ten year old kid called John McEnroe.

On arrival outside the prison Robbie had turned off the car's ignition and waited in silence. He took the time to reflect on his father's life and consider his own life as the son of a mobster. What did one have to do to turn a life's work into a legacy? Who decided what merited a legacy?

The nagging question was that, although he carried his father's name with some pride, Robbie was unsure that given the choice he would encourage the use of the Brusco name to give advantage to his children. But it looked as if he didn't have a choice. He had left it too late, Robbie's eldest, Jerry, was making his own choices. It would be a shame if the Brusco name landed Jerry with the same fate. Sonny's choices had brought both him and his second son, Robbie, to this place – sitting outside a prison on a dusty road in total silence but for distant birdsong and the occasional rustle of wind in grass. One thing was clear to Robbie as he waited for the prison gates to open and for his father to appear – however noisy a life is, it is always quiet at the end. Perhaps that was how it was meant to be. Nature's way – a built-in time for reflection at life's conclusion. Is that Life chuckling at you, Robbie pondered – life asking you, was it worth it?

Carole, Sonny's second daughter and Robbie's younger sister, was at home preparing balloons, cake and drinks for a close-knit family gathering. She was a mother to three teenagers and the wife of a city lawyer, Antonio. As lawyers go, Antonio was not a high-flyer. He had tried to be, but didn't have the depths of ruthlessness (in the legal sense). For the first ten years of marriage to Carole, he had managed to avoid becoming involved in the family business, but on realising his full potential (or lack of it i.e. hitting a career wall), Antonio had weakened. He had given in to the family's requests to sort out the occasional bit of paperwork for the family business. As everybody does, he had succumbed to the promise of easy money. That's not say it was not difficult at first, but he soon began to rationalise his way out of it. He didn't know if people were getting hurt, but he concluded it wasn't much different to the hurt dispensed by the pin-striped lawyers downtown. He might have felt his were hands clean, but only because he was wearing thread-bare gloves.

As Sonny was driven back towards the city, the conversation was light.

'How's business?' grunted Sonny from the back of the people carrier.

'Business is, you know…. Not like the old days,' Robbie sighed.

Robbie's response was partly inspired by his wish that his father might bathe in the memories of the good ol' days while being privately flattered that the family business had not thrived in his absence. Yet it was also in the hope that business talk could wait for at least one day. Robbie had no intention of bringing up the low return of the 'vice' business, the failure to secure additional cab licences from the New York port authority, the high loss-leaders trying to gain access to Brooklyn's tech city. He didn't want to talk about how they had lost some of their trusted enforcers to Las Vegas, how recruiting new blood to keep ahead of the authorities (whether it be moving money, telecommunications, tech security systems) was proving to be a challenge. In the 2000s his father had taken an interest and given direction when possible, but he guessed that on this occasion Sonny would just want to take in the sights of the world not seen for fifty years. Not only had the skyline changed in those fifty years, it had changed multiple times. In 1969 only twenty floors of World Trade Centre 1 had been completed, on Sonny's release from Egdon Heath those twenty floors had collapsed into dust 18 years earlier. Looking at his father in the rear view mirror, Robbie watched his father captivated at the sight of the new models of cars passing them on the highway. When Sonny had been jailed he had been the proud owner of a second-generation Plymouth Barracuda fastback. Only the best. Now, the only Barracuda you might see would be rusting in a gully off the highway and home to family of goldfinches or providing occasional shelter to a raccoon during a rain shower.

Watching the new world pass by, Sonny's feelings were mixed. He had long come to the realisation that times had changed and as the day of his release from prison approached he knew he wouldn't have the wherewithal to take a legitimate and authoritative interest in the family business. That said, it was still in his DNA to think of a solution to a problem and his 'solutions' tended not to be lawful. Life in New York City was tough. Survivors had to be mean. Merciless. It was a truth that brutality engendered respect, power and protection. You or your family were protected if everybody knew you meant business. In fact 'hurt' was your business. Small fortunes had been expended on large, heavy-set men who were not too bright and willing to take a dollar to enforce the will of Sonny.

That is not to say Sonny hadn't softened over the decades. He wouldn't describe it as a softening though. In private he might grudgingly admit to an increasing appreciation of his family. Having been locked up inside, all he had to look forward to were the visits from family members. He had seen his kids and then his grandkids grow up through a metal grill or, if he was lucky, across a metal table with two guards no more than four yards away. In the 1970s, when he was still fully in command of the business, even though locked up in jail, he had had visits from his enforcers and partners. He was feared both within the prison and on the outside. But over time his criminal partners had become fatter and slower in mind as well as body. Some of them just got tired of the struggle and then got fatter, only to acquire a desire to retire and move to Florida. Many of his mobster colleagues had developed illnesses, cancers. All had eventually died.

There was Jimmy Mack who hobbled into prison on a visit in July 1977. He rocked from side to side as he walked, manoeuvring his not inconsiderable body mass to the table. As Jimmy sighed in relief as he sat down, so would the chair let out a piercing squeak as his weight was transferred to the light, metal, chair frame. Sonny would then watch as Jimmy struggled to regain his breath from the exertion of moving those twenty yards from the door to his seat. As Jimmy regaled Sonny the possibility of moving into the Manhattan taxi business (not only for cash returns but to move goods) Sonny had to be patient. Jimmy's stories were littered with pauses as the visitor caught his breath. If pauses could sweat, there would be a puddle under Jimmy's chair within minutes. It was almost more difficult for Jimmy to talk that to walk as he puffed through updates on Sonny's disintegrating gang. A few weeks later Sonny heard that Jimmy had collapsed on 74th Street while berating a food stall owner. He had been admitted to hospital with emphysema and was dead within four days. Jimmy's son had tried to carry on his father's legacy and visited Sonny for two years before upping sticks himself and moving to California.

Then there was Fat Andy, an enforcer in the 1950s and 1960s. In his prime, he was the man to whom Sonny would turn if corruption was suspected in the organisation. When the director of Sonny's boutique accountancy firm retired to Florida in 1986 to be closer to his daughter and her kids, some of Sonny's money had could not be accounted for. This was closely followed by Sonny's accountant, Frankie the Wop, reporting that he had had a heart attack. Frankie then disappeared – rumour had it – to the Bahamas. Cash flow in Sonny's business interests subsequently took a dive as further problems came to light. As a result Sonny got a message to Fat Andy from prison only to learn that his enforcer's knees had been playing up. Not wanting to leave Sonny in the lurch, Fat Andy had tried to make alternative arrangements for other enforcers to 'conduct investigations' – knocking on a few doors or heads. Unfortunately, Sonny couldn't (or wouldn't) cough up the required deposit. The rates charged by the Las Vegas enforcers had outstripped Sonny's resources. Just as Fat Andy was looking to other parts of the country for yet more muscle, he had a heart attack while fishing on his boat. He fell overboard and drowned. He was 67.

And so it was that, from the early 1990s onwards, it was only Sonny's family who visited him. But all was not lost, Sonny had involved both of his sons in the business and (with help from his sons) ensured that his daughter Carole married well (and usefully) – to Antonio, the lawyer. Brothers Michael and Robbie had tried to trade on their father's name, but neither had the instinct for violence. They had to delegate the brutality. But delegation leads to dilution. In their formative years the two brothers had had nannies and bodyguards. By the time their father was sent to prison, Michael and Robbie were too soft. They never had to carve out a presence on the streets themselves. If they hadn't been Sonny's sons, they might have turned out to be perfectly law-abiding citizens, probably working in insurance or real estate. Similarly, Sonny's daughters liked the comforts and security that money could buy, but weren't interested in a life of crime either. They had no taste or time for the grubbier side of life that supported the watches, bags, spas, apartments, school and college fees. And so they remained passive partners and beneficiaries. But the funds accumulated during Sonny's years on the outside had dwindled. That said, there were signs the upcoming generation had potential to reinvigorate the family's business. Robbie's son, Jerry, certainly had the ambition.

The dwindling of fortunes were not all down to the absence of Sonny's brutal expertise from the streets. There had been death by old age – the crooked accountants, lawyers, police officers, judges and politicians who had all facilitated the business. The family's wealth had also succumbed to the cruelties of bad investments and stock fluctuations. The family had been slow to move into the online world, then tried to catch up too fast in the late 1990s. They were hit badly in the dot com crash of the early 2000s. Who do you punish for a dot-com crash? Some nerd in California? Some banker in London? More recently attempts to move into cryptocurrency systems were proving unreliable and losses had been made.

So, business aside, Robbie was pleased with the plans for his father's first twenty-four hours on the outside. Sonny had known the plan was to head to Carole's place, but to lessen any shock or irritation to the old man, Robbie explained that the first meeting was with family only – though possibly a slightly larger gathering than the old mobster might have expected or wanted. He didn't want his father to think he had been forgotten having been met by just one family member on leaving the prison.

They entered the outskirts of the metropolis and the conversation slipped into nothingness. Sonny was soaking in yet more new sights – the clean streets, the new clothes, the mobile technologies. He had missed the flares, beards and walkmans of the seventies, the perms and mullets of the eighties, the mish-mash of the nineties and the emergence (then grip) of mobile telephone technology and social media in the 2000s and the return of (hipster) beards.

To alleviate the weight of the silence as both men reflected on the significance of the shared journey back to New York, Robbie picked up the newspaper on the passenger seat next to him and handed back to his father. He had been in two minds whether to hand it over. There was a rustle of paper, then he waited.

'Page 38? Two sentences?' mumbled Sonny from the back a minute later. 'I used to be page one.'

'There's more here.' Robbie said handing back an iPad in the full knowledge that his dad didn't know how to operate it.

'You go in as a headline, you leave as a footnote,' tutted Sonny.

Neither man knew whether the obscurity was a blessing or an insult.

'That's fifty years for you,' the old man muttered.

– III – Manhattan

Robbie parked up just down the street from Carole's Manhattan apartment. They were early so Robbie took the opportunity to have a few quiet moments with his father, there wouldn't be an opportunity to talk once they headed upstairs – the family occasion would take over. He turned to face his father behind him. It was a little strange to remember the tyrant that left a city only to return as a shadow hunched over in the wheelchair decades later – old, weak, but still sharp. At least the retired mobster would have a few years to wind down after a century of giving and taking.

With twenty minutes to kill, Robbie decided to update his father on who and what to expect at the welcome gathering. He did not want the old man to be confused by the fuss made over him. He was also aware that he didn't want his father to be thrown by not knowing who was who. With a flat of nearly sixty people the old gent might be overwhelmed. To move, within a few hours, from living out an existence in a small cell – a home for five decades with every moment of one's day monitored by the government – to being the centre of attention in an environment of bustling family members would surely be a shock to anybody's system. So, in the safe, muffled cocoon of the people carrier, Robbie ran through who would be at the party.

There was Sonny's eldest son, Michael, and his wife and three adult children – all of whom were involved in shady business to some degree. Michael Jnr. was running a print firm that had in fact been procured by blackmailing and pushing out the original owner in the late 1980s. The print firm laundered money for the family businesses which included Diana's (Sonny's sixty-four year old eldest daughter) real estate company that regularly used corrupt surveyors and a bit of family muscle to lean on sellers. Only Jerry (Robbie's son) was regularly involved in violence, but only then in a managerial capacity. All enforcement requirements were passed through Jerry. He kept things simple by outsourcing the beatings to heavies, many of whom came from overseas. Russians were particularly gifted. They asked no questions, took the money and delivered a service promptly and efficiently. Robbie had set up a boxing gym in the early nineties but it was Jerry who had developed it into a Mixed Martial Arts training gym in the

2000s. The 'MMA' gym allowed the easy come-and-go of aggressive-looking men. These 'athletes' would come over for 'training camps' for six or eight months before heading back home. They made good money; they weren't around long enough to land on any federal agency's radar. Conveniently, the Internet and social media had dramatically increased the efficiency of bringing over the thugs and setting up the jobs. In fact, Jerry would never meet the thugs themselves. Encrypted messaging systems kept things efficient, especially the Russian messaging applications that Jerry had now mastered. It was another layer of security – keeping ahead of the Feds. Funds were securely exchanged through other online applications and everyone was happy.

If not directly involved in the family business, the next generation was indebted to their grandfather – regular incomes and respect from the local 'business community'. They were not turned away like any other member of the public from any door upon which they knocked. Besides, how else do you pay for apartments, sports cars, college fees, regular trips to the beach resorts? That said, some were keen to partake in the grubbier Brusco family traditions. In addition to Jerry's rising star there was Diana's son, David. It had all started with a DUI that had been overturned as a result of a few back alley chats. David had been grateful and his eyes had been opened. He saw potential and decided to work with his uncle, Robbie, to learn the ropes. Robbie had initially been reluctant thinking it best that younger family members ease themselves out of the business, but David sold it as a re-booting of the business by reaching into the tech generation. Although he had dropped out of Columbia University, David had connections and was pushing to expand the family business by exploiting the opportunities that the tech world had to offer. There were other siblings and cousins who were also ever so slightly implicated in the family business whether it be through their work in the law, accountancy, Wall Street or the blue collar trades. Introductions could be made, hands shaken and a deal made. There was potential and Robbie knew especially the upcoming generation were keen to meet and thank the man who had started it all.

Not that he was expecting Sonny to remember names or family relationships, Robbie ran through the names of the other members of the family including the teen and pre-teen great grandchildren who were expected to be present at the welcome home party. As he did so Robbie was reminded that he was quietly grateful for the occasion. It was rare that so many family members would be gathered together in one place. Like all modern day families they were all rushing about doing their own things. It was occasions like this that brought them all together. The trouble with weddings, half the guests were a bunch of strangers. And funerals were gate-crashed by so called 'friends' of the departed. No, Robbie concluded, his father's homecoming was an excellent occasion for all the blood family to get together and catch up, not only that, it was right that they give thanks to the man that had started it all – the godfather, Sonny Brusco.

The other 'family business' would be put aside for an afternoon to allow for the business of family. Sonny asked about as many members of the family as he could; he too had no wish to talk about business today. It could wait. Today was all about catching up with family. Besides, secretly he knew he would not be able to participate in business matters, but he could enjoy watching his family enjoy the fruits of his own hard labour. In fact, although he would never admit it, in recent years he had been coming to the conclusion that his family was his greatest achievement, his life's work.

With family news concluded and the time of the party imminent, Robbie phoned up to his sister. The call went through to voicemail after eight rings. Robbie sighed, rang off and re-dialled. After another failed attempt, he dialled again and left a recorded message.

'Hey, we're here. Get your ass down here. We're outside.'

He apologised to his dad.

'The thing is, if I leave the vehicle here too long it will be towed. Cameras everywhere.'

His father looked at him pitifully.

'Parking fines done by camera now. All automated. It's a different world.'

Frustrated after a ten minute wait and a further two unanswered calls, Robbie swore and climbed out of the vehicle.

'I'll go and see what's going on. I'll be two minutes.'

And with that he disappeared.

Not that Sonny would have known, but Robbie did not return after fifteen minutes. Suddenly, there was a knock on the window and the vehicle's door beside him slid open. Sonny was met with the sight of a small smiley crowd of three men and three women.

'Hello, Sonny. We're here to help,' somebody said.

Sonny didn't recognise any of them and, with the speed that they moved, he didn't have time to ask any of them.

Two men lifted Sonny in his wheelchair out of the people carrier and placed him on the sidewalk.

'Change of plan,' a woman said. 'The welcome home party got bigger. We're changing venue.'

'What?' mumbled Sonny, irritated by the sudden flurry of activity and noise and with a niggling sense of concern. Who were these strangers? Should I worry? Perhaps another part of the surprise.

'Let's go, the whole family's waiting,' said one of the men who wheeled Sonny to a shiny, black, nondescript van. Within minutes the old man was safely buckled up inside and the vehicle moved off.

– IV – Welcome Home Party, Arrivals

The van had darkened windows so he was unsure where he was heading, but Sonny knew it was out of the city. He was of an age he didn't need a bathroom visit. That was all managed by a bag on the chair, so he was comfortable sitting in his wheelchair in the back of the vehicle by himself. Nobody had joined him in the back of the van. A man and a woman sat in the front seats that were separated from Sonny by a tinted screen and large headrests. The others who had surprised him outside his daughter's apartment had disappeared into another vehicle. During the journey Sonny barked a few questions at the strangers up front, but his driver and the passenger just waved and piped some music through to the back.

It must have been mid-morning when they turned off a highway towards woods. They drove deep into the woodland then turned off a track only to travel another fifteen minutes off road deeper in the trees. The van slowed and drew to a stop on the edge of a clearing among many other parked cars and vans.

Sonny listened as the van door was unlocked and watched as it slid to the side revealing a smiling man whom Sonny didn't recognise. Behind the smiling stranger was a crowd of perhaps three hundred people, all standing to attention in a semi-circle and similarly smiling politely. No one was holding a balloon and there were no "welcome back" signs. Not that Sonny was expecting any theatrics, but the view of the gathering from his throne in the van looked oddly downbeat. Were they here for him? He scoured the crowd trying to pick out any faces he would recognise, but without success. There were certainly no family members present who had visited him in prison in the last ten years. Perhaps these were the cousins, or families of past work acquaintances or people he had been helping with a bit of cash here and there over the years? Perhaps the main family – Carole, Diana, Michael, Robbie – were all out of sight ready to make a grand entrance? Sonny's eyes returned to the politely smiling, fifty year old man standing in front of him while a few other helpers busied themselves with attaching a ramp to the van for Sonny's wheelchair, all done without meeting Sonny's gaze.

'Who are you?' Sonny said to the smiling man a little too gruffly for a guest of honour.

'Patience, Sonny,' replied the smart, but casually dressed, man. 'Introductions to follow. Right now, you just need to know I am today's Master of Ceremonies.'

'What's the ceremony?'

'Your welcome home party, of course,' the MC replied. We've all been waiting a long time for this.'

And with that, Sonny was rolled down the ramp out of the van and onto the floor of the forest. The location truly was lost in the middle of nowhere and completely hidden from the world. The old, confused man gazed up at the high canopy of pitch pine and fir trees. The ground was soft and bouncy under the wheelchair. Sonny's attention was brought earthwards when a woman stepped forward and, with a warm smile, wrapped a thick woollen shawl around his shoulders.

'It's going to be a long day, we don't want you to catch cold,' she said kindly.

Sonny appreciated the thought and nodded in thanks, but was trying to place her face. She wasn't a blood relation that was for sure. She had a dark Central or South American complexion, probably Mexican.

'So who are you?' he grunted.

She laughed.

'Patience, Sonny. As our MC said, all will be revealed. So, glad you are here,' she added with a gentle stroke of his arm.

Now confused, Sonny let himself (not that he had a choice) be pushed further into the forest clearing. The crowd parted as he was slowly wheeled forwards. Some nodded and again smiled politely (rather than warmly), others were emotionless. Not a word was said. The silence was broken only by the sound of his chair being pushed over the forest floor and distant birdsong. It was odd because the crowd members weren't even talking to each other. If they knew each other surely they should be talking? If they *didn't* know each other, then surely they would be making polite small talk?

Strange party, he muttered to himself.

On balance though, it felt good to be outside, even to be out of the city. The air was fresh. He had had no idea that there were so many people wanting to meet him. He didn't know the size of Carole's apartment but he was convinced it could not have accommodated so many people. Strange though, he noted, there were no children present. Robbie had said there would be lots of great grandchildren. The crowd seemed to be comprised of middle-aged or elderly people. Professionals too, all wrapped up warmly in outdoorsy, hiker clothing.

'Can I have a drink?' asked Sonny, thinking he might have been neglected.

'Of course, how silly of us,' the Mexican woman disappeared only to return a few moments later not with a glass of wine or a cold beer, but a plastic bottle of water. She twisted the cap, broke the seal and handed it to Sonny. He gave her a look – is that it?

Sonny was rolled fifty yards before coming to a stop on the edge of a large, but very shallow, leaves-covered depression in the ground forming a natural arena. The three hundred attendees quietly took their place in a circle on the edge of the arena perhaps three or four people deep. The circle was only broken by a large irregular-shaped object with large protrusions (possibly a piece of machinery about the size of a large van) covered completely by a dirty tarpaulin. His attention was pulled away from the object and the crowd as the Master of Ceremonies joined him at his side.

'Sonny, without further ado. Let's begin,' said the MC. 'Lots to get through.'

'Damn right,' spat Sonny, surprised to find himself a little disconcerted.

'Well, firstly, I should let you know that your family will be with us shortly. As you have probably guessed, we are not your family members – all sorts of creeds and colours here. Wouldn't work,' the MC chuckled. 'But we are family members – just not yours.'

'Just get on with it,' Sonny said.

'Of course. To explain: we are representatives of past associates of yours.'

'All my business associates are dead,' Sonny snorted.

'Exactly right, Sonny. Exactly. They are dead. All of them. But you had two types of business associates. The "willing" associate and, secondly, the "unwilling" or "involuntary" associate. But, as you say, they are all dead. Alas, death comes to us all. Usually it is Mother Nature (working with Father Time) that takes us and we have to just accept that, but I think it is fair to say that we are at least grateful for the opportunity to swim in the seas, climb the mountains and walk in the woods. But (and it is an important 'but') the one other thing that inspires joy alongside the swimming, the walking and the climbing is that we can partake in such activities with family and with friends. However, sometimes Mother Nature is not involved in the extinguishing of a life. No, in fact Mother Nature abhors the untimely taking of a life. It goes against Her Nature. And it is something that we all have an awareness of, isn't it?' said the MC to the people gathered around the woodland arena.

A murmur of approval and wave of nodding ran around the circle.

'No, as I said,' continued the MC, 'the second type is the business associate who *never agreed* to be part of your business – never agreed to be involved with you in any shape or form. This is where you come in, Sonny.'

'I get it,' Sonny replied. 'You're going to kill me?'

'No, Sonny, no. We are going to *share* with you. Share with you our stories.'

'And then you are going to kill me?' spat Sonny.

'Absolutely not, Sonny. You will be returned to your daughter's (Carole's) apartment by nightfall whereupon you will spend the weekend with your family.'

'Where is my family?'

'Not far away. Don't worry, as I said, you'll have the whole weekend to spend with them. You'll have ample time to celebrate and reflect on your life.'

Sonny quietened down. The MC and others didn't look like the aggressive, lying type. Sonny nodded in acknowledgement, muttering. 'Okay, let's get on with it.'

The MC added, 'But that is not to say some of this afternoon might not be uncomfortable,' before straightening up and announcing to the gathered, 'But first, we promised you introductions and introduce ourselves we shall.'

– V – Welcome Home Party, Introductions

'Hello, I'm Danny,' said the sixty-five year old woman stepping forward. Danny was normally quiet and shy but once the planning of Sonny's welcome home party had taken off, it became clear that there was no other person who would be the first to speak at the event.

'"Danny"?' huffed Sonny. 'Do I know you?'

'In fact, if I may, Sonny,' interrupted the MC, 'Danny is the reason we are all here. It was her idea, so it was only right that she should start proceedings.'

The MC turned to Danny, 'Please, Danny, continue.'

'I'm Danny. I am sixty-five years old and I was fourteen years old when you went to jail. We have never met, and no, you don't know me. But you knew my father, Jack Regan.'

Sonny face scrunched in thought for a moment, then relaxed having concluded that he had never heard the name and shrugged. 'Never heard of him.'

The MC put a hand on Sonny's shoulder. 'Let her speak.'

'You won't remember him. In fact, you probably never met him or knew his name. My father was a police officer in the Bronx. In 1962, when I was eight, he was making a routine traffic stop, a suspected DUI in fact. Trouble was, two of your willing 'business associates' were in the car. My father busted them for possession and the DUI.'

Danny paused, she was struggling.

'I could talk for hours about what happened, but I know there are so many other people here who want to speak and we have so little time. I will keep it brief. Your associates walked unhindered out of lock-up within an hour of my father booking them in the police station. Later that night they turned up at our house, smashed the door in and shot my father three times. My mother, screaming, was punched repeatedly into unconsciousness to shut her up. So, this is why I'm here.'

'Oh, well, thank you for sharing,' said Sonny rolling his eyes.

'I was upstairs hiding under the bed,' Danny continued. 'I can say those five minutes have been the life-defining moment of these last fifty seven years. I kissed my father goodbye that night as he took his last breath and promised myself that I would meet you one day. My mother died in the September 1977 a broken woman. If it hadn't been for all these lovely people, I wouldn't have connected, made friends and eventually discussed plans for this.'

'And what is "this"?' Sonny asked.

'Your welcome home party, of course,' MC said.

'Can I have a beer then?'

'Not yet, there's more,' said the MC with jovial smile before turning to his left and a figure in the front row of the circle. 'Jim, please.'

A man stepped forward. He appeared more nervous (or was it emotional?) than Danny.

'Hello, I'm Jim,' said Jim. 'I am forty-seven years old and have lived in Brooklyn Heights all my life. I never left. Part of me thinks I might have left if things had been different. I think deep down I was unable to leave the city because part of the fabric of my early life is in these streets. 'Those' streets,' Jim corrected himself, waving off to the east. 'Nicole Branton was my cousin. She lived across the street and was four years older than me. In 1979, as was common practice on your patch, children were forced to transport guns and drugs around the neighbourhood. Nicole, at the age of 12, was forced to carry weapons for your gang. She was shot dead at a hold up with the McKenzie crew at the age of fifteen.'

'Well, I hope you are talking to McKenzie family.'

'Anyway, it's good to be here,' said Jim, ignoring Sonny's quip.

The MC turned to his right and nodded at a grey-haired woman standing in the second row on the edge of the arena. She nodded back in acknowledgment and stepped through the line to the front. As she did so, those on either side parted to make way for her and as she took a deep breath her neighbours rested their hands on her shoulders. She introduced herself as Ellen and began her short story. She was the aunt of Lily who, she told Sonny, was raped as a fifteen year old girl in 1968 by one of Sonny's henchmen. Lily went to the police but both the police and the prosecuting authorities dragged their feet and the case went nowhere. Witness statements were lost, police officers openly doubted Lily's accounts and those of witnesses. In fact, a number of witnesses suddenly had cause to leave the city. Lily overdosed aged seventeen. Ellen had been her sponsor on the day of Lily's benediction at St Patrick's Catholic church – the same day Lily was raped.

The stories continued. There was the story of Max Diggory (as told by his cousin's nephew, Max Jnr). Max had been a taxi driver who had refused to help in a get-away on a bank job by one of Sonny's henchmen in 1966. The taxi driver, Max, was tracked down a few days later (once enough money had transferred hands and after a few knees had been broken). Max himself was beaten to death. He was unmarried, so had no immediate family, but the murder had become firmly embedded in extended family folklore. Max Jnr (there were lots of Maxs in his family) had always been intrigued by the story of his namesake – a tale of woe that had subsequently consumed him with a deep sense of injustice. So when he had been alerted to the existence of the group (through his therapist who herself had a sister similarly obsessed with the injustice of one of Sonny's crimes), Max Jnr had made it his mission to use his social media skills to widen the network to further connect with victims' families.

Then there was the granddaughter of Tom Venn who had been providing legal representation to an informer (identity unknown) on the Sonny family business in 1959. Tom's identity and work were blown by a bent cop under Sonny's pay. The then-forty year old mobster had sent his henchmen round to the lawyer's home to discover the identity of the informer. Having had his wife tied up and threatened with torture, Tom Venn was persuaded to drop the case. Ashamed, he lost faith in the justice system, turned to drink and moved to Buffalo. Miserable, he ended up giving up his legal practice and becoming a car salesmen eventually opening car repair shop. The informer was eventually unmasked by Sonny's mob. The informer's was body never found.

Thomasin Yeobright stepped up to tell the story of a family friend – a ferry driver – who used to dump bodies in the Hudson River for Sonny. Repeatedly bribed and threatened, the ferryman sunk into a deep depression eventually refusing to cooperate with Sonny's demands. He lost an eye in a beating that resulted in him losing his job as a ferryman. After months of joblessness he took a gig as a long distance truck driver having lied about his eyesight. He was killed in a crash at night six weeks later on the Interstate 95 to Baltimore in December 1967.

'Pussies.'

'Of course,' replied MC with a patient smile looking at Sonny hunched over in his wheelchair. 'This is difficult for you and tiring, I understand, but please be patient. It is cathartic for us. Besides, we have refreshments coming up later – some sandwiches and cake to restore all our strength. We are making good time, but we want to finish before dark.'

'For Christ's sake.'

'Shall we continue?' said the MC turning his attention from Sonny to the crowd. 'William?' he called out to a young man.

'And who the hell are you?' sighed Sonny, now indeed tired, not expecting a reply.

'William Budd. Arthur Budd was my grandfather.'

'Who the hell is Arthur Budd?'

William smiled. 'As I said, old man, he was my grandfather.'

'Who the fuck are you people?'

'The current generation,' said the MC trying to soothe Sonny's irritation. 'They were children or not even born when you were locked up. People don't become more compliant as time goes on, they grow, become resilient and add to their ranks,' he muttered into the old man's ear. 'Each generation is refreshed with talent and energy. And even patience. Not something a person like you worked into your business plan, I suspect?'

Sonny glared.

'Let's continue,' said the MC turning back again to the crowd.

William described how his grandfather was framed for the murder of a cop (killed, of course, by Sonny's gang) who had not been for turning and was troubling Sonny's business. Having been sentenced to life in prison (where he died in 1999), Arthur Budd's business had been taken over by Sonny.

Over the next two hours men and women (largely middle- and old-aged) stepped forward and shared their stories of murdered family members, tortured friends, broken relationships and charred family trees. There was Mary Cotterel (her roommate pushed under a bus), Sergio Paris (his brother stabbed in a nightclub's restroom), Edwardo Lopez talking about his sister Rosana whose face was slashed after which she took her own life. Then there was Gemma Mountain, Phil Ackerley, Jim Clayton. At one point the Mexican woman stepped forward and shared her story of her father and sister who drowned in the Hudson trying to escape Sonny's bullies. And many more. The dead were accountants, police officers, probation officers, local businessmen, transport officials, city disposal officials, brothers, husbands, grandfathers. And then there were stories of the fall-out – wives, mothers, fathers, brothers, sisters, cousins, grandchildren. Family friends. Friends of friends. All led in some way back to Sonny's work.

– VI – Welcome Home Party, Friends and Family

'This is Jimmy Cadogan. You knew his great aunt,' said the MC as proceedings resumed after a thirty minute break for coffee and sandwiches and carrot cake (provided by Danny). During the break Sonny had been wheeled off to the side and was left on his own with a few sandwiches while the crowd huddled around the trestle tables of food. Apparently nobody wanted to talk to him. There had been no sign of the Brusco family members, but as the hours rolled by Sonny just gave up and surrendered himself to an afternoon of nonsense. He had spent fifty years in a cell, he could endure another afternoon of mind-numbing boredom.

'Anneka Cadogan?' said Jimmy snapping Sonny out of his distraction.

Sonny had no answer and just shrugged. He had no idea, no care.

'Or rather your henchmen knew her,' said the MC.

'She was a nurse at Brooklyn General,' said Jimmy. 'Your henchmen had put three bullets into Martin Day,' he said nodding across the circle to a thirty-something woman, 'Margot's great-uncle.'

'Trouble was, Martin survived and was put on life support. Your henchmen wanted access to the hospital to finish him off. My great aunt, Anneka, was on night duty. She rumbled them, but not before they put another two bullets in Martin. Your henchmen threatened, bullied and harassed my great aunt for a week until she couldn't take it anymore. She went to the police. She was found dead beside her apartment building two hours later having 'fallen off' her fire escape on the eleventh floor.'

'Perhaps there was a fire,' Sonny smirked, before mumbling in boredom, 'I have no idea who she was.'

'Precisely, that's our point,' said Jimmy. 'So, as a reminder, she was my aunt.'

'Look, I get it,' said Sonny addressing the MC but loud enough for others to hear. 'But what is the point of all this? I can't change anything now.'

'Maybe you can't, but we can,' replied the MC calmly.

'My family will be missing me,' growled Sonny, but his advanced years had lessened the effectiveness of the once-feared mobster's grunts and growls. 'They'll be asking questions.'

'No, not quite, that is all in hand, but I am glad you brought up your own family. Having listened to how you have irrevocably impacted so many families so negatively over the decades we gave thought to it. We concluded that as you would not break the cycle, it would be left to us to break the cycle. So, now that we are nearing the end and before we move on it would be a good opportunity to advise you of what we have set in motion. As you said, about your family we have concerns too, so we have arranged for the youngest members of the Sonny family to be saved from the Sonny Brusco cycle of violence.'

'The kids?'

'Don't worry, they won't be harmed,' said the MC before nodding across the circle at a frumpy woman.

'We have already identified adoptive parents in Delaware, Wisconsin, Caspar City,' said Francesca Martinez stepping forward and introducing herself.

'And Houston,' added Annie Winters, a woman standing next to Ellen (the aunt of murdered Lily). 'All very respectable families. They will be well looked after. Their names will be changed, of course. But they are all leaving the state of New York.'

Sonny was stunned.

'The name 'Brusco' will be wiped from the records,' Francesca added as an aside. 'Technology can do that. It's not written down on cards anymore.'

'Please be assured that we will do everything we can to immerse them in the lives of their new families. Unfortunately, they...,' continued Annie.

'Who the fuck are you?' interrupted a suddenly agitated Sonny.

'I'm Annie, I'm the manager of New York City's Adoption Services,' said Annie. 'But, of course, I couldn't have done it without the assistance of not only Francesca, but also Mark, Max and Sarah, Jonny and Zia. They've all been invaluable.' Francesca nodded across the circle at individuals as she relayed their names, they, in response, nodded back or raised a hand in acknowledgement and thanks.

'You don't know Annie, Sonny,' said the Master of Ceremonies, 'but you know her grandparents – Mickey Dee and his wife Gemma.'

The names did not provoke a reaction from Sonny.

'Well, I tell a lie,' the MC continued, 'You probably didn't know them by name. Mickey Dee was an accounts clerk at Lehman Brothers in the 1950s. In 1954 your crowd was bribing his boss to fiddle the assets of Deputy Assistant Attorney General Mark Ross. Mickey inadvertently came across the irregularity and thinking it was his boss alone that was fiddling the books, was about to take it to the local regulator. His boss guessed Mickey's move and alerted you. You sent Jonny Sams and Billy Whitelaw to deal with it. Mickey Dee was pulled from the Hudson on 25 September 1954 leaving Gemma a widow with two young kids to bring up.'

'She did a fantastic job,' said Annie. 'My mum never stopped reminding me of what we owed her mother. My one memory of my grandmother was seeing her weeping every Sunday night as she sat on the balcony. She never remarried. For me, she personified the idea of a life destroyed – the extinguishing of the liberty of spirit and hope in a human being. My own mother, who died of breast cancer, ten years ago promised me to always, always do good. To always seek justice and be resolute. That's why I'm here.'

'You won't get away with this,' snarled Sonny. Whether his grouchiness was from dog tiredness or the stories pricking his conscience, no one knew. And no one cared. 'People would know I've been taken and they will track you, find you,' he spat. 'They've got cameras you know.'

'Er, excuse me, no, they won't. Roadside cameras along the route from outside your daughter's (Carole's) apartment are being refurbished,' said a young man stepping forward somewhat sheepishly. 'And to be sure,' the young man continued, nodding at another young slim man in the crowd who nodded back in acknowledgement, 'there was a software update that started as you approached the turnpike. It took the east side offline for an hour.'

'I'm still going to get somebody to look into this and I still know people,' said Sonny a little less confidently.

The MC smiled and turned to look across the circle searching for a face.

'Firstly, you won't and secondly, it's already taken care of,' said a thirty something man stepping forward. Under his plain leather coat a police officer's uniform could be discerned. 'I have already drafted the report and those people you speak of – we already have it sorted. We have identified seventeen. Some are being arrested this evening on various charges, some quite legitimate. Others are taking early retirement while others will be pleased to hear that you and your family are being retired. It is remarkable how many friends (or, should I say, "business associates") you have when you stop paying them.'

'Well, they'll get you for something with this DNA shit,' said Sonny now not really knowing what he was talking about.

'You don't give up, do you?' smiled the MC. 'Although DNA hasn't been relevant up to this point in the afternoon, we have it covered for all aspects of the day's activities. The MC turned to his left and addressed a tall slim man in the circle. 'Jon, if you please.'

The forty-something, smartly dressed, bespectacled man stepped forward.

'Hello, I'm Jon,' said Jon, 'and no, in fact this 'DNA shit' will not get us.'

'As a professor of DNA forensics at New York University which supports the research and development of DNA techniques used in FBI investigations, I can confirm that the treatments (including an active ingredient of sodium carbonate peroxyhydrate and hydrofluoric acid) that we will be using today as we continue our activities and clean the scene are more than adequate to destroy any DNA evidence.'

'And I suppose you are holding me responsible for another one of your family members?'

'Not one, but four, in fact. Anthony Black was a builder contractor in 1962. He, along with his three brothers, Tony, Joe and Bernie, set up a company refurbishing dilapidated properties on the Upper West Side. The second property they invested in was situated on 123rd street. As they were stripping the property down they came across four decomposing bodies wrapped in plastic hidden behind the wall. They reported the find to the local cop – one on your payroll – who got in touch with you. The house went up in flames on Friday May 3rd, 1962, with Robbie, Tony, Joe and Bernie all inside. You bought off the judge, Judge O'Neill, and the building inspector who concluded that it was faulty electrical work by my uncles. Needless to say, the deaths destroyed my extended family and because the court found fault with their work the insurance company wouldn't pay out.'

'So you *are* going to kill me?' said Sonny, not caring.

'No, no, of course not,' interrupted the MC with the sincerest of smiles. 'We'll leave that to nature, but we can give you something to think about as you live out your final days. We want you to reflect on your work. And, as I've said, we're breaking the cycle.'

And so it continued. Dozens and dozens more stories. Sonny hadn't realised quite how busy he had been over his lifetime. He became convinced that they would kill him but whenever he protested, the MC would reassure him that he would not be harmed. Although having lived a hundred years practising deceit, he could find no reason to doubt the MC's words.

– VII – Home at Last

It had indeed been a long day. Sonny was finally home (his daughter's Manhattan apartment in fact). The sun had gone and darkness hung over the city broken only by the twinkling lights of New York city visible beyond the expansive glass windows of the apartment in the high rise building. The living room itself was illuminated by one wall lamp kindly left switched on by the departing MC. Sonny would have called someone but didn't have any telephone numbers and had no cell phone. After fifty years in prison and fifty years of killing he had been returned home with the remains of his family.

The afternoon had continued with what they called 'testimony' about his life of crime. As the hours had passed he had become bored and bewildered. More from an indifference than a failing memory, he had forgotten much of what was said he had done during his one hundred years. He had recognised names (mostly of his "business associates" as they had been described all afternoon), but he had not thought of many of them in years, even decades. Most had died (some in grisly circumstances) in the 1970s, 1980s and 1990s. Of the remainder he had no idea. He had also recognised the names of a handful of the individuals referred to in the stories, but only when they were put in the context of their association with his business. There had been so many, it had all become a blur. If he had been given more time he might have been able to reflect on (and perhaps acknowledge) some of his actions. He protested at times – saying he was old, he didn't remember, saying the 1950s and 1960s were a different time – but his protests did not slow proceedings.

After what must have been four or five hours of 'sharing' stories Sonny was getting tired of it all. He had asked where it was all going. Again and again he assumed he was going to be killed. He wasn't afraid. Just tired and resigned. It would have been nice to spend some time with his family and then after that, a bullet to the back of the head was the preferred route. He would rather not be drowned. Perhaps they would leave him in the woodland to die overnight. At least he could look at the stars.

And so it was that as the light was fading earlier that afternoon six mini-vans drew up and over fifty hooded and silent figures were helped out of the vehicles and made to sit down on the damp, leaves-covered ground covered. The hoods were removed one by one revealing dazed-looking men and women of different ages, mouths gagged by tape. Sonny was informed they had been sedated by qualified nursing personnel. The prisoners didn't look as if they could understand their surroundings. Once everybody had been seated, the figures were introduced. Some didn't need introductions – there was Michael, Jerry, Carole and Diana. Sonny recognised Michael Jnr, Antonio (the lawyer husband of Diana), David, Jerry and a few others. But most did need introductions – they were the grandchildren, the cousins, the great nephews and nieces.

It was then that Sonny had detected a sinking feeling deep inside him. Were his captors going to share their stories with his family members? Provide personal testimony to his exploits? Hadn't they done that already? Or worse? Were they going to execute Sonny in front of his family? No.

After all the stories had been told. The tarpaulin covering the irregular-shaped object was pulled back. It was indeed a large piece of machinery, a tree shredder or 'wood chipper'. Not an uncommon sight in a wood and, being the mobster type, his mind assumed the worst. They *are* going to kill me, he thought. I don't blame them. But no, there still had been no indication that they would do such a thing. The MC had explained that the BrownMax-X1's blades turned at 1,800 revolutions a minute. It could reduce a twenty-foot tree trunk to wood chips in less than fifteen seconds.

In a manner he might have recognised from his younger days, Sonny was informed of the plan. They were not going to kill Sonny. He was going to watch as his family (of over fifty adults) were killed.

Without much ado, instructions were given and the gathered men and women went about their business. The BrownMax-X1 was switched on. After a few clunking seconds the motors started. The 'tub grinders' and blades began to turn then spin in a deafening noise that drowned out any further explanations or protests.

It took about thirty minutes to process all his family through the machine. There was little ceremony to each death. Whether Sonny shouted, cried out, pleaded for them to stop, Sonny didn't recall; the machinery drowned out everything. Each detail of the process had been methodically thought through. Seemingly working in coordination with a man with a clipboard who appeared to be organising the bound and gagged family members, the MC pulled out typed-up numbered cards. Each card had the name, photo and a short bio of the family member printed neatly in large readable font. As each prisoner's was lifted to their feet and escorted the wood chipper, the MC handed a card to Sonny. The family member was ceremoniously lifted up high above the heads of their captors and fed feet first into the funnel of the machine. Followed by another, then another in a relentless show of butchery.

The machine made short work of its inputs. Viscous liquid and crushed solid remains were spat out the other end of the machine and collected in heavy-duty bin bags held by Max Jnr and Billy Budd and others working in teams. Once full, the sacks were tied and carried back to the vans. Each input took about a minute to process – from standing in front of the machine to being placed in the mini-van. The fifty-plus inputs took nearly fifty minutes. All those gathered and who had shared their stories were involved in some way with managing

Sonny's family members, operating the machine or tying and transporting the sacks to the vans. Nothing was said (there was too much noise), everything was communicated by hand signals. It was methodical, precise and quick. As an old man sitting in a wheelchair, he could do nothing. With a remarkable efficiency Sonny's family was juiced.

And so, here Sonny was, back in the flat at midnight. The thirty-five sacks piled around him on the floor and couches. The New York skyline twinkled outside the window. The only sounds were traffic and car horns – the distant chatter of a city teaming with millions oblivious to the day's events.

With all the sacks stacked up safe inside in the apartment around the old man, the MC told him the sacks would be collected and disposed of a few days later. There was no point in calling the authorities, all bases had all been covered. The MC reiterated that those under the age of eighteen had already being transported out of the state with new identities to new homes. They wouldn't know what had happened that day and any later attempt to track down anybody in the Brusco clan would meet dead end after dead end.

Before the MC and his team left the apartment, Sonny looked to him for answers. The MC crouched down beside the old mobster and explained.

'Technology and time: the wonders of social media and a different (generational) mindset – one not based on fear. It's a different world. I was never one of the technology's early adopters, but I was slowly drawn into it once I saw its potential. It was simple – some of us connected, got interested, did research and connected with yet more. I surprised myself. What it connects, it can also disconnect – the youngsters formerly of your family will have a chance at life. The technology that is beyond your understanding will ensure that there will be no records for them to follow up later – they will soon lose any memory of Sonny Brusco and his family.'

The MC stood and nodded to his few colleagues to leave the apartment. Their job was done.

'It's bizarre to think,' continued the MC quietly, 'that all the work you did in the 1950s, 1960s and then coordinated from a jail cell, has come to this,' waving a hand at the bags piled up around the room. 'You should have invested in your future more wisely and used a currency easily understood and appreciated by the next generation.'

And with that, the MC turned and walked to the door.

'And what about you?' Sonny called after the MC.

The MC turned and smiled politely.

'What family member or friend of yours was I supposed to have killed?' Sonny rasped. 'You never said anything in the woods.'

'Oh, nobody, thankfully. I'm just the Master of Ceremonies for today,' the MC replied. 'I'm a trained actor and regularly host corporate events. That said, I do see merit in what has been done for the city today. I'm a "willing associate", if you like.'

And with that the MC departed, closing the door behind him leaving Sonny alone with the heavy duty sealed black bin liners lying about him on couches, under tables and gathered on the floor at his feet. Each one packed heavy with oozing human remains. It had been a long and busy day. In fact, a long and busy life.

DAVID O ZEUS

Acknowledgements

Many people including DMAG, AFG and family, PJB for reading, Sonja Nagy and Marion James (Marion Creative Freelancer) for artwork, Liliana Resende and Grace Fussell for paperback cover and e-book designs, David for photography.

About the Author

Born in the UK, David O. Zeus was tutored at the Old Granville House School before having a short spell at University, after which he joined the army (11th Hussars) where he saw action at the Battle of the Hornburg. While recuperating from his injuries on the remote island of Nomanisan he began writing. He is married to Donna Mullenger and lives for most of the year in the place of his birth, Little Hintock.

<u>www.davidozeus.uk</u>

Available Titles

Collected Stories – Volume I

Upcoming Titles

Collected Stories – Volume III
Collected Stories – Volume IV
Nigel (trilogy)

DAVID O ZEUS